Above all else, Maya wanted a man she could depend on.

A man who would be there for her, no matter what. One who would climb mountains, swim oceans, if that was what it took to be there. A man who would be honest and loyal and true as…as some TV cowboy. What she didn't want was a drifter or a liar or a cheat.

And yet this man—who was already hiding something, keeping some secret behind his blue, blue eyes, and who was obviously a drifter and poor as a church mouse—this man was the one to come along and cause her circuits to overload.

It must be the physical attraction. But whatever it was, it was powerful. Especially when she'd only just tonight been bemoaning the fact that she was almost thirty and still a virgin. Untouched. Untempted.

Until now.

Dear Reader,

Have you noticed our new look? Starting this month, Intimate Moments has a bigger, more mainstream design—hope you like it! And I hope you like this month's books, too, starting with Maggie Shayne's *The Brands Who Came for Christmas*. This emotional powerhouse of a tale launches Maggie's new miniseries about the Brand sisters, THE OKLAHOMA ALL-GIRL BRANDS. I hope you love it as much as I do.

A YEAR OF LOVING DANGEROUSLY continues with *Hero at Large,* a suspenseful—and passionate—tale set on the mean streets of L.A. Robyn Amos brings a master's touch to the romance of Keshon Gray and Rennie Williams. Doreen Owens Malek returns with a tale of suspense and secrets, *Made for Each Other,* and believe me…these two are! RITA Award winner Marie Ferrarella continues her popular CHILDFINDERS, INC. miniseries with *Hero for Hire,* and in January look for her CHILDFINDERS, INC. single title, *An Uncommon Hero.*

Complete the month with Maggie Price's *Dangerous Liaisons,* told with her signature grittiness and sensuality, and *Dad in Blue* by Shelley Cooper, another of the newer authors we're so proud to publish.

Then rejoin us next month as the excitement continues—right here in Intimate Moments.

Enjoy!

Leslie J. Wainger
Executive Senior Editor

Please address questions and book requests to:
Silhouette Reader Service
U.S.: 3010 Walden Ave., P.O. Box 1325, Buffalo, NY 14269
Canadian: P.O. Box 609, Fort Erie, Ont. L2A 5X3

The Brands Who Came for Christmas

MAGGIE SHAYNE

~Silhouette®

INTIMATE MOMENTS™

Published by Silhouette Books

America's Publisher of Contemporary Romance

SILHOUETTE BOOKS

ISBN 0-373-27109-3

THE BRANDS WHO CAME FOR CHRISTMAS

Visit Silhouette at www.eHarlequin.com

Printed in U.S.A.

MAGGIE SHAYNE,

a national bestselling author whom *Romantic Times Magazine* calls "brilliantly inventive," has written more than twenty novels for Silhouette. Her Silhouette single-title release *Born in Twilight* (3/97) was based on her popular vampire series for Shadows, WINGS IN THE NIGHT.

Maggie has won numerous awards, including *Romantic Times Magazine*'s Career Achievement Award. A four-time finalist for the Romance Writers of America's prestigious RITA Award, Maggie also writes mainstream contemporary fantasy.

In her spare time, Maggie enjoys collecting gemstones, reading tarot cards, hanging out on the Genie computer network and spending time outdoors. She lives in a rural town in central New York with her husband, Rick, five beautiful daughters and two English bulldogs.

Prologue

Maya

Most people in Big Falls, Oklahoma, thought it must have been a case of immaculate conception when they saw me, Maya Brand—eldest of the notorious Vidalia Brand's illegitimate brood—with my belly swollen and my ring finger naked.

Personally, I thought it was more like fate playing a cruel joke. See, all my life, I had struggled to be the one respectable member of my outrageous family. I went to church on Sundays. I volunteered at the nursing home. I wore sensible shoes, for heaven's sake! I *never* aspired to notoriety. I just wanted to be *normal.*

You know. Normal. I wanted a husband, a home, a family. I wanted to be one of those women who make pot roast for Sunday dinner, and vacuum in pearls while it simmers. I wanted a little log cabin on the hillside behind my family's farm, with a fenced-in backyard for the kids, and a big front porch. I wanted to sit down in one of the pews on Sunday and not have the three women beside me automatically slide their butts to the other end.

And it had been starting to happen—before the big disaster blew into town. Bit by bit, I'd *felt* it happening. The PTA moms and church ladies in town had been slowly, reluctantly, beginning to accept me. To see me as an individual, rather than just another daughter of a bigamist and a barmaid. And it wasn't that I didn't love my mother dearly, because I did. I still do! I just didn't want to be like her. I wanted to be like those other women—the ones who were always asked to bake for the church picnic, who did their grocery shopping in heels, and who drove the car pools. The ones who slow-danced with their handsome husbands on anniversaries and holidays, and who took golf or tennis lessons with groups of their friends. They have minivans and housekeepers, manicured lawns and manicured nails, those women.

What they do *not* have are mothers who own the local saloon, or sisters who ride motorcycles or pose for fashion magazines in their underwear.

Still, I was certain my background was something that I could overcome with effort. And, as I said, my efforts had actually been working. Once or twice, one of those other women had smiled back at me in church. The ladies on the pew hadn't moved so far away, nor quite as quickly, and one of them had even returned my persistent "good morning" one Sunday.

Things had been going so well! Until that night…

That night. He ruined everything! Made me into the biggest (literally) and most scandalous member of my entire family! The good people of Big Falls have stopped gossiping about Kara being a jinx—then again, none of her boyfriends have wound up in the hospital from any freak accidents lately, either. They've stopped whispering about Edie, who found the success she chased to L.A. when she became a lingerie model for the *Vanessa's Whisper* catalogue. Mom just about had kittens over that one. The locals used to speculate on Selene, because of her oddball customs and beliefs. Vegetarianism and Zen were not big in Big Falls. And Mel used to generate gossip for being too tough for any man, with her motorcycle and her unofficial job as bouncer at the OK Corral. That's our family's saloon; the OK Corral. Because we live in Oklahoma. Cute, huh?

But the point is, no matter how much I wished that my sisters would conform, or that my mother would suddenly sell the bar and open a sewing shop and cut that wild black hair of hers to a style more suitable to a woman her age, none of their antics did as much damage to my standing in the community as that one night of insanity with that man. That drifter with the eyes that seemed to look right through my clothes. Right through my *skin*.

I suppose, if I'm going to tell you about all this, I should probably start with him, and that night.

See it all started just short of nine months ago....

Caleb

How was I to know that one night of insanity would change my life forever? I mean, I was respectable, responsible, highly thought of. The Montgomerys of Oklahoma were known far and wide. We had money, and we had power. The name Cain Caleb Montgomery had a long and proud history. My father, Cain Caleb Montgomery II, served two terms as a U.S. senator. His father, Cain Caleb Montgomery I, served *five*.

I am, as you have probably guessed by now, Cain Caleb Montgomery III. And already my political career was well underway. I had just stepped down from my second term as mayor of a medium-sized city. On the day all this insanity began, my entire future was being planned for me. My father and grandfather, and a half dozen other men—men whose faces you would recognize—sat around a large table plotting my run for the U.S. Senate.

They discussed when and how I would declare my candidacy a little before the New Year. They discussed what I was going to stand for and what I was going to stand against. Not with *me,* mind you. They discussed it with each other. I was an onlooker. A bystander. They went on, telling me what I was going to wear, eat, and do on my vacations, as I sat there, listening, nodding, and growing more and more uneasy.

And then they went too far. There we all were, in my father's drawing room. Eight three-piece suits—seven of them straining at the middle—all around a long cherry wood table that gleamed like a mirror. The place reeked of expensive leather, expensive whiskey and cigars of questionable origin. And all of a sudden, one of the men says, "Of course, there will be a Mrs. Montgomery by then."

"Of course there will!" my father says, smiling ear to ear.

And I sat there, my jaw hanging open.

"Got anyone in mind, son?" A big hand slams me on the back, and a wrinkled eye winks from behind gold-framed glasses.

"No? Great. Even better this way, in fact. We can start from scratch, then."

And suddenly they were all talking at once, growing more and more excited all the time.

"She should be blond. The latest analysis shows that blondes hold a slight edge over brunettes or redheads in public opinion polls."

"Of course, there's always dye."

"Medium height."

"Yes, or she'll have to wear heels all the time."

"And of course, she has to be attractive."

"But not *too* attractive. We don't want any backlash."

"Educated. Not quite as well as you, though, but that goes without saying."

"Well versed. She should have a good voice, nice rich tones. None of those squeaky ones. And no gigglers."

"Oh, *definitely* no gigglers!"

"Sterling reputation. We can't have any scandals in the family. That's probably most important of all."

"Absolutely. No scandals."

"We can run background checks, of course. Just to be sure. And—"

"Wait a minute."

They all fell silent when I finally spoke. Maybe it was because of the tone of my voice, which sounded odd even to me. I placed both my palms on the table and got slowly to my feet. And for the first time in my entire adult life, I let myself wonder if this were what I really wanted. It had been expected of me, planned for me, even from before I was born. Everything all laid out, private school, prep school, college, law school. And I'd gone along with it because, frankly, it had never occurred to me to do otherwise. But was it what I *wanted?*

It shocked me to realize I wasn't sure anymore. I just…wasn't sure. Giving my head a shake, I just turned and walked out. They all called after me, shouting my name, asking if I were all right. I kept on going. I felt disoriented—as if, for just one instant there, a corner of my world had peeled back, revealing a truth I hadn't wanted to see or even consider. The fact that there might be more for me out there. Something different. Another choice.

Anyway, I went out that night looking to escape my name. My reputation. My identity, because I was suddenly questioning whether it was indeed *mine*. Everyone who knew me, knew me as Cain Caleb Montgomery III. Hell, without the name and the heritage, I didn't even know who I was.

I shed the suit. Dressed in a pair of jeans I used to wear when I spent summers at my grandfather's ranch. God, I hadn't been out there since my college days, and they barely fit anymore. I borrowed the pickup that belonged to our gardener, José. He looked at me oddly when I asked but didn't refuse.

And then I just drove.

Maybe it was fate that made me have that flat tire in Big Falls, Oklahoma, on the eve of Maya Brand's twenty-ninth birthday. Hell, it had to be fate…because it changed everything from then on. Although I wasn't completely aware of those changes until some eight and a half months later.

But really, you have to hear this story from the beginning.

It all began nine months ago, on the day I began to question everything in my life….

Chapter 1

April Fools' Day, 2000

Maya had always been of two minds about working at the saloon. Of course, it wasn't a five-star restaurant, or even a respectable club. It was where the ordinary folk liked to come to unwind. You would never see the church ladies or the PTA moms on the leather bar stools munching pretzels and sipping beer at the OK Corral. But they didn't have to see Maya waiting tables to know she worked there. It was a small town.

Everyone in Big Falls knew she was a barmaid.

And it probably didn't do her efforts at becoming respectable much good at all. But the thing was, this was the family business. It put food on the table. And it was an honest business, and one her mother had worked hard to make successful. It meant a lot to Vidalia Brand. And respectability or no, family came first with Maya. Always had. That was the way she'd been raised.

So she helped out at the OK Corral, just as her sisters did. Well, all except for Edie. Edie was off in L.A. chasing her own dreams. And respectability didn't seem to be too high on her list.

Anyway, April Fools' night started out like any other Saturday night at the Corral. Kara helped in the kitchen, where her frequent accidents were heard but not seen. Selene waited tables, so long as no meat dishes were ordered. Mel tended bar and served as unofficial bouncer. And Maya did most of the cooking, and gave line dancing lessons, as she did every Tuesday and Saturday.

In fact, the only thing that truly set this particular Saturday night apart from any other was that it was Maya's last Saturday as a twenty-eight-year-old woman. On Sunday, she would turn twenty-nine. And twenty-nine was only twelve months away from thirty. And she was still single, still alone. Still an outcast struggling to make herself acceptable. Still living with her mother and working at the Corral. Still...everything she didn't want to be. Still a virgin.

So she was depressed and moody, and she'd sneaked a couple of beers tonight, which was totally unlike her. As a result, she was just the slightest bit off the bubble, as her mother would have put it, as she walked out of the kitchen. Wiping her hands on her apron, she strained her eyes to adjust to the dimmer light in the bar. Dark hardwood walls and floor, gleaming mahogany bar, sound system turned down low for the moment. Just enough to create a soothing twang underlying the constant clink of ice and glasses, the thud of frosted mugs on the bar, and the low murmur of working men in conversation. The light fixtures were small wagon wheels suspended over every table, a bigger one way up in the rafters dead center. Dimmer switches were essential, of course. The only time the lights got turned up to high beam was when they closed the doors to clean up. The row of ceiling fans over the bar whirred softly and tousled her hair when she walked underneath them.

And then she looked up.

And *he* was there.

He'd just come through the batwing doors from the street outside. He stopped just inside them, and he looked around as if it were his first time at the Corral. And as Maya looked him over, she thought he seemed just about as depressed and moody as she was.

"Now that looks like a cowboy who's been rode hard and put away wet one too many times," Vidalia said near her ear.

Maya started. She hadn't even heard her mother come up beside her. And though she tried to send her a disapproving glance for her choice of words, she found it tough to take her eyes off the man. "Who is he?" she asked. "I don't recognize him."

Vidalia shrugged. "I don't, either."

He wasn't tall, but he wasn't short, either. Not reed thin or overweight or bursting with muscle. Just an average build. He had dark hair under a battered brown cowboy hat that bore no brand name or markings she could detect. His jeans were faded. His denim shirt unsnapped, untucked and hanging open over a black T-shirt with a single pocket. Even his boots were scuffed and dusty. But none of that was what made her so unable to look away. It was something about his face. His eyes, scanning the bar as if he were looking for something, someone...there was a quiet sorrow about those eyes. A loneliness. A lost look about the man...and it touched off that nurturing instinct of hers from the moment she saw it.

She walked closer without even knowing she was doing

it, and those lonely eyes fell on her. Blue. They were deep blue. So blue she could see that vivid color even in this low lighting. His lips curved up in a fake smile of greeting, and she forced hers to do the same. But the smile didn't reach his eyes. They still looked as sad as the eyes of a motherless pup as they latched on to hers as if she were his last hope.

"Can I help you with something?" she asked him at last.

He shrugged. "Can I get a beer?" he asked.

"Well now, this *is* a saloon." She took his arm for some reason. Kind of the way a mother would take hold of a lost child to lead him home. "Mister, your shirt's wet through."

"That's because it's raining outside."

"Yes, but when it's raining outside, most people stay inside." She took him to a table near the fireplace. It was in the area where the line dancing lessons would be starting up in a short while, but the man was chilled to the bone. He had to be.

He took the seat she showed him and looked at her sheepishly. "I had a flat on my pickup. Had to change the tire in the rain."

"I'd have let it sit there until it let up."

"I hear it hasn't let up in days."

"I suppose you have a point." She signaled Selene, who came right over. "Hot cocoa. Bring a whole pot."

"Um, I asked for a beer."

"Beer will only make you colder. You want to catch your death?"

He blinked up at her, then shrugged in surrender.

"And see if you can find a dry shirt kicking around, will you, Selene?" Maya added.

Selene nodded, tilting her head as she examined the

stranger. Of them all, she was the most strikingly different. A throwback to their father's family, Maya supposed. Her hair was long, lustrous, perfectly straight and silvery blond. Her eyes were palest blue, so they, too, often seemed silver. They seemed silver now, as she narrowed them on the man.

"You new in town?" Selene asked him.

"Just passing through," he told her.

Selene's gaze slid from his face, to her sister's. "That's odd. I got the feeling you were here to stay." She shrugged, tipping her head sideways, and said, "Oh, well," as she turned to hurry away.

The stranger sent Maya a questioning glance.

"This month she's convinced she has ESP," she explained. "Last month she was exploring her past lives in Atlantis."

He grinned widely. "Your sister?" he asked.

"How'd you guess?"

"There's a resemblance."

Maya smiled back at him, feeling warm all over just from the light in his eyes. "I'll take that as a compliment."

"You were meant to."

There was something in his eyes that made her heart quiver. She cleared her throat, searched for something to say, and came up with the lamest line in any bar in any town ever. "So, where are you from?"

His smile died. All at once, just like that. He lowered his eyes. Cleared his throat. "Umm…a long ways from here. You wouldn't know it."

"Try me." She wasn't sure why she said it. Curiosity, she supposed. She wanted to know his story. What had hurt him. What had sent him out into the dark rainy night, to a strange town, a strange bar, a strange woman…

He looked up again. Seemed about to say something. Then seemed to change his mind. "Tulsa. I'm from Tulsa."

"Well, now, Tulsa's not far away. And I'm pretty sure everyone in this room has heard of it." She smiled gently at the way his eyes widened, and he looked around. "Hey, don't look so nervous. I'm not gonna tell anyone where you're from if you don't want me to."

His gaze met hers again. Burned into hers. "I appreciate that."

"Are you in some kind of trouble?" she asked.

He shook his head slowly. "I'm not wanted or anything, if that's what you mean."

The reply that popped into her head was that he most certainly *was* wanted. Right now. By her. But she bit her tongue and didn't speak. The fire snapped, and its scent made her nostrils burn. The glow from the flames painted his face in light and shadow, and she took advantage of the chance to explore it more thoroughly. He had a straight nose that began high and was on the large side. It made her think of royalty, that nose. His jawline was sharply delineated, and he hadn't shaved in several hours. A soft dusting of dark whiskers coated his cheeks and his chin. Reaching up, she took off his hat, again moving without thinking first. It was unlike her to be this forward with anyone. But she took the hat off, and it was wet. His hair underneath, though, was dry. Brown and fire-glow red in places, when the firelight hit it. It was thick, wavy, but short. If it grew long, she thought, it would look crimp-curled. But short it couldn't. He kept it that way to keep it tame, she mused. He liked control.

And now who was pretending to have ESP?

"Stealin' my hat, ma'am?" he asked, his voice very

soft, very deep, and stroking her nerve endings like callused fingers on velvet.

"Umm...it's wet." Turning away to hide the rush of heat to her face, she hung the hat on one of the pegs beside the fireplace. Then she spoke to him over her shoulder, avoiding his eyes. "Might as well hang that shirt up here, too," she told him.

His reply came from close beside her. "If you say so." A second later, his damp denim brushed her arm as he leaned in close to her to hang it up beside his hat. His shoulder was pressed to hers, his hip...and he looked down slowly, and his mouth was only inches from hers as he turned toward her....

"Ahem!"

Maya jumped, and the stranger spun.

"Your cocoa is here," Selene said, her mysterious silver eyes sliding from one of them to the other. She put the pot on the table, set a cup beside it, and tossed a Denver Broncos sweatshirt over the back of the chair. "It belongs to a friend of mine, so make sure I get it back."

"Thanks," the man said. He took the sweatshirt and pulled it on over his T-shirt, arms first, then poked his head through and pulled it down around him. He sat down.

Selene stood there watching the two of them intently.

"That'll be all, Selene," Maya said.

Sighing, looking very deep in thought, Selene turned and left them.

"Selene, hmm?" the stranger said. "Fits her."

"You think?"

"Sure. Mystical. Lunar. Isn't it the name of some Greek moon goddess or something?"

"Could have been. Mom used to read lots of mythology."

"So?"

She blinked, saw him looking at her, and, finally, read his eyes. "Oh. Maya. My name is Maya Brand."

His brows went up.

"As in the Earth Mother goddess," she explained.

"And does it fit?"

"Oh, I'm a long way from being anyone's mother. I'm still...that is, I..." She bit her lip. "You haven't told me your name yet."

He averted his eyes. "Caleb."

"Just Caleb?" He didn't answer.

Then she looked at her watch. "I have to go start the line dancing lesson."

He met her eyes, held them. Then, slowly, he got to his feet. "That's great. I've always wanted to learn line dancing."

Oh, hell.

This was not good, whatever it was. She was waiting for a respectable man, with a position of authority. Someone so established that being his wife would set her firmly into the midst of the "good people" of Big Falls and no one would ever think of brushing her off again. She didn't want to get involved with a dirt-poor drifter who couldn't even afford a decent pair of boots. And especially not a man who was just passing through.

Above all else, Maya wanted a man she could depend on. A man who would be there for her, no matter what. One who would climb mountains, swim oceans, if that were what it took to be there when she needed him. A man who would be as honest and loyal and true as...as some TV cowboy. What she didn't want was a drifter or a liar or a cheat. A man like her father, who had never once been around for her mother when the chips were down. A man whose exploits had shamed his entire family so much they were still trying to live them down—even though he'd been dead for over twenty years.

And yet this man—who was already hiding something, keeping some secret behind his blue, blue eyes, and who was obviously a drifter and poor as a church mouse—this man was the one to come along and cause her circuits to overload. Go figure!

It must be physical attraction, she reasoned. But whatever it was, it was powerful. And its timing was damn near uncanny. Especially when she'd only just tonight been bemoaning the fact that she was a year from thirty and still a virgin. Untouched. Untempted...until now. Now she was extremely tempted to forget her morals and her ethics and her goals in life for one brief fling with a man whose eyes told her clearly he would be willing to oblige.

She'd never been so powerfully drawn to a man in her life.

Or maybe it was just the beer.

Chapter 2

Maya Brand, he thought as he watched her across the table, pouring his cocoa and stirring it absently and looking at him as if…as if she couldn't look at him enough.

Caleb knew he was running away. Shirking his responsibilities, worrying his father sick, more than likely, and letting a lot of people down. He knew that. And he knew it couldn't go on. He had to go back. To pick up the legacy and carry it forward. It was what was expected of him. His life plan. He'd worked for these goals for years, and it was all coming together finally. In just under a year he would announce his candidacy for the U.S. Senate. He would step into the shoes of his father and grandfather. He would fulfill his destiny.

He didn't know why the hell he'd put on these clothes or borrowed José's pickup or driven clear out into some hole-in-the-wall town. Last minute jitters? A sudden attack of nerves? A desire to sabotage his own success?

Whatever it was, he'd arrived at the door of this little

saloon angry, wet, and confused. But this...this was something different.

Maya Brand was an exceptionally beautiful woman. Oh, not the way most people would think of beauty. Her hair, for example. It just hung there. Not "done" or sprayed. Its color was a deep mink brown. It was very long and wavy, but not curly, exactly. It fell over her shoulders. She didn't fuss with it. Her face...was clean. So clean he could see the slight sprinkling of freckles across the bridge of her nose. Very slight. But there, not covered by makeup. Her shape was not bone thin. She was curvy. Wider at the hip than most women would probably like to be or see as ideal. On her it was good, especially in the snug-fitting jeans she wore. He wanted to rest his hands just above her hips and hold her close to him.

But the most attractive thing about her, he realized with the part of his mind that was still functioning on some rational level, was that she didn't have a clue who he was. She didn't look at him and see Cain Caleb Montgomery III, heir to millions, former mayor, future senator. She didn't see anything but a man in dusty boots and worn-out jeans. And it seemed to him, that she liked him anyway.

Why?

It puzzled him and drew him. What was there about him that she could see to like? He'd been Cain Caleb Montgomery III for so long he wasn't sure who plain old Caleb was anymore. And he found he wanted to know. And he thought maybe this woman might be able to show him.

She went to the center of the floor, where a small crowd had already gathered. Men in their "good" blue jeans and western shirts with pearl snaps. Women in flouncy skirts and cowboy boots. Caleb had never line danced in his life. He figured he would probably make a fool of himself. But it would be worth it just to have an excuse to get close to Maya Brand.

She stepped to the front of the room, looked around, and then glanced at him almost reluctantly. Everyone else had a partner. Everyone but him.

He shrugged. "Looks like you're stuck with me."

She smiled, not just to be polite, he thought. "You say that like it's a bad thing. Come here."

Damn, he liked when she said "Come here."

He moved to stand beside her at the head of the class. Maya waved to the woman at the far end of the bar. The woman at the bar waved back. She looked like a shorter, curvier version of Cher. Exquisite bone structure, dark coloring. Mexican, he thought. She had a head of raven curls that reached to her waist and a few laugh lines around her eyes that only added to her appeal.

Maya called, "Crank it, Mom. Let's start 'em with the Boot Scoot."

Caleb blinked and looked at Maya. *"Mom?"*

"If you're gonna look so shocked, Caleb, you really ought to do it when she's up close enough to enjoy it," Maya told him.

"She's your mother," he said, still not believing it.

"Vidalia Brand, mother of five, and the most notorious female saloon owner in seven counties," Maya told him, and there was an edge of pride in her voice and in her eyes.

"Wow."

The music cranked up, and he had to focus on Maya's instructions and try to imitate her footwork for a time. It was okay, though, because he had to get up close beside her and, every once in a while, hold her hand or slip his arm around her waist, so he didn't mind at all.

And every time he looked down at her, her eyes were sparkling and staring right up into his. And those cheeks were pink with color, lips full and parted as she got a little breathless. He hoped not entirely from the dancing.

Once he had the moves down, they ran through the dance again, without stopping after each step to explain the next one this time. And though he lost himself once or twice, he had it down soon enough, so he could resume the conversation.

"Mother of five, you said."

Maya nodded.

"So the cute one with the short, raven hair, who's tending bar and sending me daggers would be…?"

"That's my sister Mel. She's kicked the stuffing out of some of the baddest men in town. Some of them for far less serious offenses than calling her cute."

He lifted his brows. "But she's so small."

"She's strong, and she's fast, and most importantly, she's mean. Hot tempered anyway. Rides a motorcycle and takes karate lessons. Goes rock climbing. She's a year younger than me, but she kind of sees herself as the protector of the bunch. Guess she figured if our father wasn't around to do it, someone had to."

He nodded, searching her eyes. There had been a flash of pain when she'd mentioned her father. "Would I be out of line if I asked what happened—to your father, I mean?"

She smiled up at him as they moved to the music. "Stick in town more than five minutes and you'll hear all about it. It's the juiciest gossip Big Falls has ever had."

"Yeah?"

"Oh, yeah."

"I'm intrigued."

"Most everyone is."

The music stopped, the dance ended. Maya turned to her group. "Ten-minute break. You know the drill." Some of them wandered off to tables, the rest room, the bar, while others just stepped closer together and wrapped their arms around each other as a slow, sad song came wafting from the speakers.

Before Maya could turn to go, Caleb slid his arms around her waist and pulled her close, started moving her slowly in time to the steel guitar. She tilted her head curiously but didn't pull away. She put her arms around his neck and smiled a little nervously.

"Tell me about your father," he urged her. He wanted to know all about this woman for some reason. Why did she so intrigue him? Was it because she was exactly the opposite of the political wife his father and the others had described to him? Or was it something more?

She shrugged. "Okay. It's public knowledge, anyway. My father met my mother when she was seventeen. They had a brief affair, and then he went his way and she went hers. By the time she found him again to tell him she was pregnant, he was on the East Coast with a wife of his own. Still, time passed, and he came back. Told Mom things hadn't worked out with his first wife, that they'd split up, and he asked her to marry him. She did."

"Doesn't sound so scandalous to me," he said. He was listening as much to the sound of her voice as to her story. Her tone was deep, rich. Erotically husky.

"Well, that's because I haven't gotten to the scandal yet. See, Daddy wasn't divorced from his first wife. For ten years he managed to get by with two families. He traveled all the time on business—or we thought it was on business. What he was doing was dividing his time between the wife he had in Silver City and the one he had here in Big Falls, Oklahoma.''

"He was a bigamist?"

She waggled her brows. "Told you it was scandalous."

"So what happened?" he asked. "Where is he now?"

Maya lowered her head. "He got involved with a bad crowd in Silver City. In the end he tried to mess with the wrong people and was murdered, along with his wife. I never did learn what became of the two kids he had with her. It was only after he was dead that we found out about his other life. By then my mother had five daughters, every last one of us illegitimate. I was young at the time, but I remember it like it was yesterday. It damn near destroyed Mom.'' She lifted her head, looked across the room with admiration in her eyes. "But she came through it.''

"She must be one hell of a woman," he said.

She looked up at him. "She is."

"And she's raised one hell of a daughter," he said.

She lowered her head quickly. "You don't know me well enough to say that."

"I know you well enough to know that I'd like to know you better, Maya Brand. I'd like that a lot."

Thick lashes lowered; then she glanced up from beneath them. "I...think I'd like that, too."

"I'm awfully glad to hear that." He leaned in closer, intending to steal a kiss, but she artfully turned her face away before he could accomplish that. When he lifted his head again, he felt eyes on them from everywhere in the bar, and he thought maybe that was why. Her sisters, her mother—and for some reason, every customer in the place—seemed to be watching them intently.

Okay. So he was going to have to get her alone if he wanted to do anything more than dance with her. It shouldn't be a problem. Nothing he'd ever wanted in life had been difficult for him to have. Especially women.

He stopped himself then. This was different. Always before he'd been Cain Caleb Montgomery. Everyone knew the Montgomerys always got what they wanted. It was a patriarchal dynasty, practically his birthright.

Here, tonight, he was just Caleb. And she was like no other woman he'd ever met.

"I'm sorry," he said. "I was out of line."

She lifted her face to his, and he was tempted to get out of line again. "I can't kiss a man who hasn't even told me his last name, Caleb," she said.

And he got a feeling—a feeling that the way he answered that one, simple question might easily have some great impact he would feel for a long time to come. It was one of those moments when you just sense things looming—like a crossroad. More than anything, he wanted this delicious anonymity to go on. He'd learned more about her—and about himself—in the last couple of hours than he ever would have or could have as Cain Caleb Montgomery III.

So he made his choice. He chose to lie to her.

"Cain," he said. "My name is Caleb Cain."

She thought he was looking less heartsick than he had when he'd arrived.

And she hadn't minded dancing with him at all. Sure, he was a drifter, on the skids, and from out of town. Sure, he barely had two nickels to rub together, from the looks of him. But tomorrow was her damned birthday, and he was drop-dead good-looking. His touch made her tingle, and she really was getting tired of being good all the time.

No steady boyfriend, no prospects in sight. Hell, one more year and she would be a thirty-year-old virgin. Being the good one was not turning out at all the way she had hoped it would. So if dancing real close and real slow with a handsome stranger was bad, well, then she would be bad. Just for this once.

She ignored the look of surprise on her mother's face when she lifted her head from his shoulder to see her across the room. She ignored the way Vidalia elbowed Mel and pointed at her, and the way Mel's brows came down hard, and the way Selene folded her arms and nodded knowingly. She ignored everything except the man she was with. And how good and strong his arms felt wrapped tightly around her. His breath tickled her ear and her neck, and she grew warmer. Because she might very well be good, and respectable, and pure. But she was also a woman. A Brand woman. And never had she felt it more than she did in this stranger's arms.

At some point later, she realized she was laughing. Laughing out loud up at him, and he was laughing, too. Her skin was warm, and her heart was racing, and she felt incredibly alive.

He walked her back to his table, eyed the now cold cocoa and said, "Am I allowed to have a beer now?"

"Sure you are. In fact, I think I'll join you." She held up two fingers, not even looking toward the bar.

"Think someone saw you?" he asked.

She winked. "Believe me, they haven't taken their eyes off me since you walked in." Then she pursed her lips. "On second thought, I'd better get that beer myself. They're liable to water it down or bring us nonalcohol or something."

He looked surprised but said nothing as she went to the bar.

When she came back, he was deep in conversation with one of her regulars, a local fellow by the name of Jimmy

Jones, but they stopped talking the minute she arrived, and Jimmy tipped his hat to her and skulked away, never meeting her eyes.

She set two foaming mugs and a filled pitcher on the table, then sat down and sipped from one. "So what was Jimmy telling you about me?"

"What makes you think he was talking about you?"

She thinned her lips, lowered her brows, gave him *the look*. She'd learned *the look* from her mom, and she was pretty good at delivering it, in her opinion. All the Brand women were.

He smiled. "Okay. You win. He was. He said you come from a wild family. That you Brand girls are the talk of the town."

"Oh, but I already told you about our notoriety."

He smiled. "You left out some things."

She sat down, grinning. "I'm dying to hear. What did he say?"

Tilting his head to one side, Caleb's smile faded. "I don't want to say anything to ruin the night for us, Maya. It's been...too nice."

She drew her brows together, turning to look at Jimmy, who immediately looked away. "My goodness. It must have been pretty bad."

"No, it really—"

She reached across the table, clasped his hand and said, "I've been putting an awful lot of effort into making my-self...respectable in the eyes of the good people of this town, Caleb. It would help me a hell of a lot if you'd be honest with me right now. What did Jimmy say about us?"

He cleared his throat, turned his hand over and closed it around hers. "He seems to think Selene is either a Communist, a Satanist, or both."

She laughed. It came out in a burst, and she clapped a hand over her mouth. Then she took a long drink of beer and said, "She's a vegetarian and a feminist who believes in UFOs, Bigfoot and reincarnation. I suppose that does make her a Communist and a Satanist in Jimmy's eyes."

"You have a beautiful smile, you know that?"

She felt her face heat. "Stop changing the subject. What else did he say?"

He drew a breath. "He seems to think one of your other sisters is…uh…cursed somehow. A 'jinx' is the way he put it."

Again her smile didn't falter. "That would be Kara. She's somewhat accident-prone—and, I have to admit, the men she dates seem to have a tendency to…get hurt. But it's just a string of bad luck." She frowned. "I hope the jerk doesn't let her hear him say something like that."

"If he does, I'll punch him in the nose for you."

She smiled. "You won't have to. Mel will."

"Mel. Right. Jimmy thinks she's a sex fiend. He didn't say it flat out, but he implied she was into whips and dog collars. A dominatrix type."

She rolled her eyes. "It would serve Jimmy right if I told Mel what he said. He's still pissed because she broke his nose last year when he got fresh with Mom."

He nodded. "Then it's safe to say you don't have a sister who's a porn star?"

Her jaw dropped. "Edie is a lingerie model in L.A. Quite a successful one, too. But no, she's no porn star."

"Probably a big relief to your mom," he said lightly.

"Not really. To Mom, there's not that much of a distinction between the two. They haven't spoken since Edie left home."

She pursed her lips, then sipped her beer and set the

mug down. "So? What did our friend Jimmy have to say about me?"

Caleb's eyes shifted away from hers. "Nothing."

"Oh, come on, Caleb. Of course he said something about me. What would have been his point in talking to you at all if not about me? Hmm? You're not with Edie or Mel or Kara or Selene tonight. You're with me. So what did he say?"

He shook his head slowly. "He…told me I might as well give it up and go look elsewhere for fun tonight. Told me you don't date, don't even like men."

She leaned back in her chair, took a long pull of her beer. "Well now, this is interesting. I've been wondering what the locals are thinking and saying about me."

He licked his lips, looked away from her.

"What?" she asked, coming upright again. "What's that look?"

"What look?" he asked, still not meeting her eyes.

"*That* look! There it is again! Jimmy Jones said something else, didn't he? He told you what they've been saying about me around town. Didn't he, Caleb?"

Sighing deeply, he finally looked at her. "You don't want to know, hon. Trust me on this one."

"Of course I want to know. I've been bending over backward to become socially acceptable around here. Hell, this is the first real chance I've had to find out how my efforts are panning out. So spill it, Caleb. Tell me what he said."

Caleb pursed his lips. "It's not gonna make you happy, Maya. And it seemed to me you were starting to enjoy yourself a little bit. You sure you want to ruin all that?"

"Tell me."

He nodded, took a drink of beer, licked the foam off his lips. Made her tummy tighten in response. She took another drink of her own, and he spoke. "He said that as near as anyone can figure, you must be one of two things. Either you're frigid or you're gay."

Maya choked and sprayed beer like a geyser. It hit Caleb square in the chest and rained down on the table between them.

He jumped up automatically, arms out at his sides as the beer dripped from his borrowed sweatshirt.

Maya grabbed a napkin and lunged at him, dabbing his chest, wiping his chin. "God, I'm sorry. I didn't mean—"

He stilled her hands, took the napkin from them and lifted it to gently wipe the beer from her lips. Maya went still, lowered her eyes.

"I shouldn't have told you," he said softly.

"No. No, I needed to know the truth."

"If it helps any, I told Jimmy that if he said another word, I'd knock his teeth out."

She smiled, but it felt weak. "I appreciate that."

"Why does this hurt you so much, Maya? Why do you care what some ignorant fool like Jimmy Jones thinks of you, anyway?"

Closing her eyes, she shook her head slowly. "I've been trying to be the good one. The responsible one. Trying to be good enough for the upper crust residents of Big Falls." She closed her eyes, shook her head. "Trying to be something I guess maybe I'm not and never will be." She sat back down. So did he.

"Hey. Maybe you don't fit in with those kinds of people, Maya, but don't ever think it's because you aren't good enough."

She looked across the table at him, smiled a little. "Thanks for that."

"I meant it. But for the rest of it—I know what you're going through."

"You do? You've been trying to be respectable, too?"

He shrugged and seemed to think about it. "More like I've been trying to live up to other people's expectations of me."

"While I've been trying to live them down."

He smiled at that. "And the results so far have been pretty lousy."

She drew a breath, sighed. "I'm a saint. I live like a nun, but nobody gives me any credit for it."

"I'm expected to live my whole life according to someone else's plan. I've never even questioned it, so they assume I never will."

She drank her beer, surprised to see the bottom of the glass so soon. She was even more surprised when he refilled it for her. "I, um...I don't drink very often," she said.

"Me neither," he said. "But tonight I'm going to do what I want, instead of what other people want me to do. If I want to drink, I'm going to drink. So there."

She pursed her lips, tilted her head. "Yeah. You know what? Me too."

She took a nice long drink. Then she glanced out at the floor, where her dancers were getting ready to begin again. "Ready for round two?" she asked him.

"You lead, lady, and I'll follow."

She did lead. She led him out onto the dance floor, then back to the table for two more beers when the line dancing was done. And then she was on the dance floor with him again when a slow song came on, and everything was different.

He held her closer, tighter, than she had ever been held in her life, and he said softly, "I'm liking this way too much, Maya."

She said, "I am, too."

"Yeah?"

She nodded, looking up into his eyes, liking what she saw there. Feeling the sting of all her efforts to be respectable having failed, the depression over her impending birthday and the effects of too much beer, she knew she was in trouble tonight. And she didn't even care.

"You want to get out of here?" he asked her.

She nodded. "Yeah...I do."

His smile was slow, but gentle somehow. "Your family...?"

She glanced toward the bar. Her younger sister, Mel, was looking decidedly violent just now. Leaning on the hardwood, watching them through narrow eyes. Her short, dark hair and pixielike features hid an explosive temper and a body to match.

Maya felt warm all over in spite of that cold surveillance. Then she frowned at Caleb as a thought occurred to her. "Are you okay to drive?"

"I've only had two beers all night, hon. And the second one's still half full." He nodded toward his mug on the table. "But how about you?"

"It's my birthday," she said, and that was her only reply.

He frowned. Then he looked at her empty mug on the table, and she could almost see him mentally counting how many beers she'd had tonight. Then, licking his lips and sighing deeply, he looked at her again. He said, "As much as I hate to say this, Maya Brand, I think we ought to call it a night. Tell you what. You show me where I can get a room for the night, and we'll continue this tomorrow."

She lowered her head, thinking that she didn't want the night to end so soon. But it was a good sign, she thought.

It said a lot about his character. "You're a real gentleman, aren't you, Caleb Cain?"

"I try to be."

She nodded. "Okay, it's a deal."

"So who, exactly, is that stranger?" Mel asked, when Maya carried the empties back to the bar. Caleb had gone to the fireplace for his hat and his shirt, and gone out to start up his truck.

"Hell, sis, he was just a man. Had a flat, changed it in the rain and came in to get warm."

"Well, shoot, since when do we have body heat on the menu?"

"Melusine Brand, you hush up!" Vidalia said. She came out from behind the bar, slipping an arm around Maya's shoulders. "You okay, hon? You look a bit flushed and flustered."

"Fine. Tired, but fine."

"That young man...he new in town?"

She sighed. "Just passing through," she said. And if her regret were audible, she couldn't help it. "He's looking for a room. I said I'd show him the way to the boarding house."

They all looked up at her, silent, eyes wide.

"I'll show him the freaking boarding house," Mel said, balling up her apron and slamming it down, starting around the bar.

Maya grabbed her shoulder, halting her in her tracks. "I'm pushing thirty, Mel. If I want to spend some time with a man, it's my choice to make."

"But...but..."

"She's right, Melusine." Vidalia spoke with authority, and Mel calmed down. She didn't like it. But she backed off.

Then Kara popped out of the kitchen and said, "What's going on? Did someone call a family meeting and forget to tell me?"

"Maya met a handsome stranger," Selene said. She was sitting on a bar stool to the right, playing around with one of those decks of cards she was always messing with. "And now she's going to show him the way to the boarding house."

Kara's eyebrows went up. "The one I saw you dancing with, Maya?" she asked.

Maya nodded.

"Wow. What a hunk."

"Shut up, Kara," Mel snapped.

"He's your soul mate, Maya."

They all turned at once, to see Selene leaning over and staring down at her tarot cards, which she'd laid out in some strange pattern on the gleaming mahogany bar.

"Oh, for the love of..."

"The cards don't lie," Selene said softly.

Maya rolled her eyes. "I'm going now. You all have given me a headache."

Each and every one of them eyed her speculatively as Maya grabbed her coat off the peg near the door, put it on, hoisted her purse and sent them a final wave. She knew what they were thinking...and she didn't particularly care.

"Be careful, sweetheart," she heard her mother say just before she stepped out into the rain. "Don't do anything you'll be sorry for later on."

Those words echoed in Maya's mind and sent a little shiver down her spine. She shook it off, ignored it, pretended not to hear her mother's words over and over again in her head as she tugged her collar up around her, ducked against the rain and ran across the wet parking lot to the battered pickup that waited with its wipers flapping madly and its headlights shining through the rain onto the road sign that said Leaving Big Falls. Come Back Soon!

Chapter 3

He got out of the truck to run around to her side, open her door and help her in. It was no small distance from the pavement to the pickup floor, after all. And she wasn't long legged.

Funny, he hadn't noticed that before. He usually liked leggy women, taller and thinner than this one. More coiffed. More "done." Or maybe he only thought that was what he liked because he hadn't met Maya Brand.

He stood there watching her the way a scientist would watch an unknown species. She settled into the seat, flipped back the hood of her dark blue raincoat, thrust her fingers into her hair and shook it. He had no idea what that little ritual was, but he liked the result.

Then he realized she was staring at him.

"You're getting all wet again, standing there in the rain, Caleb."

He was, he realized. His shoulders were damp, and a steady drip was running from the brim of his battered hat.

He closed her door and ran around to the driver's side to get in. Then he put the truck in gear and prepared to pull out of the parking lot, into the wet, shining, deserted road. "Which way are we headed?"

"South," she said.

He frowned at her, and she smiled. Damn, what a smile she had. "That way," she told him, pointing a finger toward his side of the vehicle.

He turned the wheel to the right, and they were off.

He hated being this noble. But she had been drinking a little bit tonight. And then there was her reaction to the remark that jerk had made about her sexuality. Caleb had been all prepared to take Maya Brand somewhere private and explore that question for himself. But he couldn't do that to her now. So he'd just stick around in this town for a day longer, see her again when she was clearheaded and he could be sure she was with him because she wanted to be.

She told him where to turn off the main road, and he found himself driving over what was little more than a muddy path, barely wide enough for one vehicle. He worried where he would go if another one came along.

"Are you sure this is the right way?" he asked her.

"Uh-huh. I sure am. Just keep going."

He flicked the wipers down a notch as the rain seemed to ease off, and he kept going.

"See that turnoff there?"

"You mean that deer trail?" he asked, sounding skeptical.

She laughed. It was a deep and throaty sound that made him squirm with awareness. "Trust me," she said.

She had, he mused, an honest face. So he turned. But he didn't find a boarding house when he drove in through the tall red pines lining the path. What opened out before him was startling enough to make him hit the brake pedal. Then he put the truck in Park, shut it off and just looked.

He'd driven right up to the face of a waterfall. So big that about all he could see through the windshield was a wall of froth. He didn't say anything, and after a moment, he realized he was holding his breath.

"No one should come to Big Falls without see-ing…well, the big falls," Maya said. As she spoke she was opening her door, sliding out of the pickup truck.

Caleb followed suit, stepping out of the truck onto a flat, stony bit of ground that seemed solid enough. Tipping his head back, he looked up to where the falls began, high above. In front of him, about ten feet, the ground ended, and when he looked down over the drop he saw a river unwinding a few yards below. That river was all that stood between him and the massive waterfall.

"This is incredible," he told her.

"I thought you might like it." She walked away from him, and he turned to see what she was up to. He watched her as she looked around, then she frowned, shaking her head.

"What's wrong?"

"Look."

He did, seeing what she was pointing out. A ring of stones, surrounding the charred remains of someone's campfire. Around that, on the ground, a dozen or more beer cans and soft drink bottles were scattered. She bent and started picking them up. "This is a favorite spot for partying." She carried an armload of cans to the truck and tossed them in the back. "We can dump them in the bin back in town."

"Sounds like a plan." He went to pick up the rest of the cans and took them to the truck. Then they both stood there, beside the pickup. He pretended to be looking at the falls, but mostly he was stealing sideways glances at her. He didn't really know what to do next...what she'd had in mind when she'd steered him way up here.

Licking her lips, seeming just as nervous as he was, she said, "The rain's letting up."

He tipped his face up to the sky, then took off his hat and shook the water off it. "Looks like it's stopped altogether." He opened the pickup door, tossed the hat inside, didn't bother closing the door again. Maya was right, it had stopped raining. The only moisture hitting his face now was the spray from the falls. He watched the clouds skitter away from the tiny sliver of the waning moon above. A few stars managed to shine, too.

When he looked down again, it was to see Maya staring at him, her face tipped up to his. Licking his lips, and knowing he shouldn't, Caleb slid his hands around her waist anyway. "I'm going to kiss you now, Maya Brand," he said.

"It's about time, Caleb Cain," she replied, and her palms slid up the front of him to curl around his shoulders.

He lowered his head and pressed his mouth to hers, pulled her closer, kissed her. It was good. He'd been wanting to kiss this woman for hours now, and it was every bit as good as he'd imagined it would be. Her lips were soft and willing to do whatever his suggested. So when he nudged them apart, she complied right away. She shivered against him just a little when he touched the soft curve of her upper lip with his tongue, and he felt the breath stutter out of her mouth into his. Encouraged, he delved deeper, tasted her fully. She tasted like beer. And that was a reminder to him that none of this was a very good idea.

But then her hips arched against him, and he groaned and kept kissing her. His hands slid down to cup her backside, and when he squeezed her closer, she wriggled against him in a way that almost made him roar as loudly as the falls were doing.

He lifted his head and stared down into her glittering, heavy-lidded eyes. "If you want to stop, Maya, now would be the time to tell me."

She shook her head once from side to side and shucked off her jacket, letting it fall to the rain-wet ground.

"You…you've had a few beers."

"Not *that* many." Her hands came to his chest, her fingers flicking the snaps of the denim shirt open and pushing it down over his shoulders.

"You were upset by what that redneck said in the saloon."

"Was I?" Her hands went to her own blouse now. It was white, button-down, clean. She undid the buttons one by one, opening the blouse. She wore a white cotton bra…which she filled to overflowing.

"It's…it's cold and d-damp out here."

The blouse came off. She tossed it to the ground with the coat. The bra came next. "You're right, it is."

"Oh, hell." His hands covered her breasts before he could give them permission. Weighty and full, nipples taut with the bite of the chilly air. He ran his thumbs over them and watched her catch her lower lip between her teeth and close her eyes.

"You're an adult woman," he said. "Who the hell am I to tell you what's good for you?"

Her hands again, tugging his T-shirt over his head, and he didn't want to let her breasts go long enough to take it off, but he did, and when he touched them again he used his mouth. The hell with nobility. She'd only had three beers. He'd counted several times in his head since they left that bar. Three beers. She was not incapacitated.

And she was not young or innocent or naive. And he was only human.

Warm flesh and stiff nipples on his tongue made him hungry for more, and when her fingers tangled in his hair to hold him to her, he suckled her harder, nipped with his teeth, tugged and pulled at her nipple until she made whimpering sounds and fell back against the side of the pickup. Her nails dug into his back. He attacked her other breast, pressing her back to the cold metal of the truck as his hands tugged at her jeans, found the button, found the zipper, shoved them down hard and fast, baring her from waist to ankles in one hurried motion. She kicked the jeans off, tearing free of her boots at the same time. He looked her over and shivered. Then he closed his hands at her waist and lifted her, set her bare bottom on the seat of the pickup, shoved her legs apart and bent to bury his face in between. He tasted her. Salt and woman coated his tongue, and he delved deeper, spread her wider, tasted every part of her, until she was quivering and moaning and tugging at his hair and shaking. So close to ecstasy. But he didn't take her there...not yet.

He fumbled with his jeans, freed himself, and again clasped her waist and lifted her, pulling her forward this time, and down. Wrapping her legs around his waist and settling her over him, he managed not to move for one brief moment. Teeth grated, he whispered, "You sure, Maya?"

Her answer was a pleading sound from deep in her throat as she rocked her hips. So he pulled her lower, sheathed himself slowly inside her heat. And it was so good his knees nearly buckled. And when she moved lower and cried out, his knees did buckle, and he lowered them both to the ground, because he couldn't do otherwise.

Her coat was his bed as he fell backward, pulling her with him. They moved together, and he forgot to think, to perform, to do anything, as they rolled and clung and twined around each other. Until at last he lost himself to his climax as she trembled and murmured his name and then screamed it out loud.

Breathless and weak, he enfolded her in his arms, and they lay there on the damp ground for a few moments, sated. But then their body heat cooled, and she shivered in his arms.

"Let's get you out of the cold," he told her.

She didn't reply. He pulled back so he could look at her face. Closed eyes, relaxed features, maybe a hint of a smile. And another shiver.

"Sound asleep," he muttered. "Guess that says a lot about my technique, doesn't it?"

He got to his feet, and began to put her clothes back on her. Her pretty white blouse was stained with mud here and there, but he pulled it over her arms as she hung like a ragdoll in his. Then he buttoned it up with no small amount of regret. Her coat was going to be a real mess, once they got off it and picked it up off the wet ground. But before he could do that, he had to replace her panties, which were easy, and her jeans, which were not.

She stirred when he wrestled her into the jeans, opened her eyes and smiled crookedly at him. And it occurred to him for one, panicked moment that maybe she'd had more than three beers tonight after all. Maybe she'd been drinking before he'd ever arrived on the scene.

A rush of guilt swamped him, and he closed his eyes. Please, fate, he thought, don't let me have taken advantage of a woman too inebriated to consent. He was a lawyer before he'd ever been a politician. That was the way it was done in the Montgomery family. And he knew damned good and well what a rape charge would do to his political career.

"Caleb," she muttered.

He looked at her, at the pure honest goodness of her. "I'm an idiot. You're not the vindictive type, are you, Maya?" He asked the question as he put on his own clothes.

"Hmm?"

He cupped her chin. "Tell me you wanted this."

She smiled. Then she hiccuped. Caleb closed his eyes tightly and felt a bit ill. "Oh my God," he whispered. "How much have you had to drink tonight, Maya?"

She shrugged. "I don't drink," she said.

"Not ever?" He blinked in surprise.

She shook her head. "It wouldn't look good...you know, to the church ladies."

"Church ladies, huh?"

He wrapped his arms around her and helped her get to her feet. She leaned against him as he picked up her coat, but it was soaked almost clear through. So he put the denim shirt he'd been wearing around her shoulders, and walked her toward the passenger side of the truck.

"Caleb?"

He looked down at her. "What, hon?"

"Is sex always...so...so...you know? Good?"

Caleb stopped walking. "Well...no. Not always. At least, it hasn't been for me. How about you?"

Her grin was shy and beautiful as she lowered her head. "I wouldn't know," she said very softly.

She might as well have picked him up over her head and tossed him into that river. "What do you mean, you wouldn't know?" She reached for the door handle. "Maya? Are you telling me that this was...that you were a...a...?"

"Virgin."

She said it flatly.

"Oh, hell."

She shrugged. "Tomorrow's my birthday," she said. And she smiled a smug little satisfied smile as if that were supposed to mean something quite profound. Then she stepped up into the pickup, only she missed the step and almost fell face first—would have, if he hadn't caught her.

What the hell had he done here? He could see the headlines now.

Senatorial Candidate's Night On The Town:
Montgomery Deflowers Virginal Good Girl After
Getting Her Too Drunk To Say No!

"Oh, hell," he said again. He helped her into the truck. Closed the door. Then he went around to the other side and got in himself. He started the engine, then sat there a minute resting his head on the steering wheel.

"Are you all right, Caleb?" she asked him.

He glanced sideways at her. Wide eyes just as blue as the sky on a clear summer day. That sprinkling of freckles. The look of pure relaxed contentment. She was *not* a political disaster waiting to happen. She was an angel who'd given him a night he would never forget. Smiling crookedly, he reached out, cupped her face with his hand, and said, "Probably you'd do well not to tell anyone about this."

She smiled back at him. "I might be tempted to…. I mean, just to prove that the current theory is wrong."

He knew what she meant. What that redneck at the saloon had said, that she was either frigid or gay. The jerk didn't have a clue. Maya Brand was made for loving.

"I won't tell, though," she said. "Caleb…tonight was

about proving something to myself, not so much to the rest of this town.'' She shrugged. ''Besides, I really think I'm starting to make some inroads with the church ladies. No sense blowing it now.''

He nodded. ''No regrets, Maya?''

She shook her head, then tilted it to one side. ''Not a one. You?''

''Not a one.''

''You're a good man, Caleb Cain,'' she told him softly. ''I can tell.''

''You really think so?''

''Uh-huh.''

He backed around, drove down the path from the falls, and turned onto the road to head back the way they'd come.

''Whoever is trying to tell you what to do with your life...don't you let them. I get the feeling a man like you won't be happy unless you're doing what you want to do...not what someone else thinks you should.''

''What did you do, Maya? Catch your sister's ESP?''

She shrugged. ''Maybe I did. Turn right down here.''

He did, driving in silence along Main Street. It was charming, small. Rockwellesque, with an Oklahoma twist.

''That building there on the left—that's Ida-May's boarding house. Our place is another five miles along this road. Think you can find your way back alone?''

''I think so.''

''Good.''

He kept driving. She was silent, but he got the feeling she wanted to ask him something. Finally he pulled into the driveway of the old-fashioned farmhouse, white with red shutters. Every light inside blazing. A small red barn stood off to the left. Maya turned to him and said, ''You *are* staying the night at the boarding house, aren't you, Caleb?''

He smiled at her. ''Of course I am. I'm going to want to see you again, lady.''

She brightened. Then he pulled her close and kissed her, long and slow. And even while a little voice told him this was not possible, his heart kept whispering that it was. That it had to be.

When he lifted his head she flung open her door, jumped out and ran all the way to the house, not even giving him a chance to walk her to the front door. She waved once, then went inside.

Caleb turned the truck around and drove away.

It was late. He was feeling guilty. Decidedly guilty. Running away like a child was a selfish thing to do. Not that he regretted it. But maybe it was time for him to do what Maya had suggested. Figure out what he wanted his life to be, instead of continuing to live by the expectations of other people.

Maybe it was time he made his own decisions.

He flipped open the glove compartment and pulled out his cell phone. He'd had it turned off, until now. But he supposed the right thing to do would be to call his father, tell him that he was having some doubts about his future, and that he would be back just as soon as he decided what *he* wanted to do with the rest of his life.

Maybe he didn't want to tie himself to the city. To a senate seat. To a political alliance instead of a marriage.

He hit the power button on the phone. Glanced down at the lighted number pad. Before he could punch the first number, the phone bleated in his hand, startling him so much that he damn near dropped it.

Frowning, he brought it to his ear. ''Hello?''

''Caleb! Thank God we've finally reached you!''

His heart iced over at the tone of the voice even before he recognized it as that of Bobby McAllister, his longtime friend and adviser. And even before Bobby said the last words Caleb had expected to hear.

"You're father's had a stroke, Caleb. We need you to get home right away."

For a moment he couldn't speak. He was too stunned to speak as the information registered. And when it did, his first instinct was to deny it. To accuse Bobby of lying, but of course he knew better. "My God," he finally managed. "Is he…?"

"We don't know anything yet. He's in the hospital. It's…it's serious, Caleb. Please. Get home."

"I'll be there in two hours," he said. He tossed the phone down and pressed the accelerator to the floor.

Chapter 4

Maya walked into the familiar comfort of the farmhouse with a crooked smile on her face. She sailed past her mother and her sisters, ignored all their questions and demands, and floated up the stairs to her bedroom. She was asleep almost before her hair dampened the pillows.

Twelve hours later, she gradually came to. It was a dull, foggy sort of awakening, and it came with a pounding head and a queasiness in her stomach that grew worse by several degrees when she tried to move.

"Damn," she moaned. "Why am I so...?"

And then memory came. And she sat up fast, despite the rush of dizziness. "Oh my God, what have I done?"

"That's the best question I've heard in a while."

Maya turned toward the sound of her mother's voice. Vidalia had been sitting in a chair by the window, but she rose now. Her waist-long ebony curls were pulled around to one side in a ponytail that trailed down over her shoulder. She wore jeans that showed off a figure no woman her age ought to still have, and a denim blouse with flowers embroidered at the shoulders.

"Oh, Mom." Maya put her hand to her head and fell back on the pillows limply.

"You wanna tell me about it?"

Tears burned at the backs of her eyes, and she kept them squeezed tight. "I don't know what got into me."

She heard soft steps as her mother crossed the room, felt the shift of the mattress as Vidalia sat down on its edge. A comforting whiff of her mother's violet-scented talc reached her senses. As fresh as all outdoors. "Come on, sit up. Sip this," the soothing voice said, and a cool hand stroked her hair away from her face. "I had a feelin' you'd be sick this morning. As little as you touch the stuff, even a beer or two can make you sick."

Maya forced her eyes open and saw that her mother's other hand held a glass of what looked like tomato juice and smelled like the spice aisle at Gayle's Grocery. She grimaced, but she sipped. And when the tiniest relief seemed to coat her stomach, she sipped some more.

"Now I want you to stop beatin' yourself up over whatever happened last night," Vidalia said.

"You wouldn't say that if you *knew* what happened last night."

Her mother smiled. "Well, now, let me take a stab at it, hmm? You got the birthday blues. Lord knows, child, I've had 'em, too. They hit you any time you turn an age that ends in nine. Except for nineteen, of course, which doesn't count."

Maya frowned and lifted her head.

"Drink," her mother said. So she drank. And Vidalia went on. "Oh, people tend to think these crisis points hit us at the round numbers. Thirty, forty, fifty. But they don't. It's the dang nines. By the time you turn thirty, you'll have had a year to get used to the idea of turning thirty. But twenty-nine—well now, that's a shocker. All of a sudden you're looking at thirty seriously for the first time.''

Draining the glass, Maya set it aside.

"Better?" Vidalia asked.

"Stomach is. Head still aches though."

"Give it time to work. Old family remedies never fail. Now, where was I?"

"Trying to make me feel like I haven't done something horrible.''

"Oh, right." Again, Vidalia smiled. "So you had a couple of drinks last night. And a handsome cowboy came along, and you had a good time with him. It's not the end of the world, you know.''

Swallowing hard, lowering her gaze, Maya said, "I took him up to the falls, Mom. I…we…" She bit her lip. "God, what was I thinking?"

Stroking her hair, which was her specialty, Vidalia said, "You had sex with him?"

Maya nodded, feeling as guilty as a schoolgirl caught cheating on a final exam.

"Hon, you're twenty-nine years old. And sex is a celebration of life. It's acknowledging that you're not just a good, decent, upstanding, respectable person, but a woman. A real live red-blooded glorious woman. And that's okay. There's nothing wrong with that.''

Maya looked up, sniffling. "You really think so?"

"Of course I do. It's part of bein' alive. So long as you used protection, there's not a thing in the world wrong with a grown woman…" She let her voice trail off, probably because Maya's eyes had flown suddenly wider and her hand had clapped to her mouth. "Maya? Honey? You…you did use protection. Didn't you?"

Her mother pulled Maya's hand from her mouth. *"Didn't you?"* she repeated.

"I...I don't...know. I mean, it was dark, and I was..."

"You were what?"

Maya swallowed hard. "I was...drunk."

Vidalia blinked. "How drunk?" When Maya didn't answer, she slammed her hands to her thighs. "Maya, I'd have never let you leave with him if I thought you'd had more than a beer or two!"

"I just...wasn't thinking last night. God, Mom, I don't know if he used protection or not!"

Closing her eyes slowly, her mother sighed. "I think that's something you might want to find out, child."

Nodding hard, Maya got out of bed and looked down to see that she was still wearing the same clothes she'd had on last night. Her white blouse had mud stains here and there, and her jeans were wrinkled. But there was a new addition to her ensemble. Caleb's denim shirt. "I'll shower, and then I'll go talk to him. He's staying over at the boarding house." Then she paused, and a smile tugged at her lips. "He said he wanted to see me again."

Her mother bit her lip, saying nothing.

"I really like this man, Mom. I mean...he's not what I thought I wanted...not well-off or respectable or any of that...but there's something about him."

Sighing softly, Vidalia managed a smile that looked shaky. "Well now, that's nice, hon. That's real nice. You go shower now. Go on."

Nodding, Maya hurried into the bathroom.

She used the hair dryer, so her brown hair was bouncier and seemed thicker than usual. She wore a pastel blue dress with an A-line skirt and a tab collar. And she even added a hint of makeup, something she so seldom did that she had to borrow it from Selene's room. She looked in the mirror and nodded in approval. She looked perfect. Respectable. Good. Even pretty. If she had time, she thought, she would bake some cookies or something, but that would have to wait. Surely Caleb would be staying on for a little while. Even though she'd been drinking last night, she'd still felt something—something extraordinary—between them. He had to have felt it, too.

He had to.

She took the beat-up station wagon and drove into town, taking her time, humming a little along with the country song on the radio. Then she pulled into the tiny lot at the boarding house. And the first whisper of doubt crept along her spine when she didn't see his rusty pickup parked there.

Still, she got out and went through the front door to the big screened in front porch, and across that to the inner door, where she rang the bell.

Ida-May Peabody answered in a moment, greeting her with raised eyebrows. "Why, Maya Brand. Aren't you looking nice today! Whatever brings you here first thing in the morning?"

"A guest of yours…left something at the saloon last night," Maya said, holding up the shirt. "I've come by to return it."

Mrs. Peabody blinked. "But, hon, I've only got two folks staying here. Maddy Sumner's cousin, Lois, who's here for the wedding, and Ol' Hank."

She shook her head. "This man would have just checked in last night, late last night," she said. "Caleb Cain?"

The woman shook her head.

Fighting a rising sense of unease, Maya rushed on. "He's about so tall, dark hair, blue eyes, early thirties or so...." But Mrs. Peabody just kept on shaking her head from side to side, very slowly. "Are you *sure?*"

"Sorry, Maya. No one like that has been near the place."

Closing her eyes slowly, drawing a deep breath, Maya said, "Thanks, anyway, Mrs. Peabody. I must have misunderstood him. Sorry to have bothered you."

"No trouble, dear." Mrs. Peabody closed the door, and left Maya standing there, holding the stranger's shirt and feeling a little bit used. A little bit betrayed. And a whole lot disappointed.

"I have no one to blame but myself," she muttered, drumming up the will to turn and walk back to her car. She got in, tossed the shirt into the passenger side and told herself she shouldn't be crushed over this. She should chalk it up to experience, hope to God there would be no life-threatening or life-altering repercussions, and move on.

She should.

So why did she have the feeling that wasn't going to be as easy as it ought to be?

Three weeks later, her mother dragged her to an appointment with Dr. Sheila Stone, an ob-gyn in the nearby town of Tucker Lake. And while she knew these things were necessary, Maya hated every second of it all the same. Still, the doctor—a stern, handsome redhead with close-cropped hair and wire-rim glasses—took blood and urine samples, and subjected Maya to a thorough exam and a handful of advice.

"I assume you realize the chance you took by having casual sex with a man you didn't know," Dr. Stone said. "I'm not here to lecture you on morality or even stupidity, Maya. But for the love of God, use a condom next time."

"I told you, I was drinking. This is totally out of character for me, and it won't happen again."

Her face softening, Dr. Stone nodded. "We all do dumb things sometimes, I suppose. Are you worried?"

"Shouldn't I be? Wouldn't you be, Dr. Stone?"

"Yes, I guess I would. And my patients call me Dr. Sheila."

"I don't plan to be one of your patients," Maya said. "This is a one-time visit."

Removing her gloves, Dr. Sheila went to the sink to wash her hands. "Actually, Maya, the truth is you're going to have to come back a few more times."

Maya blinked. "I am?"

"I'm afraid so." She tugged paper towels, wiped her hands dry. "Certain venereal diseases or pregnancy should show up right away, of course. But for HIV…well, you're going to have be tested again in six weeks, and after that in six months, and after that—"

Maya held up a hand. "This is insane."

"That's what I try to tell people. It *is* insane—especially when a ninety-nine-cent item in a foil wrapper would prevent all the worry. Well, most of it, anyway."

Sighing, Maya said, "What if I can find the man?"

The doctor shrugged. "Well, *if* he were willing to be tested, and *if* his test came back clean, and *if* he was the only person you'd had sexual contact with—then we could rest assured you hadn't contracted the virus."

Maya drew a deep breath, held it a long moment, and sighed. "Then I suppose I should swallow my pride and contact him."

"I suppose you should." Turning, she walked to the counter and glanced down at the urine sample to which she'd added chemicals. She was very still for a moment.

"Dr. Sheila?" Maya asked, sliding off the table to pull

on her jeans and button them. "What is it? Is something wrong?"

Turning, the woman looked at her. "We're going to need to confirm this with the blood work, Maya...but, um...according to this...you're pregnant."

Maya stopped moving. She was standing there with a paper gown on top and a pair of jeans on the bottom, in her sock feet, and this woman was saying something in a foreign language. It made no sense. It did not translate. It was not comprehensible.

Dr. Sheila came forward and gripped Maya's arms. Gently she led her to a chair and eased her into it. "Are you okay?"

Blinking against the shock, Maya tried to talk, but all that came out was a whisper, and it wasn't what she'd planned to say at all.

"I want my mother," she rasped.

"I'll get her."

Caleb spent several tense days at his father's bedside, racked with guilt over having been out of town when his dad needed him most. But he was back home now. And if this episode had taught him anything, it was that you couldn't run away from your duty. Your heritage. Your responsibilities. He was expected to play a certain role in life, and he damn well would.

Running away in search of something simpler, something better, had only brought on disaster. And the pipe dreams he'd been indulging in that night? About settling down, about setting up a law office in a little one-horse town. About living there in a farmhouse with vines up one side, and a big dog, and maybe a duck pond in back. About marrying a daisy-fresh wife who had freckles on the bridge of her nose and looked great in blue jeans. They were just that—pipe dreams.

It was just as well this had happened when it had, if it had to happen at all. Before he did something foolish. Before he forgot who he was.

Still, every now and then he would find himself staring out at a rainy night sky and remembering…thinking again about that incredible woman he'd met and the night they'd spent together. Maya Brand. Even her name was one of a kind.

Had she been disappointed to find him gone the next morning? Or just angry? He wondered if he'd hurt her— and hoped he hadn't. A little voice told him he knew damn well he'd hurt her. It had been her first time. Women took things like that to heart. Still, she would be fine, a woman like that. Smart, capable. Surrounded by family. She would be just fine. And sooner or later she would find a man far better for her than he was. Far better.

It was good he'd had to come home, before things got too complicated between them. As it turned out, it had been just a brief interlude. One night of…

What?

That was what bugged him. Try as he might, he couldn't quite think of that time with Maya as a one-night stand or a meaningless sexual encounter between two consenting adults. He couldn't.

Maybe someday he would go back there and…

But no. No. It wasn't meant to be. He had to be here, taking care of his father's interests. Setting his own future into motion. She had to be there, in that little town, with her sisters and her mom. He would probably forget her soon. She would forget him, too.

It was for the best.

Damn, why did that sound like such a lie?

* * *

Maya spent the next five weeks just trying to absorb the unavoidable facts. First, that she was pregnant, unmarried and destined to become the most scandalous member of her notorious family. All she'd worked for—the image she'd tried so hard to cultivate as the respectable one, the responsible one, the sane one—all of that was gone—or would be the second word got around town about her condition.

The second fact staring her in the face became cruelly obvious when Mel insisted on trying to locate Caleb Cain of Tulsa to tell him that he was going to be a father. There was no such person. He'd lied to her.

So there it was. And she wallowed in it for those first five weeks, and even for a while after that. She stopped going out, stopped helping at the saloon. She stopped dressing, for the most part. Spent her days in sweats or her nightgown. In the mornings she was too ill to feel like dressing, and in the afternoon, she figured, why bother? She did all her usual domestic tasks, which gave her some comfort. Baking cookies and bread. *Eating* cookies and bread. Sewing and quilting and knitting. But, for the most part, she moped.

Until one bright, sunny morning on the first day of June, when Vidalia marched through Maya's bedroom door, flicked on the bright overhead light and said, ''Time's up, daughter. Now get out of that rocking chair, get a smile on that face and put some clothes on.''

Looking up, her knitting in her hand, Maya blinked in the light. She liked it dim. Dark. It was easier to dwell on her ruined life that way. ''Leave me alone, Mom.''

''I will not leave you alone.'' Vidalia went to the closet, flipped hangers until she found a sunny yellow dress, then tossed it onto the bed. ''I've left you alone for long enough already. Thought I'd give you time to absorb this. And like I said, that time's up.''

She walked to the rocking chair, took the knitting from Maya's hands and placed it in the basket on the floor. ''No more feeling sorry for yourself, girl.''

''What would you suggest I do instead?''

''Get up on your feet and act like the daughter I raised instead of some watercolor wimp. You're a Brand, Maya. And you've been given a gift more precious than any other you'll ever know. A child. You should be down on your knees giving thanks, not pouting as if you've been cursed. You want my granddaughter to think she's unwanted? Hmm?''

''How do you know it's a girl?'' Maya asked.

Her mother drew her brows together tight and tipped her head to one side, giving Maya the look that said she'd asked a foolish question. Then she gripped Maya's arms and drew her to her feet. ''Come on. In the shower. If I can handle five of you all by myself, you can certainly deal with one when you've got all of us to help you.''

''I know that.''

''Then act like it. You don't need any man to get through life, daughter. You're all you need. *You.*'' She poked Maya's chest. ''And her,'' she said, laying a gentle hand on Maya's belly. ''That's all. Your sisters and I are an added bonus. Now march in there and shower, then dress and get your tail down to the saloon. Wound-lickin' time is over.''

Her mother was right, Maya realized. She had been wallowing in a nice thick mire of self-pity. She'd been lied to, used and left behind. She was pregnant and alone and scared to death, and everything she'd ever wanted out of life suddenly seemed impossible.

But it wasn't. Not really. She could bounce back from this. Somehow.

She pressed her palms to her belly. There was the baby to think about now. What kind of a mother would she be? Depressed, moody, sullen all the time? Or alive and loving and happy?

Sighing, she looked down. "Your grandma's right, little one. Mamma's all through sulking now. Promise."

Vidalia nodded in approval. "Good girl." She left Maya to get her act together.

So Maya showered, and she dressed. She was glad her mother had chosen the sunny yellow dress, rather than something snug fitting, because she felt as if her belly was already beginning to swell just a bit. Her mother insisted that was all in her imagination, but she felt it all the same.

There was a tap at the door, and Maya turned, yellow dress in place, hair still bundled in a towel. Selene stepped in, grabbed her hand and pulled her into the hall. "You've gotta see this!" she said.

"Slow down. Selene! What's going on?"

But Selene ran, tugging Maya behind her, down the hall, into her own room. Then she stopped and pointed at the little table in the corner. It was covered in odd items, that table. Shells, rocks, candles. And, right now, those tarot cards Selene was always playing with. Two of them lay face up on the table.

Maya eyed the cards, because Selene seemed so excited about something, but they made little sense to her. One looked like a clown juggling, and the other was a nude woman with some sort of baton in each hand.

"So?" Maya asked, looking at Selene.

"Maya! You're having twins!"

Maya tried not to laugh, she really did. But it escaped her anyway, in a big gust, when she couldn't hold it in any longer. She held her belly, and snorted and roared so hard her sides hurt. So hard her eyes watered.

"This isn't funny!" Selene said. "I'm telling you, it's twins, Maya. Look at the cards!"

Maya glanced at them again, still trembling with laughter, but neither card had any babies on it, much less two of them. She got her laughter under control, gave her sister a gentle hug and said, "I love you, you flaky little weirdo. Twins." And, laughing some more, she went back to her own room; then, grabbing her shoes, she headed downstairs.

It was good to have a family, even an oddball crew like this—or *especially* an oddball crew like this. She'd needed a good laugh to snap her out of her well of misery. It was time to take charge of her life again.

She needed things. Baby furniture and clothes, a bigger vehicle, just for starters. She needed to get a nursery ready in this old house. There was so much to be done. So many plans to make.

For the first time she began to allow herself to get a little bit excited about the notion of being a mother. And the image her mother had painted for her, of another little girl in the family, warmed her inside. She missed having little girls running around this old house. She'd been a second mom to her sisters, being the oldest of them.

And now maybe she would have a little girl of her own.

Man, one thing was for sure, this baby would be the most spoiled child in seven counties if Maya's sisters and mother had anything to say about things. The most protected, too. And the most loved.

She smiled, shaking her head yet again at Selene and her silly notions. But between the two of them, Vidalia and Selene had managed to snap her out of her state of melancholia. There was so much to be done! She'd wasted far too much time already.

Chapter 5

Eight and a half months later...

Sighing, Maya walked, belly first, to the kitchen window, parted the red-checked curtains and stared out at the snowdrifts and blinding white sky. It was crispy cold outside. In here it was warm and fragrant. She had molasses cookies baking in the oven, a nice stew in the slow cooker. No husband to cook for—not that she needed one. No children. Yet. She really was going to be a fantastic mother, she thought, pressing her palms to her expanded belly. And as long as she lived, she would never, ever do anything to embarrass her children. Not ever. And eventually she would prove to this town that a woman could be a single mother *and* an upstanding citizen. They would accept her into that exclusive club of the respectable and socially acceptable. They *would*.

The back door opened, admitting a rush of frigid wind

and bundled bodies. Vidalia stomped the snow off her boots, and whipped off her red-and-white striped scarf and matching hat, an act that set the mass of jet black curls free. She was far too old, Maya thought, to keep her hair so long. Much less dress the way she did. Then again, her mother wasn't old. Not even fifty yet. Vidalia's coat came off, revealing skintight designer jeans and a black spandex top. She kept herself in great shape for a woman her age. She had every right to be proud of her looks. If only she wasn't so determined to be loyal to the memory of her long-dead husband, she might even find love again.

And if she said that out loud, her mother would probably smack her.

"Mmm, molasses cookies, Maya?" Vidalia asked, sniffing the air. "Hot damn, they smell better than a hard man on a hot day."

"Mother."

Vidalia shrugged and sent her a wink, her black eyes sparkling. "Still miserable, I see. Just checking."

"I'm not miserable. I'm tired, and my back is killing me, and I keep getting horrible leg cramps that make me want to claw the flowers off the wallpaper, but I am not the least bit miserable." Maya went to the oven, opened it and bent to check the cookies, but couldn't bend very far. Sighing, she gave up and reached for a pot holder.

"Let me get them," Kara said, hurrying off with her coat and coming forward. Towering over them all at five-eleven, she snatched the pot holders from Maya in spite of Maya's protests. Kara was too tall for her own good, and her feet were too big, and she was always tripping over them. Kara the Klutz was the nickname bandied around town, but never in front of her sisters—at least, not since the time Mel had overheard it and left the unfortunate speaker with a bloody nose and a split lip.

"Really, Kara, I can manage," Maya said.

"You should be sitting down with your feet up," her sister argued.

"Kara's right, hon." Vidalia took Maya's arm, and urged her toward a chair. And Maya could only look grimly back at the damp coats hanging on the peg near the door, snowy boots dripping all over the mat underneath them, and then at Kara and whatever mess would come next. With a sigh of resignation, she sat down as her mother instructed, even as Kara got the tray of cookies out, burned her finger, tripped over her foot and sent cookies flying everywhere.

Vidalia pressed her lips together to keep from saying a word, as poor Kara stared helplessly at the cookies falling to the floor. Then she tossed the cookie sheet toward the sink, turned and ran gracelessly out of the room. Maya heard her feet pounding up the stairs.

She looked at the mess, then at her mother. "What's wrong with her? She usually laughs it off when she does stuff like that."

"Kara had a bad day, hon. Or…her latest beau did anyway." She clicked her tongue. "Poor Billy."

"Oh, no." Maya closed her eyes. "What happened to this one?"

"Bus hit him when he was crossing the street." Vidalia bent to begin picking up the fallen cookies. Her jeans were so tight Maya was amazed the woman could bend at all, but that was her mother. She was nothing if not flexible. "Billy was blaming it on the snowy roads until one of those damned nurses over at General started telling him about Peter and Mike. By the time Kara got to the hospital to see him, he was showing distinct signs of cooling toward her."

Maya started to get up, but her mother held up a hand

to stop her, so she settled back in the chair. "So you think he's going to dump her?"

"He dumped her before they even finished his CAT scan."

Maya's lips thinned. "Coward."

"Darn straight."

"How bad did he get hurt?" Maya asked.

Vidalia shrugged. "No worse than he deserved. And not nearly as bad as Peter or Mike did. Couple of busted ribs and a few stitches where his head hit the pavement. But it's Kara I'm worried about." Dumping the cookies into the wastebasket, she brushed off her hands, set the cookie sheet down and turned off the oven. Then, turning, she leaned back against the counter, folded her arms over her chest. "But she'll be all right. She's a Brand, and my daughter. Now, how about you, Maya? Any twinges today? Any signs?"

She might be notorious and outrageous and tactless, but Vidalia Brand loved her daughters, Maya thought, smiling inwardly. "Not a one," she said. "These babies seem determined to stay right where they are."

"Well, hon, you're gonna have to stop letting them hear the weather reports out here! I don't blame them for wanting to stay put!" As she spoke, Vidalia came away from the counter. She pulled a chair into position, then lifted Maya's feet onto it. "And speakin' of babies, where's mine?"

"Selene is upstairs in her bedroom doing...whatever it is she does up there. I smelled some godawful incense burning, and she was playing that drum of hers, so I didn't bother her. But tell her when she comes down that those cookies are completely vegan-friendly." Her mother looked at the wastebasket and cocked her brows.

"Not those cookies, Mom. The ones in the cookie jar. I've been baking all afternoon."

"Oh." Then her mother looked at her. "Why?"

Maya shrugged. "Resting all the time makes me tired."

Vidalia grinned. "You sure do look tired now."

"I am. I'm bushed."

"Well, you go on now and have a nap. I'll get dinner, and Mel will be along any time now to help me. Go on. You know I won't take no for an answer."

"I wasn't going to give you no for an answer." Maya put her feet down and got out of the chair, belly leading the way. One hand immediately went to the small of her back, but she took it away to give her notorious mother a hug. "Thanks, Mom. And as for dinner, it's already made. In the slow cooker."

Her mother released her and hurried to the pot to remove the lid and sniff the steam. "Girl, you ought to be cooking in Paree."

"Yeah. I hear they love stew and biscuits in Paris, Mom." She sent her mother a wink and a smile, then headed through the large living room and on up the stairs. In the hallway she passed her youngest sister's room and smelled the familiar herbal scents coming from beyond the door. The door itself had Selene's idea of a Do Not Disturb sign hanging from it. It read Out Of Body, Back In Five Minutes.

She walked slowly down the hall, past the next door, which bore a sign that used to be funny but today seemed to sting: "Enter at your own risk." Maya heard Kara's voice coming from inside her room. She was speaking to someone, probably on the telephone, so she didn't bother her, either. She secretly hoped the injured Billy had changed his mind about breaking things off.

Shaking her head slowly, Maya finished the trek to her

own bedroom and went inside. It was actually a two-room suite, the largest in the house. It was the master bedroom and had been her mother's, but Vidalia had insisted Maya take it so there would be room for the babies.

Already, there were two cribs flanking her own bed. They were in the process of finishing up the adjoining room, which would serve as a nursery. Wallpaper with baby ducks and chicks already lined the walls, but the linoleum floor wasn't quite finished. Carpeting, in a baby's room, Vidalia had decreed, would have been about as practical as whitewash in a chicken coop. Tiles could be washed daily if needed—and it would be, she promised. So Maya had reluctantly agreed.

Maya ran a hand over the smooth rail of one of the old cribs. Both of them had been in storage in the attic. Vidalia's five girls had been born little more than a year apart, one from the other, so she'd needed more than one crib at a time. And she'd kept everything. Growing up, Maya's mother had been very poor. The daughter of migrant workers from Mexico, she'd been named for the crop they were harvesting on the day she was born. And it was a name that suited her, because she had the thick, tough skin and sharp bite of an onion when she needed it. Damn good thing, too. It hadn't been easy, raising five daughters alone.

It was not a path Maya had ever thought she would follow. But as it turned out...

Hell. She'd never meant for it to turn out like this. Sighing, she lay down on her bed, pulled a cozy fleece blanket around her and rested her head on the pillows.

Maya opened her eyes when something tickled her face some time later.

A stuffed bunny with yarn eyes stared at her. She

looked past it and saw dark, impish Mel, curled up on the other side of the bed, also staring at her. "You okay?" she asked.

"Why does everyone keep asking me that?" Maya sat up in the bed, picked up the pink terry cloth bunny and squeezed it. It was so soft you couldn't help but squeeze it.

Mel sat up, too, her short, black hair not even messed from the pillows. "Oh, I don't know. Maybe because you're eight and a half months pregnant with twins." She reached behind her, and pulled out another terry bunny, this one blue. "I picked these up in town today. Couldn't resist."

Maya smiled. She couldn't help but smile. "I should assume you're backing Selene's prediction that the newest Brands are a girl and a boy?"

Mel shrugged. "Have you ever known Selene to be wrong about anything?"

Thinking of that long ago night, when her spooky kid sister had told her that Caleb was her soul mate, Maya said, "Yes, actually. I have."

"Well, not often enough so you'd notice it," Mel said. She frowned down at her sister. "This isn't working out the way you had it planned, is it, Maya?"

She only shrugged.

"Hell, if I ever see that no-account phony cowboy again, I'll break his arms off and use 'em to cave his head in."

"Don't worry, sis. You aren't very likely to see him again."

Mel averted her eyes. And Maya knew—she just knew—that Mel had learned something. "What is it?"

"Nothing."

Sitting up, Maya held her sister's gaze. "Don't you

know better than to test the patience of a woman as pregnant as I am?''

Licking her lips, Mel finally looked down, and sighed. ''You have a right to know. I just…didn't want to have to be the one to tell you.''

''To tell me what?''

Mel got up off the bed and reached into her sweater pocket, pulling out a folded-up newspaper. She opened it, turned it and laid it on the bed facing Maya.

Maya looked, and the babies kicked her so hard she gasped. A grainy black-and-white photo of Caleb Cain stared back at her from the page. And the caption read Will He, Or Won't He?

Blinking back tears of surprise at seeing that face again…at seeing it on the body of a man dressed in an expensive designer suit and tie, with his hair all slicked back, and no battered hat in sight, Maya read the words underneath out loud.

'''Cain Caleb Montgomery III, former mayor of Springville, is still refusing to say whether or not he plans to enter the race for the U.S. Senate, though political insiders say it's only a matter of time before Montgomery makes the formal announcement declaring his candidacy. If that's true, he'll be following in the footsteps of his father and grandfather before him. There is no doubt, that should he enter the race, campaign finances will be the least of his worries. Montgomery is ranked the third richest man in the United States. But just where does he stand on the issues?'''

Mel took the newspaper out of Maya's hands. ''Come on, Maya. Do you really care where he stands on the issues?''

Maya closed her eyes. ''I can't believe this. He let me think he was a penniless drifter.''

"Well of course he did. He didn't want you coming back to haunt him later. Now that we know who he is, however, he's got some explaining to do. When I see him, I—"

"God, no! Mel, you wouldn't. You won't, I won't let you!"

Mel went silent and blinked down at Maya. "Well, gosh, sis, you have to tell him...."

"No, I don't. I'm a Brand, and I don't have to do a damned thing I don't want to. And I don't want to tell him about these babies."

Frowning until her brows touched, Mel said, "But why?"

"My God, Mel, can't you see what would happen? I'd be the biggest tabloid target since Paula or Jennifer or Monica, for God's sake! The man's going to run for the Senate! No. No, if I thought the scandal of being an un-wed mother was bad, it's nothing compared to the scandal of being at the center of a sex and politics story. Forget about it...and for God's sake, don't tell Mom."

"Don't tell Mom what?"

They both turned to see Vidalia stepping into the bedroom. She had a newspaper in her hand. "You wouldn't mean this, by any chance, would you?" she asked, holding it up.

Maya sighed. "Mom, I don't want to be dragged out and flogged by the press. I don't want my babies born in a flurry of political scandal and tabloid gossip. I won't have it."

"I don't blame you."

Maya met her mother's eyes. "Then you...you agree with me?"

"Oh, sure, hon. But that doesn't mean the man doesn't have a right to know he's going to be a father."

Pressing her lips tight, Maya shook her head. "I...kind of thought he gave up that right when he lied about his name and skipped town without a word," she said. She met her mother's eyes. "These are my babies. Not his."

Her mother held her gaze for a long moment, and Maya knew she didn't approve. She might make a lot of tacky, off-color remarks and come off as an irreverent, outrageous woman old enough to know better—but the truth was, her mother's moral code ran deep. Finally, though, Vidalia heaved a sigh and said, "I guess I've got no choice but to let you make this decision for yourself. You're an adult. Soon to be a mamma yourself. I think you're making a mistake, daughter, but that's your right. So we'll do this your way."

Maya sighed in relief. "Thank you."

Vidalia nodded and glanced at Mel. "Agreed?" she asked.

"No. Someone ought to contact that man and make him face his responsibility."

"Mel, it's not your place—"

"I'm the babies' aunt," she said. "Anyone who wants to hurt them or slight them is gonna have to go through me to do it. Why should they be sleeping in...in twenty-year-old cribs or riding in that used minivan Maya bought, while their father sleeps in a mansion and drives around in a limo or something! It's not fair to the babies."

Maya eyed her sister. "We got by just fine without mansions or limousines, Mel. My babies will, too."

Mel pitched the newspaper onto the floor and stomped out of the room. And while Maya looked after her worriedly, Vidalia only sighed. "Give her some time. She's always seen herself as the protector of the family. She'll cool down in a day or two."

"I hope so," Maya said. But deep down, she wasn't so sure.

Chapter 6

Caleb sat in his father's office, in his father's chair, trying to keep the most prestigious law firm in Oklahoma up and running while his dad slowly made his peace with retirement. But despite the weight of the job, not to mention the decision hanging over his head, or the nip of winter in the air outside, his mind was far away....

It was in a little town in springtime. By a waterfall. With a girl named Maya Brand.

Hell, it had been months. He should have forgotten about her, about that night, long before now. She certainly must have forgotten about him. Then again, he wouldn't know if she hadn't. He'd lied about his name that night. She had no clue who he was. Hell, she'd been worried about him having enough cash for the boarding house, as he recalled.

He sighed deeply. That had been real, that night with Maya. He hadn't spent a real, genuine night with a woman since. He'd been trying, with his frequent jaunts to political functions and state events. But mostly, the women who were on his arm were after something. Prestige, standing, power. Money. Usually money. They were phony, done up, made up, cinched up, dressed up, surgically enhanced, and polished to the point where the genuine parts were too well hidden to detect.

Maya hadn't wanted anything from him. She didn't think he had anything to offer. But she'd liked him anyway. She'd liked him enough to want to spend the night in his arms. It had been so honest, and so simple, and so incredible with her....

Hell, he had to stop thinking about that woman.

He glanced at the stack of memos and unopened mail on the desk, and began flipping through it to distract himself. The sight of a manila envelope with a Big Falls, Oklahoma, postmark caught his attention.

Odd.

He grabbed the envelope, tore it open and reached inside. Then he pulled out an 8 x 10 glossy photo of a woman who looked to be about eleven or twelve months pregnant. He smiled a bit at the sight of her belly, stretched to the size of a beach ball. His gaze moved slowly upward over the figure in the photo. She stood with one hand on the small of her back, a strand of mink brown hair hanging in her face, her eyes....

And then he froze. That face. Those eyes.

An expletive burst from him without warning.

His office door flew open, and Bobby McAllister, his ambitious right-hand man and future press secretary, should he decide he needed one, burst in, looking around with wide eyes. "What's wrong!"

Blinking slowly, licking his lips, his head spinning with disbelief, Caleb turned the photo over. There was one word on the back. *Congratulations.*

Caleb's throat went just as dry as desert sand. All this time…my God, she'd been alone, all this time….

"C.C., what is it?" Bobby asked again.

Caleb bit his lips. "Exactly how long has it been since April first?" he asked.

"April Fools' Day?"

Caleb almost moaned, but instead only nodded.

Bobby thought for three seconds, then said, "About…eight or nine months. Why?"

"*About* eight or nine months? I need to know *exactly*."

Blinking, Bobby whipped out his pocket calendar, flipped pages and said, "Thirty-seven weeks and two days."

"And how long does it take a woman to give birth?"

"Nine mo—"

"*Exactly* how long?" Caleb said, stopping Bobby before he finished speaking.

Swallowing hard, Bobby turned briskly and left the room. He came back a moment later. "Forty weeks is full term. Boss, why are you asking such odd questions? What's going on?"

He looked at Bobby. Bobby read the look, turned, closed the office door. When he turned back again, Caleb held up the photo. "Thirty-seven weeks and two days ago, I spent the night with this woman."

Bobby's eyes widened to the size of saucers. He strode forward, snatched the photo from Caleb's hand. "According to the date, this was taken the day before yesterday."

"I know."

Flipping it over, Bobby read the back. "This is…this is extortion! *Blackmail.* They can't get away with this!"

Frowning, Caleb said, "Who can't?"

"Jacobson, of course. Your only real opponent for the senatorial race."

"I haven't even declared myself a candidate yet."

"He knows the game. He knows that's just a formality. This is a pre-emptive strike. Who else would want to get this kind of dirt on you, Caleb?"

Caleb shrugged. Silently, he thought perhaps Bobby was taking his candidacy a bit too much for granted—especially now. But he didn't say that out loud. No sense sending the ambitious young genius into panic mode. "I don't think it's blackmail, because they don't ask for anything. And if it were Jacobson—well, I rather think this envelope would have been delivered to the press, not to me. Don't you think?"

"Well then...who is it? You think it's the woman?"

He shrugged. "Could be. I didn't think she knew who I was, but I suppose she could have found out." He sighed, lowering his head. It hurt, deeply, to think that Maya might have seen through his facade of being an unknown drifter. It had been so special to have someone be attracted to him for him, not for his name or his legacy. He gave himself a shake and went on. "Now she probably figures...I owe her. And I suppose she's right, at that."

"Oh, for crying out—are you saying you think this bull is true? You think you fathered this woman's child in *one night?* For God's sake, she was probably pregnant before you ever met her. She was probably looking for some rich scapegoat to pin it on."

He drew a deep breath, sighed. "No. No, I don't think so."

"Why the hell not?" Bobby was so upset his voice squeaked on the question. He tossed the photo down and awaited an answer.

"First, because she didn't have a clue who I was—"

"Or so she made you believe," Bobby interjected.

"And secondly, because she was…not that kind of girl."

Bobby stared at him as if he'd grown a second head. "Not that kind of girl. She was not that kind of girl? C.C., have you gone out of your mind here or what?"

"She was a virgin."

Bobby just blinked at him. Then he looked at the photo and blinked again. "But…she's…my age."

"I've got to go out there, Bobby."

Bobby's head came up, eyes wide. "Oh, no. No way. That's the worst thing you can possibly do right now."

"I'm going. Make something up. Cover for me. Say I'm sick with the flu and taking a few days off. Or better yet, say I needed some private time for the holidays. There's only a week until Christmas, so that sounds reasonable. Say anything you want, Bobby, but I have to go out there. I have to see her."

Bobby closed his eyes, shook his head. "If this leaks—"

"It won't."

Bobby groaned softly, hand going to his forehead as if to ward off a headache as he paced the office three times. Then, finally, he sighed and faced Caleb again. "Where will I be able to reach you?"

"It's a town called Big Falls," he said. "I'll call you when I get there and give you a phone number."

He tucked the photo back into its envelope, tucked it under his arm and started for the door.

"Boss?"

"Yeah?" he asked, turning.

"Don't let this woman play you for a fool."

He felt his lips pull into a bitter smile. "Don't you worry, Bobby. I'm a grown-up." But he didn't feel like one. He felt sick and queasy and lightheaded.

He left the office, taking the elevator to the basement parking garage and then driving back to the mansion. But the symptoms didn't ease up. His hands were shaking, for crying out loud! His palms were damp. He didn't know what the hell to think. He was so distracted that he drove the Lexus sports car right through two stop signs on the way home, and at the second one, he nearly got hit. He skidded to a stop in the driveway, ran straight up to his rooms and tugged a suitcase from underneath his bed. He whipped open the closet and stared in at the rows of expensive suits, the drawers full of designer shirts.

And then he thought to himself, what if she wasn't the one who sent that photo? What if she still didn't know who he was?

Okay, so it was wishful thinking. But it could happen, right? And if there was even a chance…

He thought about her eyes, the honesty in them. And how sincere she'd seemed when she'd talked about trying to be respectable, to get the town's elite to accept her. He'd believed her.

He still believed her. Damn, what must this pregnancy have done to all her efforts? He winced at the thought.

Slowly he reached for the bottom drawer and pulled out his entire collection of worn-out jeans—all three pairs. He put two in his suitcase and put one pair on. He dug for sweatshirts, found an old fleece-lined denim coat way in the back of his closet, and dug out that stupid battered cowboy hat, as well, for good measure. He wanted to see her as a man—not as a millionaire.

He finished his packing hastily, then carried the suitcase, coat and hat downstairs and set them on the floor near the back door, before forcibly slowing himself down, taking a few calming breaths.

He couldn't just walk out on his father without a word.

Look at what had happened last time. Stiffening his spine, he went to his father's study.

The wheelchair turned slowly when he entered the room. Cain didn't use it all the time—only when he was tired or stubborn. He could walk, though his uneven gait required the use of a cane. His stern face was more disturbing now, since the stroke. One side reflected his feelings—that side was looking decidedly pissed off just now—while the other side remained lax and limp.

His father lifted his good hand, and Caleb saw the photograph he was holding. He glanced quickly around the room, half expecting to see Bobby lurking in a corner somewhere, but there was no sign of him.

"No, it wasn't Bobby," Cain said, speaking from one side of his mouth, his words still slightly slurred. "But I did call him. Whoever sent this to you at the office wanted to be sure you got it. Sent a copy here, as well. And I'm glad they did. This is something I ought to know about, don't you think?"

"No. You don't need the stress of this—and I can deal with it. I'm about to deal with it."

"Sit down, son."

"Father, I've made my decision. I have to go out there, see for myself what's going on."

His father glared at him, and Caleb finally sat down. He didn't like upsetting the old man. He didn't want to set off another stroke, or worse. Mean as hell he might be, but he was also in a fragile state right now, though he would rather die than admit it.

"You were a twin, you know."

Caleb sighed, closing his eyes, wishing to God his father would deliver any other long practiced speech than this one. He *hated* this one.

"Your mother carried two of you. Two boys. One bigger, stronger, and the other small and weak. Cain and Abel. Only one of them born alive.'' He knuckled a button, moving his wheelchair closer. ''The doctors said it was just as well. One strong child was much better off than two weak ones. As it was, the stronger of the two survived. And that one was you.''

''Right.'' Caleb had never accepted this, and it was largely why he refused to go by the name Cain. But though he rejected it, hearing it dug deep. ''I've heard this story a hundred times, Father, and it has no more merit now than it ever did. Fetuses do not think or plot or conspire. I didn't kill off my weaker brother so I could survive, and the fact that I lived and he didn't is nothing more than genetics.''

''Garbage!'' his father said in a burst. ''You're my son. Your mother died giving birth to you. You carry my name. So you'll *always* do what you must to survive. You understand?''

He opened his mouth to argue, closed it again, and said nothing, getting up to leave.

''I was a twin, too, you know.''

Caleb, frowning, turned to stare at his father. ''No. I didn't know that. You never told me.''

''It never came up. My birth was just like yours, Caleb. The stronger twin survived, the weaker one didn't make it.'' He shook his head. ''It's genetics, yes, but it's also a marker, Caleb. A reminder that the strong survive, and that we, you and I, were destined for something more than ordinary men. And that sometimes sacrifice is necessary to keep the dream alive.''

''It was a quirk of fate. Not a sign from God,'' Caleb told him gently. ''Dad, you and your destiny had nothing to do with your twin dying. No more than I did with mine.''

Cain shook his head stubbornly. "Nothing can ruin a political career faster than a woman and a sex scandal, Caleb. Nothing. Now you take my advice. You pay this woman enough to keep her quiet, and then, later on, you get a DNA test done very quietly. If it's yours, you pay her some more. All it takes. Send her and the child away somewhere. But do it all through third parties. Send Bobby out there, or Martin and Jacob Levitz. They're your lawyers, that's what they're paid for. Just don't get personally involved in this."

Slowly, Caleb went to his father. Keeping his tone low, he said, "I'm *already* personally involved, Dad. It doesn't get much more personal than this. And I may be your son, but I'm my mother's son, too. God rest her soul. And I think she'd want me to do the right thing here."

His father's head came up, one eye snapping with anger, the other dull and glazed over. "She died so you could be born to carry on this family's proud tradition! She would want you to protect that legacy at any cost!"

Caleb smiled, leaned in and clasped his father's hand once, firmly. "If I have a child, won't he be a part of that legacy?" He sighed when his father didn't waver in the least. "I have to do what I think is right, Dad. I'll only be gone for a few days. You've got your nurse and the household staff, and if you need anything they can't handle, call Bobby."

Straightening, he turned and walked out of the room, even though his father's voice shouted after him all the way. He only stopped long enough to pick up his suitcase, and then he headed out.

Two hours later, tired and wary, Caleb pulled into the parking lot of the OK Corral, that saloon he remembered so well, in the middle of Big Falls, Oklahoma. He hadn't been here in the winter before. It was nothing like the city, and he couldn't help feel a little stirring of the senses as José's truck rolled over the narrow roads and in between hillsides that looked wild and ominous. They were almost bare of leaves, some of those trees. There was not a lot of snow yet. But the ground was thoroughly covered, and there had been a fresh inch or two overnight, coating everything like a powdered doughnut.

Pretty.

He wondered why there were no cars in the lot at the Saloon. Then he realized he had arrived in the middle of a Monday afternoon. The Corral likely didn't even open until nightfall.

Great. So how was he going to find Maya?

He looked up and down the road. Saw a few men in red-and-black flannel coats, and some in camouflage from head to toe, hurrying to their pickups with gun racks in the back windows and shotguns in the racks.

Hunting season. This was not the city. Here, if you were a man, you owned a gun and knew how to use it. And hunting season was the be all and end all of your holiday experience.

Swallowing hard, he got out of the truck and started on a path designed to intercept one burly hunter before he reached the front door of the ammo shop. He paused briefly to snap up the fleece and denim coat, and wondered if the thing looked redneck enough to get him by.

"Excuse me," he said, and he managed to draw the big guy's attention. Jowls and whiskers was the impression he got when the man faced him.

"You lost?" the stranger asked.

"Actually, I, uh…I'm looking for a place to get a room. I didn't see a hotel in town anywhere, so I thought…"

''We ain't got no *ho*-tel,'' the fellow said, putting the accent on the first syllable.

''That's what I thought when I didn't see one,'' he said. ''I seem to recall there was a boarding house last time I was here, but I've forgotten where, exactly.''

The fellow shrugged. ''Yep. There's a boardin' house, all right. You might could get a room there. But I don't know for sure.''

''Er…right. I might…could. If I knew where it was.'' The man just stared at him, chewing. ''Can you tell me how to get to the boarding house?'' he asked, figuring direct was the way to go here.

''End of the road, on yer left. 'Bout a mile up.'' He pointed.

''Thanks. Good luck with the hunting. I, uh, hope you catch a big one.''

''Catch one?'' The guy grinned almost ear to ear and strode away, shaking his head. ''He hopes I *catch* one,'' he muttered, chuckling to himself all the way into the shop.

Caleb stared after him, saw him speaking to the fellow at the counter, and then they both looked his way and laughed some more.

Hell. He was fitting in here in redneck land like a duck fit in a henhouse. He was going to have to do better than that.

He turned to go back toward the pickup and came face to face with a young woman with short black hair and dark eyes. For a moment they stared at each other as recognition clawed at his mind. And then it seemed to hit them both at once. She was one of Maya's sisters—he'd met her at the saloon that night.

Even as his mind grasped who she was, hers seemed

to identify him. Because her eyes went narrow and her lips thinned.

He thrust out a hand in greeting. She thrust out a fist in a right hook that caught him in the jaw and made lightning flash in his brain.

When he shook his brains back into order, he found himself on his butt in the snow, and she was revving the motor of a well-worn minivan and speeding away.

He rubbed his jaw. Hell, he hadn't expected a warm welcome, but he hadn't expected an ambush, either.

The question was, would Maya be as glad to see him as her sister had obviously been? Suddenly he was having second thoughts about finding out. Maybe he'd better try to get the lay of the land just a bit first—rather than waltzing right out to that cozy little farmhouse right away. Maybe it would be wise to make sure there wouldn't be armed infantrymen lining the driveway, with instructions to blow his head off first and ask questions later.

Swallowing hard, he nodded. To the boarding house...then he'd see.

Getting to his feet, he got back into his gardener's pickup truck and twisted the rearview mirror to get a look at his jaw.

Shoot. It was already starting to bruise.

Chapter 7

"Nothing yet?" Mel asked, occasionally rubbing her knuckles as the five of them sat down around the dinner table. Four sat in ordinary ladderback chairs. One had been prodded into the giant recliner someone had hauled in from the living room. Maya sat there, feet up, tray positioned to one side. It would have been in her lap, she supposed, if she still *had* a lap.

"No," Maya said with a scowl. "Nothing yet."

"That's okay, hon. Christmas is coming." Kara grinned, and there was a knowing twinkle in her eye. "Things are bound to get better."

"How are you feeling, Maya?" Selene asked.

"Like a beached whale. Why do you ask?"

Selene shrugged and smiled a secretive smile. "You'll feel better soon."

"I'll feel better when I have these babies," she snapped.

"Oh, come on, don't be so grouchy," Kara said. "This should be a cheerful time for you."

"She can be grouchy if she's of a mind to," Vidalia put in. "It's allowed the first few weeks and the last few weeks. And you have to admit, she's been a real trooper in between." Her mother smiled indulgently at her.

"You all just try carrying a couple bags of feed tied around your middle for a few months and tell me how cheerful you are."

Everyone went silent, and for a moment they just ate while the tension built. Maya's three sisters kept looking at their mother sort of…expectantly. Finally Maya picked up on those looks, and, narrowing her eyes, she said, "What's going on that I don't know about?"

Vidalia licked her lips. "Well, I don't suppose there's any point in waiting for you to be in a better mood to tell you this, is there?"

"Not unless it can wait until these kids are tucked in their cradles, there isn't," Maya said.

Vidalia lifted her dark, perfectly shaped brows. "Fine. Then I'll just tell you flat out. *That man* is back in town."

Her sizable stomach clenched—no small task. "What man?"

Her mother let her gaze slide down to Maya's belly and with a nod said, "*That* man. Ida-May Peabody called. She said he showed up this afternoon, got himself a room at her boarding house."

"Ohmygod."

"Watch your mouth, young lady," Vidalia scolded.

"Mother, really," Selene said. "You say more off-color things than anyone."

"But I do not take the Lord's name in vain, nor will I tolerate anyone else doin' so."

Maya was pushing her tray away and struggling uselessly to get out of the chair. And Selene, the silver sister said, "Hon, it was inevitable, him coming back here. And besides, it's for the best that he came back. He has a right to know that he's going to be a father, don't you think?"

"Right? What right? Geez, Selene, he didn't even give me his real name!" She pulled herself partway up, then fell back again. "Will someone get me the hell out of this chair!"

"Your language, Maya," Vidalia scolded.

Kara shot to her feet and hurried to her sister's aid, gripping her arms and tugging. She was really leaning into it, too, Maya thought.

"Well, I couldn't care less about his rights," Mel put in, rubbing her knuckles again. "But he does have some responsibilities here, and if you're smart, you'll make sure he lives up to them. You'll feel much better with someone else shouldering part of the financial burden, if nothing else."

Kara tugged harder.

"I don't need any help from any man. You leave him alone, Mel!" The moment she said it there was a knock at the front door, about ten feet away from the dining room.

Kara gave one last yank, and the chair sort of thudded into its upright position, launching Maya out of it like a rocket. Kara screamed bloody murder, falling backward to the floor. Maya landed right on top of her like a sack of feed, and poor Kara's scream turned into a burst of air, driven from her lungs by the impact. The others flew to their feet and swarmed, and whoever had been at the front door flung it open and ran inside, no doubt alarmed by Kara's bloodcurdling scream.

"Good God, are you all right?" a man's voice said.

"Watch your mouth, young man," Vidalia scolded.

But Maya barely heard her mother's disapproving tone. Not when that voice had sounded vaguely familiar. Not when she focused her vision to see those scuffed up and battered boots a foot away. And certainly not when two very strong hands closed on her shoulders and gently eased her off her sister, rolling her carefully until she was sitting on the floor, bent knees up and in front of her as if she were getting ready to give birth. Then he crouched in front of her, gripped her underneath her arms and easily got her up to her feet.

She looked up—right into those blue eyes that had melted her resolve nine months ago, minus a couple of weeks. And in spite of herself, the blood rushed to her cheeks and heated them.

"Hello again, Maya Brand," he said.

"Um…hi." Self-consciously, she reached up to straighten her hair. Then she realized what a wasted effort that was. He was *not* going to notice what her *hair* looked like.

"You okay?"

Her lips thinned. "Fine." She glanced down at Kara. "The more pertinent concern here is, have I flattened my poor sister?"

Kara was already picking her gangly self up off the floor. "It's my fault," she said. "I'm such a klutz."

"I'm sure that's an exaggeration," Caleb said, finally letting go of Maya long enough to reach out, giving Kara a hand up. "A pretty girl like you could never be referred to as a klutz. You look more like a swan."

Kara smiled and lowered her head, blushing furiously.

Selene launched into a "your body believes what your mind thinks" speech. But Maya ignored her. Because Caleb was turning back to her now, and his hands were curling around her shoulders, and his eyes were staring into hers. For a few seconds, anyway. But then they moved, skimming down her body, reaching her belly and widening just slightly. He didn't say "Holy cow," but she heard it anyway.

"Guess I've put on a little weight since you saw me last," she said.

"Uh…yeah, a little bit." He couldn't seem to take his eyes off her belly. So she put a finger under his chin and tipped his head upward until he met her eyes again, at which point he said, "We've got some talking to do, don't you think?"

Drawing a breath, she sighed and looked away. "You don't need to look like that, Caleb. I don't want anything from you, I promise."

He lifted his brows, even as Mel's hand came down on Caleb's shoulder from behind. He turned at her tug, facing her. "Well, hello again," he said. "Mel, isn't it? Sorry we didn't get more time to talk this morning."

"This morning?" Maya asked. She saw Caleb rub his jaw, saw the slightly bruised skin there, saw Mel's knuckles all red, and said, "Mel, what did you do to him?"

Mel ignored her, her narrowed eyes on Caleb. "Maya may not want any help with this, mister, but you can bet your—"

"Melusine," Vidalia said, cutting her off. "This is between your sister and this fellow! You stay out of it until I tell you otherwise." Then she moved forward, walked up to Caleb, who turned again, facing her this time. And she smiled and said, "But believe me, mister, if I think you're not treating my daughter right, I *will* tell her otherwise."

Kara cleared her throat. "You really don't want to mess with Mom and Mel," she said.

"You all sound like a gang of thugs," Selene said,

getting to her feet. ''Whatever is meant to happen between these two is going to happen, no matter what you all do or say or threaten. So why don't you just get out of the way and let it?''

Blinking, giving his head a shake, Caleb drew a breath as if about to respond to one or all of them. Then, instead, he just closed his mouth, turned and faced Maya. ''Can we *please* talk? Alone?''

She nodded. ''We can go—''

''To dinner,'' he said. ''I, um…made reservations.''

Lowering her head, Maya said, ''I'd really just as soon not be seen with you in public, Caleb. You have no idea how efficiently the rumor mill works around here.''

He nodded. ''I can guess. That's why I made the reservation in Tucker Lake.''

Tucker Lake, the next town over. He had thought this through, then, hadn't he? Maya pursed her lips. ''Okay. Sure. I never touched a bite of this anyway.''

''Are you sure you should be riding that far, hon? You're carrying—''

''I'll be fine, Mom.''

Her mother frowned, but nodded. ''Guess you know best, not having ever given birth before. I wouldn't presume to advise you, just because I've been through it *five times over*.''

Selene met Kara's eyes, and they both shook their heads. Mel stood beside her mother as if in full support of her opinion on the matter.

Maya glanced down at her clothes. She wore a pair of pseudo-jeans, big enough for all four of her sisters, held up with a drawstring, and a smock top that looked, in her opinion, like a Christmas tree skirt.

''I was going to say I'd change first, but I basically look the same in any of the assortment of tents in my closet, so it would be pretty much useless. Let's just go, shall we?''

"I'll get your coat," Selene said with a wink. She did so, not handing the heavy woolen coat to Maya, but to Caleb.

"Gee, you're so subtle it's scary," Maya said.

Selene sent her an innocent, wide-eyed look, while Caleb held her coat for her. She slid her arms in and didn't bother trying to button it. She could, but even this supersized coat was getting snug around the middle.

Taking her arm, Caleb drew her outside, down the steps. She glanced up at his pickup truck, made a face and said, "Listen, I don't know how much you know about pregnant women but—"

"Nothing," he said. "Nothing at all."

She nodded. "Bumpy rides have been known to induce labor. And your truck there doesn't look all that...gentle." Turning, she looked up at him. "I don't want to offend you here, but would you mind terribly if we took my van instead?"

"Hey, no offense taken."

She nodded and led him across to the old barn, some fifty yards away from the house, which served as a garage. It kept the snow off the vehicles in the winter, anyway. He held her arm the whole way. She reached for the sliding door, but he stopped her with a shake of his head, opened it himself and stood looking at the three Brand family vehicles.

"It looks excessive, to someone like you, us having three vehicles." She watched him as she spoke, knowing to him three junkers like this probably seemed like living at poverty level and waiting for him to admit it. He didn't, damn him. So she just went on. "But even now, we're often short a vehicle. The pickup there is essential out here. And the Bronco sports utility of course, is for when the roads get really nasty. And then there's the minivan. I just bought it. Used, of course, but it's not in bad shape for what I paid. Figured I'd need a reliable vehicle of my own with these...er...with the baby coming.''

He nodded. "Good thinking." He escorted her to the passenger door and held out a hand. "Keys?"

"Oh, it's not locked. And the keys are in the ignition."

He lifted his brows but made no comment as he helped her into the van, then went around and got in behind the wheel. He started the engine and drove it out, then got out and went back to close the barn door.

As he drove out the driveway, he said, "You may have to help me find this place. I made the reservations over the phone and got the recommendation from Ida-May at the boarding house. It's a place called Spellini's. Do you know it?"

She lifted her brows and looked at him. "Are you sure you wouldn't rather just stop at a diner? I mean—looking at you, I would hardly think you could afford a highbrow place like Spellini's. There's Polly's Kitchen just off the highway. You can get a whole chicken dinner there for four ninety-five."

He watched her face carefully as she spoke, so much so that she wondered what he was looking for. Had he detected the edge of sarcasm in her tone? But then he sighed, almost in relief. "I've been working pretty steadily since we...I mean, well, you know. I've got some money set aside."

So he was still lying to her. Still willing to let her believe he was some poor drifter, rather than one of the wealthiest men in the state. Why? To protect his millions from his own children?

Drawing a breath, she sighed. It had been stupid to let

that hopeful little light flare up in her heart at the sight of him. Served her right.

So she still thought he was a penniless drifter.

Either that or she was a very good actress. Good. He would let her think it a bit longer. That way he could be sure her reactions to him were based on him, and nothing else.

He was pleasantly surprised when they got to the restaurant, a giant-sized log cabin with cathedral ceilings and full-length windows. The bottom floor was littered with tables, and stairs went up to the second floor, where tables lined the perimeter, behind rails. He did not think, however, that those stairs looked like anything he wanted to see Maya trying to climb tonight.

God, she looked so different. So…big. He didn't think he'd ever seen a pregnant woman this large before. But the changes went further than that. Her eyes looked… circled and tired. Not as sparkling or full of life as they had been before. Her face seemed drawn and tight, and he imagined her goal of trying to become accepted by the good folk of Big Falls had blown up in her face, as well. The conservative residents of small towns were not known for being big on unwed mothers.

A waitress greeted them, wearing a tiny black dress with a white apron. "Oh!" she exclaimed upon seeing Maya's condition. "Your first?"

Maya nodded.

The waitress smiled ear to ear and glanced up at Caleb. "You must be so excited. And you," she said, looking at Maya again. "You look as if you're due any day now."

"Yes," Maya said, at the same time that Caleb said, "Almost three more weeks."

Maya looked at him and frowned. The waitress only

laughed. "Sure, I understand! I've had three myself, and I always spent the last few weeks wishing it would happen and get over with."

Maya slowly drew her suddenly suspicious gaze away from Caleb's to look at the waitress. "You've had three? And you got your figure back?"

"Oh, honey, sure I did. You will, too, don't you worry. Now, come on, let's get you off your feet." She led them to a nice table with plenty of room on either side, in a rear corner, with huge windows on both walls.

Caleb took Maya's coat, held her chair, braced her arm as she eased herself into it. God, it must be hard carrying so much extra weight around. She wasn't a big woman to begin with.

"My goodness, he's good," the waitress said. "Does he give you backrubs at night, too, hon?" She sent Caleb a wink. "Believe me, her back has to be screaming by now."

"I believe it."

She took their drink orders at last and promised to hurry back with their menus. But the second she left the table, Maya speared him with those gem green eyes of hers, and said, "How did you know my due date? I didn't even think you knew I was pregnant."

He blinked, searched his mind. "What do you mean?"

"I mean, you just told that waitress I was due in just under three weeks."

"You told her any day now." He leaned forward on his elbows. "So which is it, Maya?"

She narrowed her eyes on him. "Both. Full term would be January sixth—just under three weeks from now. However, my doctor has no doubt I'm going to go early."

He blinked and felt a little bolt of alarm. "You

mean…the baby's going to be premature? Isn't that dangerous?''

The waitress came back with their drinks. Milk for Maya. Mineral water for Caleb. She handed them their menus, smiled brightly and hurried on her way.

Maya was still staring at him. ''It's not early enough to be any cause for alarm, Caleb. Actually, early deliveries are common in cases like mine.''

He frowned at her. ''And what kind of cases are those?''

''Caleb…we're getting off the subject here. You knew my due date right to the day. Now how did you find that out?''

He lowered his eyes. ''Forty weeks…from the night we spent together. I was just guessing.'' Lifting his gaze to hers again, he stared hard at her, watched her face. ''It *is* my child you're carrying. Isn't it, Maya?''

It was her turn to look away. ''No.''

''No?'' Shock washed through him like a splash of ice water in the face.

''No,'' she said. ''It's my child I'm carrying. Not yours. Not anyone's. Just mine. Do you understand that, Caleb?''

He felt that ice water come to a slow simmer. ''Hell, no, I don't understand that.''

''Well, then, let me see if I can explain it. You were a stranger, passing through town. We were a one-night stand. There was no relationship. No commitment. I got pregnant, Caleb. My problem. My situation. Not yours. You're still just a drifter passing through. There's nothing for you here.''

There was, he thought slowly, one hell of a lot more going on with this woman than met the eye. He resisted the urge to lose his temper. Not only because she was in a tender state, but because he sensed it would do him no good. "Maybe I need to rephrase my question?"

She shrugged.

"You were a virgin the night we made love," he said, keeping his voice low, leaning over the table.

Her cheeks went pinker, and she looked away from him, focused on the view outside. Rolling meadows and woodlands beyond.

"And according to the town gossips, you haven't so much as had lunch with a man since. Most of them are going out of their minds trying to figure out how you got pregnant, according to the very talkative Ida-May at the boarding house. Even though a few may have seen us that night, the idea of the untouchable Maya Brand indulging in a one-night stand with a stranger seems to be beyond the realm of possibility."

"It's really none of their damned business, though, is it?"

He let his smile come, even though he sensed she wouldn't like it. He liked her spunk. "One busybody I met in the general store even put forth the theory that you visited a sperm bank and were artificially inseminated."

"Oh, for the love of—"

He covered one of her hands with his own. "Please tell me the truth, Maya. Did I father this child you're carrying?"

Staring down at his hand on top of hers, she said, "Yes." Then, lifting her head slowly, "Now you tell me the truth about something. For once."

He frowned, wondering what the hell that implied. But he said only, "Okay."

"Why did you come back here?"

Ouch. That was not one he wanted to answer. But he'd promised her the truth, and she was damned well going to hear it. "I received a photograph of you taken just a couple of days ago. On the back there was one word. 'Congratulations.'"

She only stared at him steadily. No expression on her face. As if she were waiting for him to finish the story, or to deliver the punchline or something. But when he said nothing, she lifted her brows. "But...who... how...?" Then she drew a breath, and her eyes widened even further. "You thought I sent it, didn't you?"

He sighed deeply. "Hell, I didn't know what to think. But yeah, it did enter my mind that you might have sent it."

"Well. I guess we know where we stand, then, don't we?"

"No, frankly, I don't have a clue where we stand, Maya."

"Caleb, if I'd had any idea how to find you to tell you I was pregnant, I would have called or shown up in person. I wouldn't have sent some cryptic photo with a note on the back. God, what would be the point?"

Good question, he thought. What was the point?

"Listen...it doesn't matter who sent the photo—"

"Oh, it matters. Believe me, it matters. And I have my theories on that. But the point is, I didn't know how to find you. I tried, but there was no such person as Caleb Cain in Tulsa."

He licked his lips. "I...move around a lot."

"You lie a lot."

"Regardless, I'm here now."

"So what?"

He licked his lips. "Well, hell, Maya, I don't know. You're going to be the mother of my child. I guess I'd like to get to know you a little bit. And if you think I'm the kind of man who's going to let you take full responsibility for this all alone, you'd better think again. I'm going to take an equal share of the financial responsibility for this baby.''

She leaned a bit forward—not a lot, because there wasn't room between her belly and the table for a lot—and she said, ''In exchange for what? Partial custody? Or the whole enchilada? What do you want, Caleb?''

He held up both hands. ''Hey, hey, hold on now. Is that why you're so hostile? You think I came out here to try to take your baby away from you? To fight you for custody or something?''

She blinked rapidly. ''You'd have to kill me to do that, Caleb. Just so you know in advance. You'd have to kill me. And I don't care who your father is, or how many millions you have.'' Tears pooled in her eyes.

He was stunned into silence for a long moment. And then he drew a breath, sighed deeply. ''So you do know who I am.''

She nodded. ''I found out yesterday, when I saw your picture in the paper.''

Twenty-four hours before that photo arrived on my doorstep....

He shook himself. A tear managed to escape her glittering eye, and it rolled down her cheek. And all of the sudden, not only did he doubt she would try to blackmail him—he didn't care. Moreover, if she did, he wouldn't blame her. ''Dammit, I didn't come out here to upset you.'' Reaching across the table, he covered both her hands with his. ''Please don't cry.''

Too late. The tears were streaming. She snatched up a napkin and wiped angrily at them, even as the waitress came back to take their orders. He hoped to God this entire discussion hadn't ruined Maya Brand's appetite.

Slamming the napkin down on the table, Maya sniffled and said, "I want the T-bone. The big one. Rare."

"Mashed or fries?" the waitress asked.

"Both."

Smiling, the waitress scribbled and said, "Gravy or sour cream, hon?"

"Both."

"Anything on the side?"

"Yeah. The fried chicken." She closed her menu with a snap and handed it back to the waitress, who turned to Caleb, pen poised.

"Um...the salmon?" he ventured.

"Sure thing." She scribbled and turned to leave; then, turning back, she eyed Maya's half-empty glass. "More milk?"

Maya nodded. Her tears were gone now, and as soon as the waitress was gone, she face Caleb squarely. "I did not send you that photograph."

"That is becoming painfully obvious," he said. "Frankly, I don't even care who sent me the photo, Maya. If this baby is mine, I want to take responsibility. That's all."

"Then why did you lie about who you were?"

He lowered his head, shook it. "I...had my reasons. What difference does it make, Maya? You know the truth now."

She pressed her lips together. "Not that I trust anything that comes out of your mouth at this point, Caleb, but if you want to spend one more minute with me, I want you to swear you won't try to take my babies away from me. Swear on all you hold dear, Caleb, or leave right now."

"I swear. I'll put it in writing if you want me to. I can have my...wait a minute." He frowned then. "Wait just a minute. What did you just say?"

She bit her lower lip, averted her face.

"Maya, did you just say 'babies'?"

Slowly, she faced him. Then she drew a breath, blew it out again. "Hell, Caleb, you might as well know. I'm carrying two babies, not one."

"Two? Twins?"

She nodded. "That's why the doctor expects me to go early. Twins hardly ever go to term."

He just sat there, stunned to the bone. A deep tremor worked through him, and his gaze fell to her swollen belly. "Are they both...all right?" he said softly.

"If the way they kick is any indication, they're fine."

Those words only made his stomach clench up tighter as his father's words replayed in his mind. *The strong survive, the weak don't. It's our legacy, Caleb. And it's a reminder....*

"What...what does your doctor say? Do they have any way of knowing for sure that they're both...?"

He saw her face then, clouding with worry. And he decided to shut up. She was going through enough without him saying things that would scare her to death. There was no reason to think... Hell, twins were born healthy every day. They were!

"I go in every week for a checkup," she told him. "They listen to the heartbeats, and we've done ultrasounds. These kids are huge, for twins. Over five pounds each already. And they're fine. They're Brands. They can't be anything less than fine."

"They're not just Brands, they're Montgomerys, too."

She shrugged. "So I suppose they'll have politics in their DNA?"

He smiled at her, liking her slightly lighter tone. "Maybe we should ask them to check for it when they do the blood tests."

Her expression changed. Lightness fled. Her eyes became…thunderous. He'd never used that term to describe a facial expression before. But it described hers now.

"A blood test? You…mean a paternity test, don't you? You want the babies to have a paternity test."

He blinked fast. "Well…isn't that pretty standard…I mean, in cases where the parents aren't married?"

"It's standard, all right. In cases where the mother is being called a liar." She glared at him. "Help me up."

"Oh, come on, Maya. I wasn't calling you a liar. I…you're…I…"

"Help me up *now*." She gripped the table and started to rise.

He leapt to her aid but found himself awkwardly unsure where to put his hands. He finally settled on gripping her forearms and pulling, even as he tried to fast-talk his way out of the slam he'd inadvertently delivered. "Please don't leave. Have dinner, come on. You're overreacting to everything I say here."

"I'm not overreacting. And I'm not leaving," she said, once she was upright.

He frowned. "Then…where are you going?"

Tilting her head to one side, she said, "Caleb, there are two hefty babies writhing around on top of my bladder right now. Where do you *think* I'm going?"

"Oh. Uh. Sorry."

She tossed her head and headed across the restaurant to the rest room in the rear. And despite her proud stance, she sort of…waddled when she walked away, which took all the pomp and arrogance out of her exit.

He sat back down, feeling like he'd just been through Round One of a fight with no rules and no reason. The woman was obviously an emotional basket case right now.

And no wonder. Twins. And she was alone.

But why the hell did she seem so determined to see him as the enemy?

The waitress brought the food—Maya's order took up two plates—and a whole pitcher of milk. He waited for Maya to return, and then got up and met her halfway to escort her back to the table. She sat down, looking a bit calmer.

"I did some thinking," she said, "and I've decided that you should go home."

"I should?"

"Uh-huh. First thing in the morning. Leave an address, phone number, something like that. I'll call you when the kids arrive. We'll work out a time for you to come visit them. And I promise I'll be generous about that, so long as you don't try to take them away from me." She shrugged. "And if you want to pitch in on expenses, fine. I won't fight it." She spoke as if it were all decided.

"I see."

She dug into her food as if she were starved. And as Caleb watched her, he thought she looked very smug and superior. As if she made the rules and he had no choice but to obey. He was a freaking Montgomery, for crying out loud. He was the third richest man in the country, a former mayor, and the predicted winner of the senatorial race even though he had yet to declare himself a candidate. And her attitude chafed, big time.

He picked at his food, while she finished hers. Finally she looked up at him, dabbing her face with a napkin. She'd barely left a crumb on her plate.

"So, are we agreed?" she asked him.

He pursed his lips, crossed his arms over his chest, looked her in the eye and shook his head. "Not on your life."

Blinking in surprise, she stared at him. "Why not?"

"Because you're acting like a little dictator, and I don't like it. So, no, Maya. I think maybe I'd better look into things just a bit more thoroughly before I agree to anything regarding *our* children."

Her brows rose. "Jumping the gun, aren't you? You don't have your precious paternity tests yet."

"No. But I will."

"Oooh, yes. You never know, I might be conspiring to take you for everything you have. Now that I've figured out that would amount to slightly more than a pair of scuffed boots and a rusted-out pickup truck, that is!"

"Why are you so determined to treat me like the enemy here?"

"As far as I'm concerned, you are the enemy!"

"Fine," he said, and he got to his feet. "Then this conversation is over."

"It is *not* over," she retorted, "until *after* dessert!"

His anger seemed to wash away, and something warm and fuzzy rose up to take its place. Only for a moment. But it was there. He lowered his head to hide his amusement from her and tried very hard to regain his anger and indignation. He kept trying, right through the cheesecake and coffee. But the way she tasted the chocolate syrup on the tip of her finger weakened his resolve. And the whipped cream that stuck to her upper lip annihilated it altogether.

She was angry. Okay, he figured she had a right to be angry. He'd lied to her. And now he was back, and she was afraid. Protecting her babies the way a mother bear might protect her cubs from anything she perceived to be a threat to them. That wasn't a bad thing. In fact, if anything, he ought to appreciate it. It meant she cared deeply about her babies. His babies. It meant she would be a great mother to them, protect them with everything in her.

He just wished she didn't feel they needed protecting from him.

Chapter 8

Terror was an ice-cold feeling that made him shiver more than the chilly winter wind. Twins. God, twins. Just like he'd been. The cruel joke of the name he'd inherited from his father still twisted in his gut like a blade. And the old man's words echoed like a curse. About how he'd been the stronger, and how he must always do whatever he must to survive.

Hell, he knew, with the rational part of his mind, that a child in the womb couldn't cause premeditated harm. Couldn't even harbor an ill thought. But it dug at him, ate at him. Always had.

And now he was the father, and dammit, there were two babies. Twins. He was scared to death. What if something happened to one of them? What if only one survived?

Standing stock-still in the slowly falling snow outside the boarding house, he blinked at the unfamiliar burning sensation in his eyes, the odd tightening of his throat, the hitch in his breathing.

He still didn't know who the hell had sent the photograph. It suddenly seemed like the least important thing in the world. What he *did* know was that he had to stay here until his children were born. And he had to do everything in his power to make sure they were both strong and healthy. Protected and safe. Cared for, provided for. And those jobs didn't belong solely to Maya Brand. They belonged to him. Because he was…their father. The idea made him stand a little straighter, square his shoulders, lift his chin. All of a sudden he felt…omnipotent.

"Going to stand outside all night or go on in?" a small voice said from behind him.

Caleb turned to see the youngest Brand sister standing there staring up at him. Silvery Selene, with her huge mystical silver-blue eyes and her elfin features. She wore a red hood with a scarf attached and a black wool coat. Her nose and mouth were wrapped up, just her eyes peered at him. But they were enough to identify her easily.

"I'm going in," he said. "You?"

She nodded at him. "Me too. I want to talk to you."

He pursed his lips, then shrugged and led the way up the front steps and onto the glass enclosed porch that stretched the entire breadth of the house. On the large mat in front of the door he heeled off his boots, then shrugged out of his coat and hung it on a nearby hook. Selene did likewise and looked around.

"This is nice, what Ida-May's done out here," she observed.

"It's cozy." Despite the early darkness and chilly temperature, it was pleasant here. And private. Moonlight spilled down over the quiet little town, and he thought it had an almost enchantingly picturesque appeal. Like a

Currier and Ives Christmas card. He went to the small round table in the corner, pulled out a chair. "Is this good for our...talk?"

"It's fine. At least it's warm in here." She came to where he was, sat down in the chair he held.

Caleb took his own seat across from her. "So," he said.

She drew a breath, licked her lips. "I'm not sure how to begin."

"Well, maybe I can help. You're about to ask me what my intentions are toward your sister."

She lowered her gaze. "That's...not what I came for...but since you brought it up...are you at least going to stick around a while?"

"At least."

Her gaze rose slowly, locked with his. "I have a confession to make, Caleb. I...I'm the one who made you come back here."

That shocked him into silence faster than almost anything could have. Not only that this innocent-looking baby of the family would resort to sending photographs that could destroy his career in unmarked envelopes, but that she would then come to him to admit it!

"I think you would have come anyway. In fact, I'm almost sure of it, but I couldn't take the chance I might be wrong. It was wrong to make you come back, I know that...and yet...I'd do it again. I'm sorry, though, if it messed up your life."

He closed his eyes, drew a breath, then opened them slowly. "That photograph could have ruined me, Selene. You could have just called me, you know. Anything a bit more discreet than—"

"What photograph?"

He frowned. Huge silvery eyes blinked innocently at him. "What do you mean, 'what photograph?' The photograph that landed on my desk yesterday—the one of your sister, her belly out to here, with the word 'congratulations' scrawled across the back.''

Her eyes grew even wider, if that were possible. ''Caleb...I don't know anything about any photograph. I just...gosh, I mean, I didn't think it would manifest like that! I'm sorry.''

Caleb frowned, because she made no sense. He gave his head a little shake, but that didn't help. ''Selene, if you didn't send the photo, then just what did you mean when you said that you were the one who made me come back here?''

She looked so guilty that he almost felt sorry for her. Chin lowering, she said, ''I...performed a little...rite.''

''A...rite?''

''A...spell.''

He blinked at her.

''Magic,'' she said. ''You know. You burn some herbs, light some candles, chant some words....''

Light finally dawned. This was the tarot card sister, the New Age guru. The Aquarian of the family.

''You're not supposed to mess with people's free will,'' she went on quickly. ''But I messed with yours. I just wanted to own up to it. I'll deal with the karma. It'll be worth it if....well...I mean...if things work out the way I'm hoping they will.''

Caleb smiled. She seemed really upset about all of this. Her hands fisted together and kneading on the table, teeth worrying her lower lip every little while. He covered her hands with his. ''You didn't mess with my free will, hon. If I had known about the babies...I'd have been here long before now.''

''You would?''

''Of course I would. Why does that surprise you?''

She blinked and seemed thoughtful for a moment. "Well...I guess because you used a false name and everything...you know, when you came here before. I just assumed that was a precaution to keep anyone from tracking you down if there were...consequences to that night."

He sat very still for a long moment. Then he said, "And is that what your sister thinks, too, Selene?"

She only shrugged. "I don't know what she thinks. But I think she needs you, Caleb. She's doing just fine at playing the fearless firstborn of Vidalia Brand, but deep down, she's scared to death. About carrying those kids, about delivering them, and even more about raising them afterward."

He nodded. "She should be. But to be honest, Selene, she doesn't seem any too eager to let me be a part of any of it."

Selene's eyes speared him. Deadly serious and intense, she said, "That's got nothing to do with you, Caleb. It's got to do with the past, and our father, and stuff that I don't even remember. I just know it's in her, you know? Like a deep sliver she hasn't been able to dig out." She shook her head slowly. "Maybe she thought it was all healed over, but this thing with you just jammed it in deeper and started it hurting all over again."

For a moment he thought he was going to learn something real, something meaningful, about the mother of his children. He knew the story of her father. She'd told him, and he'd heard about it again from the local gossips even since he'd come back this time. But he didn't know how Maya felt about it—how she'd felt then, how she felt now.

And it didn't look like he would know any time soon, either. Selene bit her lip, shook her head. "That's for Maya to talk to you about, not me. Like I said, I don't even remember. But I do know this much. If Maya's unwilling to let you be a part of this, you're going to have to make her let you. You have every right to be involved in the birth of your own kids, Caleb, and you need to say so. Don't take no for an answer."

"She might hate me for it," he said softly.

Selene shook her head. "Maybe for a while. But she needs you. Trust me." Her hand touched his. "I *know* things." Drawing a breath, straightening, she gave a nod. "And know that whatever happens will be real and coming from the two of you. I'm not going to interfere again."

He lifted his brows. "What, no love potions?"

"You're teasing me, aren't you?"

"No, Selene. I might, but there's something about you that makes me wonder."

She smiled, seeming to take that as a compliment. "Well, that's it. That's what I came here to tell you. Good night, Caleb."

"Night," he murmured. But he barely saw her leave. He was too busy wondering if there were secret wounds festering in Maya Brand's heart...and how he could possibly hope to get close enough to find out.

From his room that night, he called Bobby, spoke to him briefly, only to learn that no further word had come in about Caleb's impending fatherhood. No threats, no demands, no one even hinting that they knew. So if Selene hadn't sent that photo, and Maya obviously hadn't, then the question remained...who had? One of the other sisters? Mel or Kara? Perhaps Vidalia Brand herself? He hoped so. Because if it wasn't one of them, then that meant someone else must know about all of this. And if someone else knew, they were holding the fuse to Caleb's personal political powder keg.

Her back ached. Her head ached. Her stretch marks itched. Her feet were swollen. Her bladder was about to burst, and, oh, hell, she had a leg cramp. "Ow, ow, ow, ow, *OW!*"

The cramp eased. The knotted muscles in her calf relaxed. She stopped yelling and managed to get through her morning rituals without serious damage. The babies were kicking so hard it actually hurt now and then, and she was so big she had to use the long-handled back brush to wash her feet, even though she'd put a waterproof stool in the shower stall.

Ugh!

Finally she chose one of her colorful tent-sized outfits from the selection in her closet and pulled it on over her industrial-strength bra and super-support panties. A pretty kaftan and a pair of stretchy leggings. But she just didn't feel pretty in them.

She sat at her dressing table, brushing her hair, when there was a tap on her bedroom door.

"Come in," she called, not even looking up from her brushing.

The door opened, footsteps came in, falling too heavily to belong to any of the Brand women. And she glanced into the mirror to see Caleb, of all people, standing there with a tray in his hands.

"What in the world are you doing here?" she asked his reflection.

"Good morning, Maya. How are you feeling this morning, hmm?"

She eyed the tray, not answering, because she was so sick and tired of answering that same question every single day a dozen times. "What are you doing here? What is this?"

"Breakfast in bed. Or…it was intended to be. Only, you're not in bed, so I guess I'm late."

Maya set the hairbrush down and turned slowly. "Who let you in?"

"Your mother. I brought enough fresh pastries for everyone, and Vidalia was kind enough to supply the coffee to go with them." He nodded at the cup on the tray. "Decaf for you, of course."

"Of course."

He carried the tray in, right to the chest at the foot of her bed, and set it down. "I found this great bakery in town this morning, just a stone's throw from the boarding house."

"Sunny's Place. I know it."

Picking up a platter heaped with doughnuts, Danishes and muffins, he brought it to where she sat and held it under her nose.

God, they smelled good.

Hell, *he* smelled better. There was a hint of something...not cologne, it was too subtle for that. Maybe it was the soap he used. Sort of a wind and water scent. It tickled a deep part of her that hadn't been tickled in...well, in nine months, give or take a couple of weeks.

"Pretty low trick, bribing your way in here with pastries, don't you think? Why are you doing this, anyway?" she asked him suspiciously.

"Because I want to. Hey, you've been lugging those twins around for nine months now. I figure the least I can do is help you through the last couple of weeks."

"Don't say that!"

He blinked. "Don't say what? That I want to help you out?"

"No. That 'couple of weeks' part. If it's more than a couple of days, I'll die. My belly will explode, and I will just simply die." She sighed, grabbed a yummy-looking

Danish and a napkin, took a heavenly bite and closed her eyes in ecstasy as she chewed. "Oh, this is sooo good."

"I know. I ate two myself." He smiled at her.

And he was so damned charming she couldn't help but smile back. But then she thought about what he'd said a moment ago, about helping her through the last couple of weeks, and she tilted her head. "So does that mean you plan to hang around town until the babies come?"

Licking his lips, he seemed to think very carefully about his words before he spoke. "Maya, I'd really like to. I've never been a father before. This is all...well, it's special to me. Scary as hell, totally out of line with my plans...but special. I'm...I'm not the kind of guy who can just walk away from something like this...and I know you probably don't believe that, but I think you will. If you give me a chance. Get to know me...just a little bit." He swallowed hard. "I'd really like you to agree with me on this, but I want you to know that I'm staying, even if you don't. I mean...I'm their father." He looked at her belly. "I'm their father."

The second time he said it, he got a shaky, crooked little smile on his face, and his voice cracked just the slightest bit. She couldn't argue with him when he looked like that. And he was right, she knew that. She'd been feeling guilty about her attitude toward him all night long. It wasn't his fault she didn't want a man in her life.

"I was crabby with you last night," she told him. "I get that way a lot lately. But it's not my normal attitude, you know."

"I know."

She nodded. "I will not exclude you from the babies' lives. I want to make that clear, Caleb. You're right. You are their father, and you can be just as involved with them as you want or need to be. I promise you that."

He smiled broadly and blew a sigh of relief. "I'm glad to hear it." Then he glanced down at her belly. "Still nervous as hell and reeling from all this...but glad."

The babies were kicking like crazy. She had a thought, bit her lower lip, and finally gave in to it. "Give me your hand," she said, setting her Danish down.

He did. She took his hand in hers and laid his palm on her belly, sliding it around to the spot where some little foot had been repeatedly thumping her. He met her eyes, his expectant, excited. It took a moment. But finally there was a succession of rapid and rather forceful kicks.

She never looked away from his eyes when it happened. And she was glad she hadn't, because they widened; then his gaze slid down to where his hand rested, and she swore she saw moisture gather in his eyes. "My God. Oh my God," he whispered.

"You look like you're going to faint, Caleb. It's okay. Babies are supposed to kick. It means they're healthy."

"Are you sure?"

She nodded.

Caleb laughed nervously, gave his head a shake, met her eyes again. "I...it's like it wasn't quite real until just then." Then he frowned. "Does it hurt when they do that?"

"Oh, they give me a good jab once in a while. Enough to make me suck in a breath, maybe, but nothing drastic."

He stared at her for a long moment as if a little awed by her. But then he shook himself and went back to the tray, brought her cup of coffee. "Better drink this while it's still warm."

"You didn't need to do all this, Caleb."

"I wanted to, I told you."

She sipped the coffee. Finished the Danish. Grabbed a doughnut.

"Your mother says you, um…have a doctor's appointment today," he said, speaking slowly.

"Yeah. In an hour actually."

He looked at her, his blue eyes conveying a clear message. She rolled hers and sighed. "Don't tell me you want to come along."

He nodded hard. "Only if it won't make you too uncomfortable," he said quickly.

"When the stirrups come out, pal, you leave the room. Got it?"

He shuddered. "I…think I can safely promise that much." Turning, he went to the two cribs, checked them out, nodding in approval. "Why the mesh on the inside?" he asked.

"The slats were a bit too far apart on the older models. Of course, the five of us survived them, but you can't be too careful."

Nodding, he reached in to touch the soft blankets. "I've never seen a baby quilt like this before."

"That's because I made it."

He turned toward her, his brows arched, then lifted the quilt out of the crib for a closer examination. Building blocks with letters on them, and bunnies and teddy bears, all hand stitched, in various textures and colors, littered the piece. "Wow. This is some intricate work, Maya." Then, grinning at her, he said, "I guess my plan is working."

"What?" she asked.

"To get to know you better," he explained. "Already I've learned something about you. You quilt."

The sound of a throat being cleared made them both look toward the door, where Kara stood looking in at them. Her head was only a few inches below the doorframe.

"She quilts, she sews, she cooks—the woman makes Martha Stewart look like an amateur."

"Oh, cut it out, Kara. I'm not auditioning for anything here."

Kara only shrugged. "Caleb," she said, "I have a favor to ask you."

He said, "Anything at all, Kara. What do you need?"

"Well, with all that's been going on, we haven't even got a Christmas tree up yet."

He tipped his head to one side. "Hell, I can't even remember the last time I had a tree for Christmas."

"Really?" Kara asked. "Why not?"

"I don't know. It's just me and my father, and I guess we…" He shook his head. "I don't know. So, what do you need? Help getting a tree?"

"Yeah. Not that we can't do it ourselves. I mean, we do every year, but the pickup seems to be acting up this morning. It doesn't want to start. So I thought maybe you'd volunteer yours."

"Sure. When?"

"Sooner the better," Kara said with a smile. "How about right after you two get back from the doc?"

"No problem." Caleb smiled. "Actually, I'm kind of looking forward to it."

Kara's smile had enough wattage to light the entire town of Big Falls, Maya thought.

"Hey, we should probably be going pretty soon," Caleb said. "I'm going to go out and start the car, let it warm up." He glanced at Maya. "I'm assuming you want to take the van, right?"

"It's the most comfortable for me."

He nodded and headed out of the room. Maya heard his feet running down the stairs. Her sister sent her an innocent look, and then turned to go.

"Kara, hold it right there."

Stopping, but not turning, Kara said, "What?" in a squeaky voice.

"What did you do to our pickup?"

Now she did turn. She must have thought those fluttering lashes would help her cause. "What do you mean?"

"You did something so it wouldn't run, so that you could con Caleb into coming with us to get the tree. Didn't you?"

Her brows came down fast. "You have a suspicious mind!"

"And you haven't denied a thing."

Kara crossed her arms over her chest. "I *like* him." Then she tipped her head to one side. "Besides, did you see his eyes light up? Did you hear what he said about not remembering the last time he bothered to celebrate Christmas with his father?"

"That's not what he said—he said he couldn't remember the last time he got a tree," Maya corrected.

"So how do you celebrate Christmas without a tree?" Kara shook her head. "He's lonely, Maya. I can see it."

"Yeah, well...maybe."

"Aren't you even curious?"

Behind her, Caleb said, "Curious about what?" Kara gasped and whirled on him. He only grinned, gave her a mischievous wink, and looked past her to Maya. "Your chariot awaits. But you can finish your coffee first. Give it time to warm up."

"I'll take the coffee with me," she said. "The sooner we get this over with, the better." She drew a breath, preparing herself for the inevitable awkward moment when she was forced to get her bulk up out of a chair. But before she could even begin, Caleb was there. He slid one arm behind the small of her back, steadied her with

the other, and helped her up so easily anyone would have
thought she must be tiny.

She liked it.

And that scared her.

Chapter 9

Caleb caught himself sliding into a mire of sentimentality more than once on that drive to the small redbrick prenatal clinic in Tucker Lake, fifteen miles the other side of Big Falls. It was a dangerous game he was playing out here. Getting emotionally involved with the babies...insinuating himself into the family and into Maya's life before he even knew for sure that he was the father.

But hell, they were twins. *He* was a twin. His own father had been a twin, too. But, like Caleb's own twin brother, his uncle had been stillborn.

Damn, but it terrified him to think of that. It also verified that these children were his. Maybe not totally, and maybe not legally, but it was all the proof he needed.

He couldn't leave. That was obvious. He didn't *want* to leave. Exactly what he *did* want was as elusive as the meaning of life on Earth. What to do next was a question too deep to even begin to figure out. It seemed all he could do was stumble through, one step at a time. If it turned out that Maya was lying to him, then he was setting himself up for a big fall. The problem was, she wasn't lying to him. He might be a gullible idiot, but he just…believed her. Maybe because he wanted to believe her, an even scarier thought!

That worried him.

They didn't have to wait long. He was glad, because being in the waiting room surrounded by swollen-bellied women and nervous-looking men made him feel like a fraud. As if he didn't belong. As if they could take one look at him and tell he was an outsider, not a real partner to the mother of his kid. Kids.

"Come on in, Maya," a nurse said, only moments after they had taken seats in the waiting room.

Caleb helped Maya to her feet and held her arm as they were led to a small exam room.

Maya seemed to know the drill by heart. She walked in, stepped on the scale, then used a small stepping stool to get up onto the exam table. She lay back, and the nurse whipped out a tape measure and peeled Maya's blouse back and leggings downward to measure her belly. "Any problems?" the nurse asked cheerfully.

Caleb stared at the swollen mound of pink flesh underneath Maya's blouse. Her belly button was turned inside out.

"None," Maya said. "Stop staring, Caleb."

Grinning, the nurse jotted a note and proceeded to take Maya's blood pressure, then her pulse, simultaneously shooting glances at Caleb every once in a while. Curious, pointed glances, but she didn't ask.

He didn't know how much to say, so he said nothing at all.

When she finished, she said, "The doctor will be in soon," and headed out the door.

Maya remained lying down on the exam table, although she did rearrange her blouse. He assumed it was probably too much effort to get up. Caleb paced and looked around the room. Baby scales, baby pictures on the wall. A chart denoting the phases of labor, which he found himself studying intently.

"Sit down," Maya said. "You're making me nervous."

He sent her a sheepish grin and sat down, but the moment his buttocks touched the chair, the door opened, so he shot back up again. The doctor came in. Fortyish, red-headed and female. There were silver frames on her oval glasses and a ready smile on her lips.

"Maya! How are those babies doing this week, hmm?"

"Kicking up a storm, Dr. Sheila," Maya said.

"That's the way we like 'em." She turned to Caleb, offered a hand. "I'm Sheila Stone, Maya's ob-gyn," she said.

"Good to meet you, Doctor. I'm Caleb...er....Cain." Maya shot him a look he couldn't read. "I'm...uh...I'm the..."

"Father?" she asked.

He nodded, not waiting for Maya's permission.

"Well, congratulations. I'm glad to see you're here for the blessed event." She pulled her stethoscope to her ears, leaned over and moved it around until she found the spots she wanted.

"Doctor, is it normal for the babies to kick so much? I mean, they're really...active in there." He saw Maya's curious gaze on his when he asked the question. She had eyes that could hold a thousand emotions, he thought, and he wished he could read every one of them. But they tended to bubble up and swirl and sink again in such rapid succession and unlikely combinations that he thought he never would. He would glimpse something, some glimmer, but it would be replaced by another before he could get a handle on it.

"It's perfectly normal, Caleb," the doctor was saying as he plumbed the depths of Maya Brand's eyes. "It means they're strong and healthy."

Again she leaned over, listening to Maya's belly, and he dragged his eyes away from the depths of the mother to observe the doctor for signs of dishonesty or worry or anything telling at all.

"But…is it safe for them to be so active? I mean…with two babies…it is possible they could…you know, hurt each other?"

"Oh…they may poke each other a bit now and then," Dr. Stone said. "But they're very well protected, Caleb. Completely surrounded and cushioned by amniotic fluid. And while those kicks may seem pretty solid to us out here, the babies aren't strong enough to seriously harm each other. Really, with the quality of prenatal care we have today, twins are barely any more concern to us than single birth babies."

She might be lying to him, he thought. Perhaps because Maya was in the room. Oh, he *wanted* to believe her. But he knew better, didn't he? He'd been told all his life how the stronger twins in his bloodline managed to survive at the expense of their weaker siblings.

"You look worried, Dad," Dr. Stone said. "Come here, let me reassure you." She motioned at Caleb to come closer. When he did, she snagged a second stethoscope from her pocket and handed it to him.

He took it, his hand shaking, and put it on. Then the doctor guided the other end to the right spot. And he heard it. Rapid as the beat of a hummingbird's wings—a tiny, powerful patter.

"Holy…my God, is that the baby's heart?"

"It sure is. Here, here's the other one," she said, moving the business end of the thing yet again.

Caleb closed his eyes as he heard the second beat, every bit as strong and steady as the first. "Are they supposed to be that fast?" he asked, eyes closed as he listened.

"They're just right," Dr. Stone assured him.

When he opened his eyes again, they were slightly blurry, and Maya's were staring right into them. Probing and seeking and surprised and a dozen other things. "It's amazing," he said. "I…I don't even know what to say."

"So are you planning to be in the delivery room, Caleb?"

He blinked and felt his eyes widen as they shot to the doctor's.

Maya smiled. "Don't panic, Caleb. No one expects you to do that."

"But…but…"

"Well, you've got time to think about that. But for now, it's time for the internal, and you need to wait outside."

"Okay. Okay, sure." He reached up and gave Maya's hand a squeeze before he left. Then he met her eyes, held them for a long moment, and without even knowing he was going to, he leaned down and kissed her very softly. Then he straightened, realized what he'd done and wondered why. It had just seemed…like the thing to do. "I'll…be right out there…if you need me."

She stared at him as if too stunned to speak, and he turned and fled.

In the waiting room, he paced. Hell, he didn't like this. He didn't like believing her without question, and he liked even less that he knew right to his toes that he was right to believe her. She wouldn't lie to him. She wasn't up to anything. She didn't even want him around, much less want his money, and even if she did, she wouldn't have to resort to scamming to get her hands on it. She could just ask. He would give it to her. All of it. He would give her everything he had, if she wanted it.

She was carrying two babies, and they were both his. His children. His babies. He wanted to be there when they were born. In the delivery room, right there. She was incredible…that she could do this thing, perform this miracle, give life to his offspring…it was mind-boggling to him.

Minutes ticked by. He spent the time pawing through the pamphlets, of which there seemed to be hundreds. He flipped through all of them, took several. Then added a couple of parenting and natural childbirth magazines to his collection. Finally the door opened, and the doctor called him back in. "It's not going to be long," she said. "I don't think you'll go another week, Maya."

"Thank God. I don't think I can take another week." Maya grimaced at the doctor as she got herself up into a sitting position on the table. "We're going to want a paternity test done as soon as they're born, Dr. Sheila," Maya said.

The doctor lifted her brows. "Sure. But I can already tell you their blood types. Not that it would prove you are the father, Caleb, but it could eliminate you."

Caleb shook his head. "I don't need that. I don't need—"

"I want it settled," Maya told him.

"I believe you, Maya. You don't have to prove anything to me."

She lowered her head, keeping her gaze from his. He

couldn't even try to read her eyes. She said, "That... means a lot to me, that you'd say that, Caleb. Thank you."

"No. Thank you."

Lifting her head, meeting his eyes, she drew a breath. "Caleb, you're...who you are. The question of paternity is going to come up, sooner or later—someone's going to want proof. Maybe it won't be you. But it's going to happen. So I'd just as soon we get this done right away."

He thought about what she'd said, realized she was right. It *would* come up eventually. "All right. Okay, you're probably right."

The doctor flipped open the charts without so much as shooting Caleb a curious glance. He liked her. She was a pro. "Well, according to the amnio, the babies are both type O-negative. That doesn't match Maya, so it has to match the father. Do you know your blood type, Caleb?"

He lifted his head slowly. "Yeah. It's O-negative. And it's not a common blood type." He turned to face Maya. "I'd like...very much...to be in that delivery room with you, Maya. If you think you wouldn't mind too much."

Frowning until her brows touched, she sighed. "I...don't know."

Dr. Stone eyed them both. "When you make a decision, let us know, okay? The hospital needs to be forewarned."

"Thanks, we will." Caleb watched the doctor go and turned back to Maya. "I didn't mean to put any pressure on you. I mean...if it would make you uncomfortable, then—"

"We have a tree to cut down," Maya said. She started to slide off the table.

Caleb reached for her, picked her up and gently lowered her to the floor. Their eyes locked as he did, and Maya's cheeks went pink. Then he grabbed her coat and held it for her. But she shook her head slowly and glanced down.

He looked, too, and saw that she was standing there in her socks. Her warm suede shoes stood nearby. She, too, looked at the shoes. Then at him. Then at the shoes again. She kicked them closer to the chair where he'd been sitting earlier, then sat down and, biting her lip as if preparing to face some great challenge, bent to reach for the shoes.

Caleb got there first. "Let me do that."

"I can put on my own shoes."

"Lean back in the chair, Maya. You bend over any further and my kids are going to be born with no necks. You're squishing them."

"I am not." But she did lean back.

Caleb knelt down. He grabbed a shoe, then slid it gently onto a socked foot. He pulled the laces snugly and tied them up. "Just like Cinderella," he quipped, picking up the other shoe.

"Yeah, but those aren't exactly delicate glass slippers."

He shrugged. "Yeah, well, Cindy didn't have to carry her coach-sized pumpkin around with her. It carried her, as I recall." He slid the other shoe on, tied it and got to his feet.

"Last week I could reach," she said.

"Maybe next week you'll be able to reach again."

She closed her eyes fast, turning her head slightly. But not before he saw what flashed through her expression. "Hey," he said. "It's okay to be nervous about this. Hell, I'm nervous and I don't have to do anything." She didn't say anything. He caught her chin, tipped it up. "Are you? Nervous?"

For a long moment she stared into his eyes, and then she said, "I'm scared to death, Caleb." Her hands went to her belly. "I mean, what if I can't do it? One baby is hard enough. I went to the hospital one day just to check out the maternity ward. And I heard some woman screaming in the delivery room. It sounded like a Halloween horror movie on high volume. I thought she was being murdered in there."

He swallowed hard. "Did you talk to your mother about it? I mean, she's been through it so many times."

Maya lowered her head. "I don't want her to know how scared I am. Mom's...she's the strongest woman I've ever met. She thinks I'm like her."

"I think you are, too."

She shook her head. "I can't tell her I'm terrified of something as natural as giving birth. She'd be..."

"Disappointed?"

Maya nodded.

"Don't you think she was afraid the first time? Hell, I'll bet she was afraid every time, Maya. But your dad was there with her, right? And maybe that made it easier."

Maya sighed. "No. Dad wasn't there for her at all. Not for any of us. Mom...she gave birth five times, all by herself. Daddy...well, his job kept him traveling a lot. Or...that's what we all thought at the time."

Frowning as he helped her to her feet, Caleb asked, "But...it wasn't really his job that kept him away, was it, Maya? It was...his other family."

"Yeah," she said, smoothing her blouse, turning her back to him and shrugging into her coat with his help.

He waited, but she said no more.

"Will you tell me about it sometime?" he finally asked.

She shrugged. "I already told you about it, that night at the bar."

"You told me the facts. Not how it affected you or

your mother or your sisters. I'd like to hear how you felt about it, when it all came out. How you feel about it now.''

She shook her head. "It's irrelevant. It's in the past."

"Then will you tell me?"

She gave a shrug. "Maybe."

He nodded slowly, taking her elbow, steering her out the door, through the waiting room and into the parking lot where her van waited. He opened her door for her, helped her get in, then went to the driver's side.

After he started the engine he sat there for a minute. Then he said, "Tell me this much. What happened between your dad and your mom—is that why you don't trust men very much?"

"Who said I didn't trust men?"

He shrugged. "No one. No one had to, Maya. You've been suspicious of my every move, word and deed since I showed up here."

"Well, who wouldn't be?" She shook her head. "But for the record, it's not that I don't trust men. It's that I don't want to get hurt like my mother did—but, uh, by the looks of things, I didn't miss it by much. I mean, you didn't break my heart, but I sure as hell did end up with a pair of babies and no husband around."

He licked his lips and told himself not to blurt the words he blurted next. "That could be remedied, Maya."

Her eyes got wider than the rings around Saturn, and she stared at him as if he'd lost his mind. "You've got to be kidding me."

"No. No, I wasn't, as a matter of fact." Starting the van, he drove it into the road, and carefully back toward Big Falls.

She was still staring at him. He could feel her eyes on

him, huge and probing. "You're out of your mind, Caleb. My God, I wouldn't even consider marrying you!"

The barb sank deep. He felt it clear to his bones. "Why not? I mean it's not like I'm the flat-busted drifter you thought I was before. I could give you anything, Maya. Everything."

Not one word came from her lips, and when he turned to ask why, the look in her eyes almost toasted him to a nice golden brown hue.

"How dare you?" she whispered.

He shrugged. "How dare I what?"

"Try to buy me! My God, do you really think I give a damn how much money you have or don't have? I wouldn't consider marrying you for one reason, and one reason only, Caleb Montgomery! I don't love you. I don't even *know* you."

"And what if you did?"

Her brows bent low, and her eyes burned him. "What if I did what? Know you? Or love you?"

"Both. What then?"

She lowered her head, her cheeks burning red. "This is ridiculous. It's a ridiculous conversation, Caleb. Because it's irrelevant. But the fact of the matter is, if I were in love with a man—any man—it wouldn't matter to me how much money he had, or what kind of truck he drove, or what he did for a living."

He searched her face, looking for the lie, but seeing no sign of it.

"The only thing that would matter," she went on, so earnestly it was difficult to imagine she might be making it up as she went along, "would be how he treated me and the babies. Whether he...felt the same way. I'll never be one of those women tied to a man who doesn't love her. I've seen them—the political wives, the trophy wives, the ones who married because they fit the profile their husbands were looking for, and vice-versa.''

He stared at her for so long he almost veered off the road. Then he looked straight ahead again. Snowflakes, huge and soft as balls of cotton fluff, came floating a few a time from the sky.

''You're right,'' he said finally.

''I know I am.''

He glanced sideways at her. ''I had a profile, you know. Just before I left that night when we first met, my father and his advisers had been filling me in on the woman I was going to have to find and marry. Or should, if I wanted to win the senate race.''

Blinking slowly, she turned to look back at him. ''And I'll bet I missed on every point,'' she said. ''Go on, tell me the kind of woman you were looking for. Let's see, I imagine she should have at least been college educated, which I'm not. Probably her mother should not own a saloon, and I daresay her father being a bigamist wasn't on the list. I don't imagine being pregnant and unmarried showed up anywhere, either.''

He tilted his head to one side. ''I left that night because I didn't want to be tied to the woman who would fit their profile. And you're right—you would have missed it by a mile on one point in particular.''

''What's that? 'Must have class and breeding'?''

''No. It was item number seven, if I recall correctly. 'She must be pretty, but not too pretty.''' He tried a charming smile on her. ''You're way too pretty.''

She averted her face quickly, stared outside, but her cheeks went pink. ''I'd have missed on a dozen points,'' Maya said softly, her voice raspy. Then she shrugged. ''But you already know I'm not up to your family standards, don't you? Isn't that why you lied about your name to Dr. Stone?''

He stepped on the brake, stopping the van dead center in the middle of the deserted, snowy road. ''Is that what you think?''

She didn't look at him, so he gripped her shoulders and turned her until she did. ''Maya, I lied about my name to protect you and the babies and the rest of your family.''

This time the message in her eyes was clear. Doubt. Skepticism. She didn't believe a word he said. ''Protect us from what?''

''From public humiliation. Scandal. The press. A story like this gets out, Maya, and this town will become a circus. You wouldn't have a moment's peace, and what's left of your reputation would be in shambles.''

She tilted her head to one side. ''And so would yours.''

With a sigh, he nodded. ''Yes. So would mine. But that's not what I was thinking about when I gave the doctor a false name.''

''And what about the last time—when you lied about your name to me? Was that to protect me, too?''

He swallowed hard, looking away. ''I had reasons. They had nothing to do with you, Maya, I just…I was running away from who I was that night.''

''That's convenient.''

He lowered his chin, shook his head and put the van back into gear again. ''I'm telling the truth, Maya,'' he said as he drove. ''You're the one who's lying now.''

''Me?'' She shot him a surprised look. ''What have I lied about?''

''When you said you don't have any problem trusting men.''

She looked away. She needn't have bothered. It wasn't

as if he had a snowball's chance in hell of reading whatever flashed into her eyes.

An hour later they pulled in at the house, and Maya reached over to blow the horn. Within minutes several bundled-up women came scrambling out the front door. One was carrying a small chainsaw. Mel, of course. She tossed it in the back of Caleb's pickup, then came to the driver's door of the van, tapped on the window. Caleb rolled it down.

"Where do you think you are, Caleb? New York?" she asked him.

"Huh?"

"Keys," Mel told him, holding out a hand, palm up. "You've got that thing locked up tighter than Fort Knox."

"Oh. Right." He dug in his pocket, fished out the pickup keys and handed them to her. "It's not that I think anyone's going to steal that heap," he told her. "Just habit."

"Oh, yeah? I suppose it would be, for a guy used to tooling around in a Mercedes-Benz sedan." Mel wore a blue knit hat with a fuzzy ball on top over her short dark hair. Her bangs stuck out from under it, and a couple of snowflakes had landed in them and clung like glittering ornaments.

"Lexus coupe," he told her. "It's less pretentious."

"Oh, yeah, right. That's downright slumming." But she said it with a smile. "So you may as well drive the van over. I'll take Mom with me in your truck. That is, if you trust me with your wheels."

Already the side door of the van was sliding open, and Selene and Kara were clambering into their seats, snapping their belts. "Sure I trust you," he told her.

"You should," Mel said. "I figure any collisions I might have can only improve the looks of that thing, anyway." She sent him a wink and turned away.

"Hey, I saw yours in the barn, Mel. Makes mine look like a luxury car," he called.

Mel stopped, turned and eyed him.

"And, I might add, mine runs."

She grinned and sent him a mock salute, then walked away. As he rolled his window up he heard Vidalia say, "I told you he'd loosen up once he got to know us."

In the back seat, Kara and Selene were still laughing at his exchange with Mel. As he put the van into motion, Kara said, "I'm so glad it's snowing! It really ought to snow on tree day, don't you think?"

"Oh, yes," Selene said, sobering. "Snow is a great backdrop for murdering a tree."

"Oh, gee, here we go..." Maya muttered.

"Oh, come on, Selene!" Kara cried. "Don't spoil it for us!"

"I can't help the way I feel! I just don't think it's nice to chop down millions of living trees every year just for our own selfish pleasure. Hell, we only throw it out a few weeks later!"

"It's not like we're chopping down *wild* trees, Selene," Kara argued. "These trees wouldn't exist without the custom! For Pete's sake, they are planted and raised just for this purpose! Selling them helps farmers make ends meet. You're so narrow-minded!"

"I am not. Life is life. Trees have spirit, and I don't see the sense in murdering them."

"Dammit, you two, enough!" Maya shouted. They went silent as she glared at them over the seat. "We are going to be joyful and filled with Christmas spirit while we choose our tree, do you understand?" She practically growled the words through clenched teeth. "Now stop fighting and be joyful, or I'll come back there and make you sorry!"

Caleb looked at the two pouting faces in the rearview mirror, then at Maya's angry one beside him. He cleared his throat and very softly said, "Can I...make a suggestion?"

All three sets of eyes turned on him. He swallowed hard. "The ground's not frozen yet. It wouldn't be all that hard to dig the tree up, instead of cutting it down. We could wrap the roots in burlap and soil, put it into a big tub of dirt, feed and water it all winter. Then, come spring, we can take it out and plant it again."

Selene's pout eased into a smile so soft and genuine that Caleb thought she might lean up and kiss him. She looked at Kara, and Kara smiled back and nodded.

Then he looked at Maya. But she wasn't reacting at all to his suggestion. Instead she said, "What do you mean 'we'?"

"Huh?"

"You said *we* could take the tree out and plant it in the spring. I want to know what you meant by that."

"I...well, hell, I don't know."

"Do you plan to be here in the spring, Caleb?"

She said it as if she were issuing a challenge. He decided to rise to it. "Are you and my children going to be here in the spring?" he asked her.

"Well, of course we are."

"Then...then so am I." He didn't know what the hell made him blurt those words. Had he lost his freaking mind?

"Hot damn," Kara said from the back seat. "You go, Caleb!"

"Shut up, Kara," Maya growled.

Caleb glanced at Kara in the mirror and sent her a wink. She smiled, and her eyes sparkled. He shifted his gaze to Selene, whose eyes were knowing, wise beyond their years. She gave him a very slight nod of approval, but the look she sent him said she had known it all along.

Caleb was worried. He'd said something he had no intention of saying. He had no idea if he *could* be around here in the spring. He would visit, of course, but that wasn't the way his statement had sounded. And now it was said. It was out there.

Chapter 10

The truck and the van were parked side by side in the tree farm's driveway, and Maya was following the farmer up a snowy hill, surrounded by her sisters, her mother and Caleb Montgomery. She didn't know why he'd said what he had. That he would be here in the spring. He couldn't have meant it. He couldn't have. She wouldn't believe him. After all, he'd told her one night, eight and a half months ago, that he would still be here in the morning. But in the morning, he'd been gone. He hadn't so much as mentioned that to her, or offered an apology, much less an explanation. And she would be damned if she would stoop low enough to ask for either of those things. Far be it from Maya Brand to let a man think his presence or absence mattered that much to her.

It didn't. And it wouldn't. Not now, not ever.

She remembered the nights...the soft sounds of her beautiful mother crying alone in her room. She'd felt her mother's heartache as if it were her own, no matter how Vidalia had tried to hide it from her.

No. She wasn't going to let any man hurt her like that. And she would die before she'd subject her children to that kind of pain.

Besides, he couldn't very well run for the U.S. Senate from Big Falls, Oklahoma. He couldn't serve from here if he won. He was lying. Just plain lying. And all this concern for her, for the babies, all this pampering and coddling and chivalry—putting on her shoes, for God's sake—it was just an act. Joking with her sisters, respecting her mother. It was false. She didn't know what the hell he wanted from her—maybe just to win her over so he could then convince her to keep quiet about his illegitimate babies. Whatever it was, it didn't matter. She wasn't falling for it. He wouldn't be here when the chips were down, when she really needed him. He wouldn't, because in her experience, men never were.

A twinge of pressure tightened around her belly and made her lower back howl in protest. She stopped walking, her hiking shoes ankle deep in the snow. Beside her, sharp as a tack and twice as irritating, Caleb grabbed her arm. "Maya? You okay?"

She blinked slowly, took a breath, and took stock. Nothing. "Fine," she said. "Just a twinge. Not the least bit uncommon."

They were twenty feet from the van, and there were twenty more to go, up the side of a steep little hillock, to the field of perfectly shaped little trees. And in spite of herself, Maya sniffed the Christmassy scent of them, and felt her spirits rise.

"Smells good, doesn't it?" Caleb asked.

"Smells like a memory in the making," she said, not knowing why. Her mother was always saying things like that. But not her. It was a sappy, sentimental thing to say. She turned to look at Caleb, at the snow falling on his shoulders and dusting his dark hair. He was staring into her eyes and looking confused, maybe a little emotional. Hell, it was that time of year. Everyone was emotional.

"A memory in the making," he repeated. "I've never heard that before."

She gave her head a shake. "Maybe I'll go back to the truck. Sit this one out."

"Now what kind of a memory would that be?" He moved closer, brushed the snow from her hair. "Come on, before they pick a tree without us."

Without warning, he scooped her into his arms, right off her feet, and started up the hill with her.

"Caleb! You're out of your mind! Put me down!"

"No way."

"I weigh a ton! You'll kill yourself."

"Hey, there are three of you here! And hell, you've been carrying these two kids of ours around for nine months. I think I can handle it for a minute or two."

Ours. She didn't like the way the word sounded on his lips, or on the air, and she liked even less the way her tummy tightened in response to the sound of it.

They reached the top of the hill and the tree lot. Caleb stopped trudging, but he didn't put her down. She was looking ahead at her sisters, running around like excited children from tree to tree, examining them from all angles. But now she drew her gaze in, turned it upward and focused it instead on the man who held her as if she were not the size of a small hippo. He wasn't even out of breath. And he was looking at her like...like...

"You're beautiful, you know that?" he said.

She lowered her lashes. "Stop."

"You are. Snowflakes on your lashes. Cheeks all pink

and glowing. But it's more than that. I've been trying to put my finger on what's different...but it's not something I can name. It's something from inside.''

"It's a pair of somethings from inside," she told him.

He smiled at her. Then he leaned down, and he kissed her. Long, slowly, tenderly. His mouth was warm, and he tasted so good she wanted to kiss him forever. Yet the kiss terrified her, partly because she wanted it so very badly. And then he lifted his head away.

She blinked rapidly, because there was moisture in her eyes, and she stared at him. "Put me down."

"What do you want for Christmas, Maya?"

She looked away fast when he said that. Because images of her childish wishes and dreams popped into her mind. A rambling log cabin. A dog to lie by the fireplace. A cat to sit in the window. Her own kitchen to fill with the smells of baking bread and Christmas cookies. Her children's wide sparkling eyes as they watched for Santa's reindeer on snowy Christmas Eves. And a loving, devoted husband coming through the front door, stomping the snow off his boots, his arms filled with presents for the kids. His eyes filled with love—for her.

"Maya?" he asked.

She cleared her throat. "Let's go get a tree before we start worrying about what to put underneath it."

He set her down on her feet, and she trudged forward.

An hour later, a huge tree with roots enough to fill the entire back of Caleb's pickup was on its way to the Brand place. It was wrapped in burlap, and a half acre of the tree farm seemed to be coming with it. It had taken all that time for Caleb, Mel and Ben Kellogg, the farmer, to dig it up. And once they removed it, they had to fill in the hole and smooth things out as best they could. The farmer charged extra for the privilege of digging up a living tree. Caleb insisted on paying, since it was his idea.

It took a giant washtub to hold the thing. But Maya watched Selene's eyes light up when they finally got the tree home and standing upright in the living room. Her small hands were black with soil and her hair full of pine needles. She'd been underneath the tree, smoothing the soil they'd added to the tub, pouring in water and tree food, holding the base as they straightened it and tied it off to keep it in place. And talking to it as if speaking to a puppy. The tree's lush branches completely hid the baling twine they'd used to support it, thank goodness.

Maya stood back and looked at it, shook her head at the dirt all over Mel and Caleb and the living room floor.

"My, my, but that's the nicest tree we've ever had," Vidalia said, shaking her head in awe.

"You say that every year, Mom," Maya told her.

"And every year it's the truth. We just keep topping ourselves." She smiled. "Well go on, now, Caleb, Mel, Selene, get washed up. Dinner in an hour, and there's plenty to do before that. We'll need all hands on deck for hauling out the decorations. Lord knows we're already late getting them up." She clapped her hands twice.

Maya looked at Caleb, closed her eyes. "That's my mother's way of inviting you to stay for dinner."

He smiled at her. "I figured that out. But I'd feel better if you were the one issuing the invitation."

"Would you really?"

He nodded. And he looked at her with those big eyes of his like a puppy dog. She felt something soften inside her. In spite of herself, she heard herself asking, "Would you like to stay for dinner, Caleb?"

His smile was fast and blinding. "Oh, yeah."

She rolled her eyes as he raced off to the bathroom to

scrub his hands like an excited youngster. Vidalia came close to her, slid a protective arm around her shoulders. "He seems like a decent man," she said.

"Yes. He does, doesn't he?"

"He's your soul mate, Maya," Selene whispered from nearby.

"Hell, Selene, you just like him because he didn't support the tree killers of the family."

Selene shook her head slowly, coming closer, slipping her arm around Maya on the other side. "I do like that about him. But, if you recall, I told you he was your soul mate that night a long time ago, in the saloon, when you first met him."

Maya frowned and turned to the side.

"She did," Kara said, coming from the kitchen. "I remember she told me the same thing." She sidled up to her mother, slung an arm around her. So there were four now in the link.

"What made you think it?" Maya asked.

"Something in his eyes…and in yours. Plus I pulled a tarot card from my deck when I first noticed the sparks between you two. The Lovers."

"You know I don't approve of those cards, Selene," Vidalia said.

"Not now, Mom, please. Come on, it's Christmas."

Vidalia looked sideways at her, and her frown eased. She smiled and began to hum a carol, and in a few bars she began to sing the words, and they all joined in. At some point Caleb and Mel reappeared, and Mel slung an arm around Caleb's shoulders, dragged him to the tree and linked with the others. They both joined in the singing.

The timer bell from the oven pinged, and Vidalia stepped out of the arms of her children, dabbed at her eyes, and turned to hurry into the kitchen, muttering, "Lord, it's almost perfect."

When she was out of sight, Caleb sent Maya a questioning glance. "Almost?" he asked.

She nodded. "There's one more of us," she said. "I told you about her before, didn't I? Edie. Mom misses her most around the holidays."

"We all do," Selene said, eyelids lowered.

"She doesn't come home for Christmas?" Caleb asked.

Maya shook her head. "She and Mom aren't on...the best of terms."

"Not even speaking, you mean," Mel filled in.

They had broken ranks and were drifting toward chairs, the sofa. Kara bent to paw through a box of ornaments Vidalia had brought down from the attic.

"But why?" Caleb asked.

Maya had settled into the corner of the sofa, and she noticed that he didn't hesitate to take the spot beside her. Awfully sure of himself, wasn't he?

Mel said, "Edie ran off to the West Coast with stars in her eyes, Caleb. But when she got there, she found a thousand other girls just as pretty and just as bright with the same dreams. Her biggest break to date was landing a gig as a model for *Vanessa's Whisper.*"

His eyes widened just a bit. *"Vanessa's Whisper?"* he asked. And when Mel nodded, he said, "Wow, I had no idea. Maya told me she modeled lingerie, but I didn't realize she was that famous. Why didn't anyone say anything sooner?"

Maya blinked at him. "You think we go around advertising it?"

"Hell, if it were my sister I'd erect a monument in the middle of town to her success."

"Success, Caleb? My sister poses in her underwear.

And the closest thing to a monument to her in this town is Wade Armstrong's body shop, where my sister's photos, clipped from the pages of the catalogue, are the basic wallpaper pattern.''

Caleb's brows came together. "*Vanessa's Whisper* is big time, Maya. Your sister had to have competed against hundreds of models to land a contract with them. Do you know how many actresses got their starts as models? This is a big deal.''

"That's what I keep trying to tell them," Selene said. "Edie's gorgeous, and the beauty of the female form is nothing to be ashamed of.''

"Nor is it something to spread naked on the walls of body shops for dirty minded men to drool over," Maya said primly.

"She doesn't pose nude, Maya, and you know it," Mel put in.

Kara looked up. "I don't care what she does. I think you and Mom have been too hard on her, and I just want her to come home.''

Maya lifted her brows in disbelief, then slid a glance toward Caleb. "And you agree with her?''

"Well...yeah, frankly, I do. I think you ought to be congratulating your sister, not condemning her.''

Maya thinned her lips. "And how would you feel if it were your daughter posing in an eye patch and a rubber band, airbrushed, glossed over and sent to thousands of pairs of horny eyes all over the country?''

He blinked, and she knew she had nailed him on that score. "I...hadn't thought of it that way.''

"Well maybe you should.''

"Shssh! Mom's coming," Kara said.

"Dinner in a half hour," Vidalia said, smiling. "Then we'll decorate this tree.''

Maya lifted her brows and parted her lips to protest. It was bad enough her family had conspired to get Caleb to escort her to the doctor, then dragged him into their family tree expedition. And invited him to dinner. But to invite him to actually help decorate the tree was going just a bit too far.

"I'd be intruding, Vidalia. That's…that's a family thing. I've already been hanging around here too long."

He looked almost sad to have to say so.

"Bullcookies!" Vidalia squawked. "Are you the father of my grandbabies or aren't you?"

"He's not gonna answer that one until after the DNA tests, Mom," Maya said softly.

That earned her a sidelong scowl from Caleb. "I am," he said to Vidalia. "Though the idea of you being a grandmother is almost as stunning to me as that of me being a father."

Vidalia smiled and sent him a wink. "That makes you family. Period." Then she leaned closer to him and said, "That doesn't mean you need to ease up on the efforts to flatter your way into my good graces, however."

"I wasn't planning to." His smile came slowly. First one side of his mouth pulled upward, and then the other. "It's been a long time since anyone's called me family, Vidalia," he said. All humble and sweet looking. The big phony. "Thank you."

Vidalia looked as if she were going to melt right into a puddle of pudding at his feet. And as Maya glanced around at her sisters, she saw that he'd wrapped them all around his fingers, as well. Even Mel looked at him without snarling.

Hell.

"You okay?"

She frowned and saw that the man of the hour was

addressing her, still sitting beside her on the sofa. "My feet are swollen and my back aches and I have cramps in my calves that would down a bull moose."

He smiled softly and lifted her feet up off the floor, draping her legs across his lap and proceeding to rub her calves with his big hands. As he massaged the cramps away, she released a breath.

"Go on, relax. You know you want to," he said. "Lean back. Breathe, for crying out loud."

"I am breathing."

But she did lean back and let go. Hell, it felt great, what he was doing. She was only human.

"Sheesh, when did that start?" Kara asked from across the room. She stood with curtains parted, staring out the window. The snow was falling harder than before. The gently floating fluff of earlier in the day was now slanting downward at an alarming rate.

"I'd heard we might actually get an inch or two tonight," Vidalia called from the kitchen. "Come on, Kara, Mel, Selene, you three get upstairs and start bringing down the ornaments and lights, while I set the table." She glanced in at Maya, then Caleb. "You two stay right where you are," she added with a wink. "I've been trying to get that girl to lie down and relax for days but she's been just like a jitterbug on a hot plate lately...." Her brows rose, and she tipped her head to one side. "They used to say it was a sign the time was near, when a woman takes to acting all nervous and jittery like that."

"We can only hope," Maya groaned, letting her eyes fall closed.

It was nine o'clock by the time he headed back to the boarding house. In a small town like Big Falls, that seemed like midnight. The town only had a handful of streetlights, and those were dim. But it was enchanting, all the same: the moon straining to shine through the thick night clouds, giant snowflakes falling like an invasion of tiny paratroopers.

He stomped the snow off his boots, then crossed the closed-in porch area and heeled them off. He carried them inside—then stood still as the man in the living room rose from the chair where he'd been sitting, apparently having tea with Mrs. Peabody, and turned to smile at him.

Caleb almost cursed aloud. Jace Chapin was grinning like a Cheshire cat. "Well now," Caleb said slowly, wishing to God he could make the man disappear. "What's the world's sleaziest tabloid reporter doing way out here in Big Falls?"

"Came to find out what the richest candidate for the U.S. Senate is doing way out here in Big Falls," Jace replied.

"I haven't declared my candidacy, Chapin. But getting the facts straight has never been your strong suit."

The man shrugged and pursed his lips. "Oh, but the facts this time are too good to resist," he said. "I mean, the background on this unmarried pregnant woman you've been running around with is better than anything I could have invented, I gotta tell you."

Caleb tried to look unconcerned, but he kept his eyes averted as he walked past the man, stood near the fireplace, set his boots down. "You're going to have to explain to me why the background story on a friend of mine would be of any interest to your readers, Jace. Because, frankly, I'm clueless."

"Oh, come on, Montgomery. It's your kid. I have photos of you escorting this woman into the clinic in the next town. Having dinner with her. Carrying her up a snowy hill to pick a Christmas tree."

"That's quite a leap of the imagination, even for you. From dinner to fatherhood."

He shrugged. "I've got more. Just wanted to give you a chance to comment before the story runs in tomorrow's edition."

"Run this story, Jace, and I promise, I'll bury you."

Jace's brows lifted. "And what will you do for me if I *don't* run it, Montgomery?"

Caleb narrowed his eyes on the man, finally reading him. "You're slime, you know that, Jace? How much do you want?"

He shrugged. "Five hundred grand...for now."

"Fine."

"Fine? You mean you'll pay it?"

Caleb had his hand on his cell phone already. "Just tell me where to transfer the funds and I'll call—"

A click made him stop speaking. Jace had one hand in his pocket, and he pulled out a minirecorder. "That's all I need, Montgomery. If this wasn't your kid, you wouldn't be so desperate to keep it quiet. I can name my price for this story."

Caleb reached for the little weasel, but he ducked, and ran for the door. Caleb ran after him, only to stop at the porch, sock feet already damp, as he saw the man slam his car door, and lurch into the narrow street.

"Son of a—"

"Oh, my. Oh, dear. Oh, my, what are you going to do? Poor Maya! Poor, poor Maya. That dear girl..." Ida-May Peabody wrung her hands and paced behind him. "I had no idea! I should never have let that man in here. Oh, my."

"Now, Ms. Peabody, you know this isn't your fault. You had no way of knowing," Caleb assured her.

She didn't look too relieved.

He had to get to his room, call Bobby, see what could be done about damage control. And then…then he had to warn Maya.

Damn, if she didn't already dislike him enough…

"He'd make a real nice addition to this family, you know," Vidalia Brand said softly. She and Maya were sitting in front of the fireplace. Maya had her feet up. Her backache had been growing steadily worse all day, and now it was really hurting. The dishes were done, and her sisters had all gone to bed. The tree winked and sparkled magically.

"He will be a part of the family," she told her mother. "As the babies' father, he'll be as much a part of it as he wants to be."

"Looks to me like he wants to be…even more than that."

"Mother, please…"

Vidalia shrugged, sighed a surrender. "Not easy, you know. Raising a family alone."

Looking up, Maya saw her mother's eyes. The lines at the corners, the hard-worn contours. "You are a hell of a woman, Mamma. Did I ever tell you how much I admire you? No, really. I mean it. You did fine by us. No man could have done better. And I know it was hard. Probably the hardest thing you ever did in your life, raising us alone."

"No, child. The hardest thing I ever did was saying goodbye to your father."

Maya closed her eyes, lowered her head. Her father had been a two-timing slime bag. But damn, her mother's loyalty ran deep.

"I think that man could love you, girl."

Lifting her head, she met her mother's eyes. "I don't want him to.... I don't want to—"

"To believe in him? I know. You're afraid he'll let you down, break your heart, the way your father did to me."

"I don't want to talk about it," she corrected.

"It was worth it, Maya. The time we had together—it was worth the hurting later on. And just because you admire me for having survived the raising of a family without the help of a man, doesn't mean you should wish it for yourself, because it's no kind of rose garden."

Reaching out, she covered her mother's hand with her own. "There's a difference, Mamma. You had nobody. I have you. And Kara and Selene and Mel."

"And Caleb," her mother insisted stubbornly.

"No. The babies will have Caleb. I won't."

"But, Maya…"

"Mother, that's enough. I'm not going to discuss this. There is no way I'll let myself get tangled up with any man I can't depend on."

"But…but how do you know you can't depend on Caleb?" she asked, seemingly dumbfounded.

"He already left me once. Just walked out, without a word. And eight and a half months later, he waltzes back in again like nothing's happened. Just like…" She bit her lip.

"Just like your father," Vidalia finished for her.

"Oh, Mom, I didn't mean—"

"Yes, you did. I'll remind you, daughter, that you are talking about the man I love." She got to her feet and stomped away, up the stairs, and Maya heard the bedroom door slam.

Damn. She hadn't meant to insult her father or hurt her mother's feelings. What was wrong with her, anyway?

She strained to her feet and waddled through the house,

checking locks, shutting off lights. She paused at the window to glance outside. Then she let the curtain fall back into place and sent a sidelong glance at the telephone. She told herself that she was not hoping he would call to say good-night.

One hand on her aching back, she turned to go upstairs. And then the telephone rang, and she knew it was him before she even picked it up.

"Hello?"

"Maya?" he asked. "Why aren't you sound asleep by now?"

She pursed her lips. "How do you know I wasn't?"

He hesitated. Then, "Oh, God, I'm sorry. Did I wake you?"

Her lips pulled into a smile in spite of herself. "No. I was just on my way up."

"Well...well good. You, um...you need your rest."

"You sound like my mother. Why are you calling, Caleb? Is something wrong?"

"No. I mean...yes." He sighed.

She heard it and frowned. "You're leaving, aren't you?"

"What?"

"It's all right. I've been expecting it. I never asked you to stay, Caleb. Hell, at least you're calling to let me know...this time."

"Maya...I'm not going anywhere. I'm calling because... Wait a minute, what do you mean, 'this time'?"

She closed her eyes. "Nothing. Just tell me why you're calling."

It took him a moment. She wondered why. "I can't tell you how sorry I am about this, Maya, but there's been a leak. The story's out. There was a tabloid scumbag waiting here when I got back to the boarding house tonight.

Apparently he's been following us around, snapping pictures. God only knows how much dirt he thinks he's dug up on us.''

Maya closed her eyes in relief, which was so odd that she felt like smacking herself in the head for feeling it. But she felt it all the same. A wave of relief that he hadn't called to say goodbye. And while the actual news should seem far more serious than the latter would have been, it felt small in comparison.

She must be losing her mind. Maybe it was hormonal.

''Maya?''

''Yes. I'm here. I'm just…well, I'm just not sure why you're telling me this. What can I do about it?''

There was a long pause. ''I just wanted you to be warned. It'll hit the tabloids tomorrow, and the press will be stampeding into town in droves.''

''Well…then you'll be able to tell your side of the story, won't you?''

''I'm afraid my side of the story isn't exactly going to help matters.''

She sighed. ''This is liable to ruin your chances for the Senate, isn't it, Caleb?''

''I don't know. It might.''

''It will. If they go digging for dirt in my background, they won't have to dig far, Caleb. My family is…rolling in it.'' She licked her lips nervously.

''It's not me I'm worried about here, Maya. It's you, your family. I don't want this upsetting you—you're in no condition to—''

''Everything upsets me in this condition,'' she said. ''But I'm getting used to it.''

''I'm going to fix this, Maya. I'm going to find a way to make it all right again. I promise.''

"Don't make promises, Caleb. I don't like when they get broken."

"I promise," he said again. "Try to rest, Maya. I'll be there first thing in the morning."

"You will?"

"Yeah. I will."

She pursed her lips, bit them to keep from making some remark about the last time he'd promised to be around in the morning, and whispered good-night. Then she hung up the phone and went up to bed. But she didn't sleep for a very long time, and when she did, the dreams that plagued her were odd and frightening.

She wore white and walked into the church on a fine summer Sunday, with two gorgeous toddlers clinging to her hands. But she found the church doors blocked by a crowd of her neighbors, all of them pointing at her and whispering words that blended together. *Trash. Sinner. Harlot.* And then they aimed those fingers at her children, and the whispers grew louder. *Bastards. Fatherless. Illegitimate. Bastards.*

Beyond them all she saw Caleb, his suit impeccable, turning away and sneaking out the church's back door.

She looked down at her pristine children, but they wore rags now, and their faces were coated in tear-streaked dirt. And her own white dress had turned to scarlet.

She sat up in bed with a gasp and a sharp pain in her middle. But then it eased, and she lay back again. "Just a dream," she said. "This is the twenty-first century, for God's sake. They don't tar and feather fallen women anymore."

Maybe not literally, a little voice inside her whispered. No, the ways of making people feel less than worthy were far more subtle these days. The whispered remarks, the constant slights. The invitations that didn't arrive, and the distasteful looks of those who considered themselves better.

She'd grown up with all of those things. They had hurt her, because she'd been too smart a child to not be aware of them. She did not want her children to feel the sting of nasty people and their nasty attitudes.

And yet she didn't know how she could prevent it.

Chapter 11

The telephone rang at 7:00 a.m. Maya had finally fallen into a fitful sleep, but the sound woke her instantly, and even as she rolled over, covered her head and decided to ignore it, she heard her mother's voice from downstairs as she answered the call. But when she spoke again, Vidalia's tone made Maya's eyes blink wider, and all thoughts of sleep vanished.

"Exactly where do you get the nerve to call my home and ask me something like that, mister? Don't you dare call here again!" There was a bang, no doubt the sound of the phone being slammed back into its cradle.

Maya got up, tugged on her industrial-sized bathrobe and went into the hall barefoot. She was halfway down the stairs when the phone rang again. And by the time she got to the bottom her mother was slamming it down just like before.

"What is it, Mom? Who was that?"

Her mother looked at her as Maya crossed the living

room. The angry look on her face immediately eased, and she replaced it with a false smile. "Nothing for you to worry about, hon. Just some kid playing pranks on us, is all."

Her mother was lying, trying to protect her. She knew that. Maya reached the kitchen, eyed the filled coffeepot and longed for some real caffeine, and the phone rang yet again.

She snatched it up before her mother could.

"Hello, is this Maya Brand?" a strange voice asked.

"Who wants to know?" She walked to the coffeepot, took a mug from the tree and filled it.

"I'm Ben Kylie, a reporter for the *Herald,* ma'am. Do you have any response to the story in this morning's *Daily Exposé?*"

"I don't read trash, Mr. Kylie, so I have no clue what story you mean."

She eyed her mother, who was sending her a look of pure worry.

"You mean…you haven't seen it?"

"No, I haven't. And I'm very busy today, so if you could get to the point…"

"Sure. The point is the *Exposé* says you're carrying the child of Cain Caleb Montgomery III, as the result of a drunken one-night stand last spring. It claims you yourself are the illegitimate progeny of a bigamist with connections to organized crime and a barmaid, and that your family's main claim to fame is that you have a sister who poses nude for men's magazines. Is this basically accurate?"

Her mouth had fallen open as the man spoke, and now she drew the phone away from her ear to stare at it in disbelief.

A firm, warm hand took the telephone from her, and

she looked up through welling tears to see Caleb standing there. "Ms. Brand has no comment at this time. However, rest assured that her team of lawyers are even now preparing their libel suit. I would be extremely careful about what I printed if I were you." He clicked the phone down, held it two seconds, then picked it up again and laid it on the counter, off the hook.

His eyes met Maya's. "I'm sorry. My God, Maya, I'm so sorry."

She held his gaze, even though hers was swimming now. "Did the *Daily Exposé* print what that man said it did?"

"I...what did he say?"

"Don't avoid the question, Caleb. You know what he said. Have you seen the story or not?"

He licked his lips. "Yes."

"And do you have a copy with you?"

He shook his head side to side, hard. Too hard.

She held out her hand.

"No."

"Fine. I'll go to the general store and buy my own copy." She reached for the door.

"Maya, for crying out loud, you're barefoot and in your pajamas!" her mother said, reaching past her to press a palm to the door.

"So what, Mom? You afraid the neighbors will talk?" Her voice broke just a little with the irony.

"Look, it doesn't matter what that rag sheet said or didn't say, Maya. All that matters is how we respond to it."

Maya sank into a chair at the kitchen table, lowered her head onto her arms. "If it doesn't matter, then why won't you let me see it?"

Her voice sounded muffled, even to her. But he could hear her. She knew he could.

"Maya...try to understand." He sat down in the chair beside her, and his hands closed on her shoulders. "You're carrying my babies. I want to protect you from this kind of garbage. I want to stand between all that ugliness and my family."

Very slowly, she lifted her head. She knew her eyes were probably wet and red, and her hair was likely sticking up all over. She hadn't even showered yet this morning. And yet he looked at her with nothing more than kindness, tenderness, caring, in his eyes.

"Isn't that what a father is supposed to do?" he asked her.

"It's what a mother is supposed to do, too, Caleb." She sat up a little straighter. "Thanks for reminding me of that."

"Well, hallelujah," Vidalia said, smiling. "I wondered where my daughter was hiding for a minute there."

"She's back, Mom." Maya sent her mother a loving smile. Then turned to face Caleb again. "I'm Vidalia Brand's eldest daughter. I need to see the newspaper, and I promise you, I'm not going to fall apart when I do. No matter what it says."

Caleb lifted his brows and turned to glance at Vidalia. She gave him a nod. Looking as if he thought better of it, he reached inside his jacket and pulled out a folded-up tabloid newspaper. On the front page was a photo of Maya and Caleb walking into the clinic, obviously taken the day before. The headline said Front-Running Candidate's Dirty Little Secret.

She lifted her chin, folded the paper back up. "I'm going to shower and put on some decent clothes. I'll take this with me."

"Maya, don't worry. We're going to fix this. I promise."

She looked at Caleb, so strong, confident, sure of himself. "You really do care about these babies, don't you?" she asked. Because it was suddenly so crystal clear to her that he did.

He held her gaze. "I didn't know it was even possible to care this much, Maya."

She smiled a bit unsteadily. "I know."

"Do you need help...with anything?"

She shook her head. "My sisters are still upstairs. I'll, um...I'll call them if I need them." Then she frowned as a thought occurred to her. "Mom, if Mel catches any reporters snooping around, there's going to be trouble."

Her mother looked worried, then looked at Caleb. Good Lord, why was everyone suddenly turning to him for answers? They'd gotten along just fine without a man forever!

"No reporters will be near the place. I was on the phone half the night getting things set up. We've got security men stationed out front. No one's going to get past them. My top aid is on his way here with my legal team. They'll help us formulate our response. And by the time you get out of the shower, Maya, you'll have a new private telephone number."

She tilted her head. "You work fast."

"I've been in this game a while."

She got to her feet, but before she turned to go, he stopped her, placing his hands tenderly on her swollen belly. "I'll make it all right...for all of you. I promise."

She laid her hands over his. "I honestly believe you'll try, Caleb."

He was looking very deeply into her eyes just then, and there was something else. "All this...all that's been happening…there hasn't been time to talk about…anything else.''

She lowered her head. ''What else is there?'' And before he could answer, she turned and hurried away.

By the time she came back downstairs, dressed in her prettiest maternity clothes, back throbbing and clenching in protest, Maya's home was crawling with strangers. Men with radios and headsets sipped coffee and munched on crumb cake in the kitchen, and the dining room table was surrounded. Mel, Selene, Kara and Vidalia lined one side of the long oak table, while three men in dark blue suits lined the other. Caleb sat at the head, and the chair to his right was empty.

''I'm telling you, Caleb,'' one animated man in his late twenties was saying. ''I can spin this thing into solid gold, for both you and Ms. Brand.''

''She's not going to like it, Bobby,'' Caleb said.

''What won't I like?''

Everyone looked up to see her. The men rose, and Caleb pulled out the empty chair for her. ''Gentlemen,'' Caleb said, ''meet Maya Elouisa Brand, the mother of the heirs to the Montgomery fortune.''

She blinked in surprise. ''That's a far cry from my former title—'the slut who destroyed the Montgomery legacy.'''

''Thank you,'' the impeccably dressed, almost boyishly good-looking Bobby said.

She frowned at him. ''Why are you thanking me?''

''For the compliment on my work. 'Mother of the heirs to the Montgomery fortune.' That's mine. It's what I do,'' he explained. ''You're status is soon going to be the American equivalent of royalty, Ms. Brand. I'm the best spin doctor in the business. And you…well…'' Shaking his head, holding his palm up toward her, he smiled. "Hell, with you to work with, this is going to be a cakewalk."

She frowned. "I'm afraid I don't follow." She went to her chair, took it, and the men sat down.

"Well, *look* at you. You're gorgeous. And you have that clean, natural, healthy look about you."

"I'm not sure whether to thank you or offer to let you check my teeth," she said.

Bobby smiled even harder. "Perfect. Wit, too. You're perfect."

"Perfect for what, Mr....um...?"

"Bobby McAllister. Just consider me your new right-hand man."

She glanced at Caleb, who looked uncomfortable, and then at her mother and sisters, who sat there wide eyed and uneasy. "So what is this plan I'm not going to like?" She looked to Caleb.

He reached out, took her hands and drew a deep breath. "Believe me, this is not the way I would have...gone about this, given the choice, Maya. But..." He paused, looked at the men around the table, then at Vidalia. "Maybe it would be better if I could speak to Maya alone."

"Good thinking, son," Vidalia said with a smile of encouragement. "The family room is empty."

Caleb drew a breath so deep it made his chest expand. Then he blew it out again, got to his feet and reached for Maya's hand. Frowning, she took it and let him help her up. "This better be good, Caleb," she told him. "Getting up out of a chair is no small effort, you know."

He shot her a look and a slight smile. A nervous one, though. And he kept hold of her hand as he led her through the doorway to the left, into what they called the family room. It held a wall of bookshelves, a sewing machine and several baskets full of half-finished projects, a writing desk, and an air hockey table. A smaller table in the corner held a propane burner and a double boiler. Strings tacked to the walls like miniature clotheslines had hand-dipped candles suspended from them to dry. And in yet another small alcove, a TV/VCR combination sat near a rocking chair.

Caleb stood in the center of the room, looking around at the odd collection and smiling.

"It's…"

"No, no…let me. The sewing stuff is yours. My crafty, talented baby-quilt maker. The candle making setup has to be Selene's. Actually, I'm surprised it's not a Ouija board or something."

"Mom makes her keep that in her room."

He smiled. "The air hockey has to be for Mel. And the books and television must be Kara's."

"She lives for fantasy," Maya said.

"The desk is your mother's."

She nodded. "Getting to know this family fast, aren't you?"

"I hope so." He walked to the most comfortable chair in the room, turned it slightly and nodded at her to sit on it.

She did. "What's Bobby's brilliant plan, Caleb?"

He stood in front of her for a minute. Then, finally, he took her hands in his and dropped down to one knee. "Maya…"

"Oh, come on——" She tugged her hand against the grip of his and wished he wouldn't say what she thought he was going to say.

He held on tighter and said it anyway. "Let's get married."

She closed her eyes. "That's got to be the most ridiculous thing I've ever heard in my life."

He licked his lips, lowered his head. "Not *exactly* the reaction I was hoping for, Maya."

"Caleb, we barely know each other!"

"Maya, you're having my kids. Two of them. And...and, hell, if I had to choose a wife today, I can't think of anyone I'd rather marry than you."

"If you had to. The point is, you don't have to."

"No. I don't have to. And neither do you. But if you'll just listen to my argument here, I think you'll see that it's the logical thing to do."

"The logical thing to do would be to get up off the floor, Caleb."

He frowned at her, but got up. Pushing a hand through his hair, he turned and paced away, then paced back again.

"So, present your case, already. I can't wait to hear this."

"Okay. Here it is. Marrying me will be the difference between you being seen the way Bobby described you out there and the way that tabloid rag did. It is the difference between you being the most notorious member of your family or the envy of every woman in town. It's the difference between those babies you're carrying being legitimate or illegitimate. Between them being snubbed or respected as...practically as princes. And it will be the difference between our story being a dirty little scandal or a classic American fairy tale."

She pursed her lips. "And it will make the difference between you winning or losing the senate race."

He gaped at her. "My God, I don't even know if I'm going to run! Maya, that is the last thing on my mind, I swear to you."

She narrowed her eyes on him, not sure she believed that. But she did know he cared for the babies. Deeply.

"I...I don't know, Caleb. This is...this is very sudden and I...well, I don't..."

"Is there someone else?"

He asked the question so suddenly she almost hurt her neck snapping her head up. "Someone else?" she asked. "Are you out of your mind? Have you *looked* at me lately?"

He muttered something that sounded like, "In my sleep," but she couldn't be sure. "You're beautiful, smart, sexy as hell."

"I'm a heffalump."

He smiled then, broadly, widely, and came back to her. He ran a hand over her hair, cupped her cheek. "Tell me there's no one else."

She rolled her eyes. "There's no one else."

"Then why not me? Hmm? Maya, I can give you everything."

"I don't *want* everything." She bit her lip, sighed heavily. "I want to live here, not in Tulsa or D.C. or wherever you'll end up if you win this thing."

"You'll be able to do that. I promise."

"Yes, I imagine I will." But where would he be? She didn't voice the question. "I don't want my kids getting their hearts broken, Caleb. I don't want them giving their whole hearts to a father who's going to walk out on them and leave them bleeding. I can't do that to my babies."

His eyes widened, and they seemed wounded, way down deep. "That's what your father did to you, didn't he, Maya?"

She closed her eyes, nodded. "I really did love him. And Mom...oh, God, she still adores the man. But he was cheating on her, cheating on all of us, and it hurt me,

Caleb. It tore my mother apart, and it broke my heart. He was never around when we needed him, and we never knew why until he was dead and gone.'' She lifted her eyes to his, knowing they were tearing up again. ''I know it almost killed my mother. But she was a strong woman. I was just a little girl, and I can't even begin to tell you how the truth ravaged my whole world. Everything I knew, believed, had been a lie. Now I'm the mother. And I'm strong, and I can take anything this world can dish out. But I won't subject my kids to that kind of heartache, Caleb. I won't let you hurt my children the way my father hurt me.''

He stood there for a moment. Then he sank to the floor again, just sitting down in front of her chair. He drew a deep breath and sighed heavily. ''I've been meaning to explain some things to you. So much has happened that it just keeps getting pushed aside, but I can see now that it's important.''

He looked up at her. ''When I came out here that night, last spring, I was running away from who and what I was. I told you that, but I didn't explain it to you. Not really. I was running from what was expected of me. When I saw you in the bar that night, all I could think was whether a woman like you would give a guy like me a second look—without the name, without the legacy. And then…you didn't recognize me. You didn't know who I was. And you…you liked me anyway.''

She tilted her head to one side, studying him, seeing sincerity in his eyes. ''Yeah, well…what's not to like?''

''I'd never had that before, Maya. Everyone in my life wanted something from me. No one just wanted me…for me. And I needed that so badly that night. So I didn't tell you my real name. It was stupid, Maya, and I've regretted it ever since.''

She lowered her head. "And yet...you left that night. You said you'd stay...and then you left."

"Just like your father did," he said softly. He lifted a hand to her cheek, and she closed her eyes at his touch. "Maya, it wasn't like that. I got a call that night. My father had a stroke."

Her eyes flew open, met his, saw the truth there.

"You can check it out. Hospital records—hell there was even a piece in the paper about it. I rushed home...and I decided to stop running from my destiny and live it. I didn't contact you again...because I was afraid of what you'd think of me. Running out on you, lying about who I was. I figured I'd already blown any chance I might have had with you. I figured you were better off without me, anyway."

She sighed, shook her head. "You're such an idiot, you know that?" But she said it softly. "If only you'd called."

"I know. I know. I screwed it up...badly, Maya. But there was something between us that night. I know there was." He put a hand gently on her belly. "I think... there's something between us now. Something more than just the babies. And I think we owe it to them, and to each other, to find out what."

"Finding out what is a far cry from getting married, Caleb."

He nodded. "I know. But...marriage is just the legal part of this. The paperwork part of it. It's got nothing to do with what's really happening here."

She averted her eyes, felt her cheeks heat all the same as she asked, "Then...you're talking about a...a marriage in name only. Just for the sake of the babies...."

"No," he said. "Not necessarily. Unless...that's what you want."

She couldn't look at him, couldn't answer him.

"Listen, let's do this. Let's get married, officially, on paper, for the record. For the kids and the press and the public. But between you and me, Maya...let's just take this one day at a time. See where it leads." He took both her hands in his. "I can promise you this, Maya. I'd walk through fire before I'd hurt these babies. I swear it on my mother's grave."

A tear finally fell onto her cheek and rolled slowly down. She wanted to believe him more than she had ever wanted anything. But she was so afraid he would let her down. All the same, she knew his solution made perfect sense. "Okay, then," she said. "Okay."

"Yes!" someone shouted.

Maya and Caleb both turned their heads sharply. The door was opened just a crack, and Selene smiled sheepishly at them and, backing away, pulled it closed.

A second later it burst open again, but this time it was Bobby, in his extremely expensive suit, who appeared, smiling and rubbing his hands together. Maya could almost see his mind clicking away behind his eyes like some high-tech piece of equipment.

"It's agreed, then?" he asked. "That's great. Listen, neither of you talks to the press. Not yet. We'll go the righteously indignant route for today. Of course, I'll arrange a couple of leaks. Get people wondering. Then we'll grant some lucky reporter an exclusive. Meanwhile, we need to get our story in place. So..." He paused there, probably because Caleb was frowning at him, and finally Bobby glanced at Maya. "I'm sorry. Um...congratulations, Ms. Brand. I don't mean to come on like a steamroller here."

She wasn't sure what he meant to come on like, but she was thinking more bulldozer than steamroller. "I'd just as soon leave the plotting to the two of you, if that's okay," she said. "Maybe you could just fill me in later?"

Getting to his feet, Caleb nodded and gave her a nervous, encouraging smile. "We'll handle everything. Just don't worry. It's not good for the babies."

She nodded, and hurried—as much as a woman her size and shape *could* hurry—out of the room. Her sisters and her mother were waiting in the dining room, all of them on their feet, all of them grinning ear to ear, and only her mother's eyes shadowed by a hint of worry.

"I guess you already know the big news," she said.

Vidalia came forward then, pulled her close and hugged her tight. "My baby. Are you sure this is what you want to do, hon?"

Forcing a brave expression, she pulled away just enough to look her mother in the eye. "I think it's...I think it's the right thing, Mom." And then she waited for the reassurance she needed to hear right now.

"No you don't, girl," her mother said. "You're scared to death. But, honey, I think you're doing the right thing. I do, Maya. I honestly do."

"Oh, yes, of course you are!" Selene chimed in, coming closer. "You wait and see. It might not seem perfect right now, but...oh, it will be."

"It better be," Mel said, eyeing the closed family room door. "He hurts you or those babies, and I'll personally kick his—"

"Melusine!"

Mel frowned at her mother, then sent Maya a wink. "But don't worry. I think he might be an okay guy."

"I think this is the most romantic thing in the world!" Kara said, wiping at her eyes.

"There's nothing romantic about it, Kara. We're doing

what's best for both our sakes and for the babies'. That's all.''

"Landsakes," Vidalia said, slapping her hand to her forehead. "Do you have any idea how much there is to be done? Why, there's the dress, the church, flowers and food—and here we are standing around.... Do we even have time for invitations? These babies could come at any moment!''

Chapter 12

Her mother, her sisters and Bobby seemed to have bought every newspaper in print the next morning. It was the day before Christmas Eve. A time when she should be bustling around in excited holiday preparations. Not worrying about the press. At first Maya was almost afraid to look at the newspapers scattered across the table. The ones she'd seen the day before had been horrible. Mean-spirited, and filled with attacks on her character and personal life. Some went so far as to suggest she'd deliberately sought Caleb out and gotten pregnant with his child, all as a means to get her hands on the coveted Montgomery fortune.

Hesitantly she picked up one paper, glancing at the headline.

More Than Meets the Eye?

Her gaze skimmed to the lines someone had highlighted.

Sources close to Montgomery suggest there is far more to this story than meets the eye, and that it is, in fact, more a tale of star-crossed lovers than a political scandal.

Frowning, she set that paper aside and glanced at the one beneath it, which also had lines highlighted in yellow.

The Reverend Robin Mackensie, of the Big Falls Christian Church, claims that despite what the press has had to say about Miss Brand, her character is beyond reproach. In fact, all the residents of the small town seem to have positive opinions about Maya Brand. Far from the party girl some sources have depicted, residents claim she has rarely even been seen in the company of a man, much less dated one. She goes to church every Sunday and is good to her mother and sisters. Doesn't drink, doesn't smoke, doesn't swear. So what is the real story here? At the moment, Montgomery remains stoically silent on the issue, refusing any comment at all.

She set the paper down atop the rest of the stack on the kitchen table when she heard the now familiar pattern of Caleb's footsteps. Heavy steps, trying hard to be light. Measured, but not hesitant. Pausing, always, when he got a certain distance from her. She wondered about that.

"Morning," he said softly.

She looked up. He was whiskery this morning. His hair tousled, his eyes sleepy. He'd been up half the night plotting with Bobby and the two lawyers her mother insisted on calling Oompah and Loompah. Not to their faces, of course. The lawyers and Bobby had taken up residence at the boarding house. Caleb had spent the night here, in Edie's old room.

"Morning," she replied. Then she held up her coffee mug. "You want some?"

"I'd love some, thanks." He took her mug, took a sip, licked his lips and handed it back to her with a smile that told her he knew full well that wasn't what she'd meant. "That's so good I think I'll get a cup for myself."

"That was the whole idea," she said.

He crossed the room, poured his mug full, sipped again and said, "Caffeinated?"

She turned to look at him. "Half. I swear it won't hurt the babies. But I might have collapsed without it."

He frowned at her. "Not sleeping well?"

"No."

He lowered his head fast. "It's all this stress. I knew it would be bad for you—"

"It's only partly because of the stress, Caleb. Mostly, it's these kids of yours, wriggling around. I swear they're break-dancing in there."

Smiling at her, Caleb returned to the table, set his mug down and moved behind her chair. "It won't be much longer, Maya." His hands closed on her shoulders, squeezed, pulled, released. "Lean forward, hmm?"

She sighed deeply and, folding her arms on the table, laid her head on them. "You don't have to do that," she said, and didn't mean a damn word of it.

He rubbed between her shoulder blades, then down her spine, and finally made small, delicious circles right at the small of her back where it seemed all the tension of the past eight and a half months was centered.

"Oooh, yesss," she moaned very softly.

His hands stilled, but only for a moment. Then he went right back to rubbing again. "We, um...we've got an interview scheduled with Dirk Atwater, today at noon. He's with the *Oklahoma Times*. They're putting out an evening edition, and we're the lead story."

She lifted her head a little. "Do I have to be there? I mean, you're the celebrity here. Can't you do the interview?"

He stopped rubbing. "I can. Sure I can, if you want."

"Keep rubbing."

She almost heard him smile, but he started massaging her again.

"It would be better if I was there, though, wouldn't it?" she asked.

"It'll be fine either way."

"Is that what Bobby would tell me if I asked him?"

He hesitated. His hands stopped moving on her back. So she sat up and turned to look over her shoulder at him. "You don't have to protect me, you know. If it's better for me to be there, I can be there. It's not my dream come true, but it won't kill me, either."

"I just...don't want you doing anything you'd rather not be doing right now."

She smiled. "Tell me that when I'm in labor. Speaking of which—I'll make a deal with you."

His brows went up. "A deal?"

"Yes. I made a little appointment of my own for us today. You come to mine, and I'll come to yours. Okay?"

He narrowed his eyes on her. "Do I dare to ask what I'm agreeing to here?"

"You said you wanted to be in the delivery room, didn't you?"

Very slowly, he nodded.

"Well, then you should come with me today."

He didn't realize what he was agreeing to. And he didn't regret it, exactly, he just hadn't been prepared. He drove. And he pretended not to notice the number of vehicles that fell in behind the rather weather-beaten van as he left the Brand farm behind.

"We're going to have to get a new van," he commented.

She swung her head toward him. "What's wrong with this one?"

"Nothing!" he answered quickly, because she sounded slightly defensive. "I mean, it's just odd, the wife-to-be of a multimillionaire, driving around in a...er...an older...vehicle."

She pursed her lips, crossed her arms over her belly. "I worked hard for this van. It's a *nice* van."

"I know you did, and I agree. It's a *very* nice van."

She pouted a little, then sighed. "I suppose a newer one *would* be safer. For the babies, I mean."

"Oh, yeah. Lots safer. Side impact protection, built-in baby seats—you know, they say a lot of kids get hurt because their car seats aren't fitted correctly for the kind of vehicle they're in."

She frowned at him. "Where did you hear that?"

"Read it. One of those parenting magazines I got from the clinic. See, the seats of various vehicles are shaped differently, so the baby seat that's perfect for one car might be totally unsafe in another."

"You actually read all those magazines you took home?" she asked him, her eyes curious.

"Sure I did. Research. I bought about a dozen books in town, too."

He glanced at her as he pulled to a stop at a red light, the only red light in town. She was smiling. "I'm really glad you believe in doing your homework, Caleb."

"Why?"

"Because that's what we're doing now. Turn right here. It's at the house around the corner."

"We're going to someone's house?"

"Uh-huh. Nancy Kelly. She's the nurse who gave the natural childbirth classes I attended. I called her, and she agreed to give us a quick refresher course, since you missed the first round."

He felt his eyes widen. "Childbirth...classes?"

"You want to be in the delivery room, don't you?"

He nodded mutely.

"You want to know what to do while you're in there, don't you?"

"I kind of thought being there would be the extent of my...duties."

"You thought wrong, then."

She said it with such a sweet smile that he almost stopped being nervous.

Fifteen minutes later, though, the nervousness was back and then some. He was sitting on some woman's living room floor, legs stretched out in front of him, with Maya reclining in between them.

"Come on, Maya," Nurse Nancy said with a scowl. "Lean back and relax. You know how this is done."

"It was a hell of a lot different with Mom as my partner," Maya said, but she did lean back.

She reclined against Caleb's chest, and her hair was under his chin, and the scent of it reached up to tickle his nose and his memory. It smelled the same as it had that night, all those months ago. But wait a minute, he wasn't supposed to be thinking thoughts like that. Certainly not at a time like this.

"Put your hands on her belly, Caleb. No, no, like this." Nurse Nancy bent to take his hands and place them strategically on the lower part of Maya's swollen middle.

Then she paused and looked up. "My goodness, Maya, the babies certainly are riding low today."

"I thought something felt different. Does that mean anything?"

Nancy smiled. "It might mean you're getting ready to deliver."

"You think?" she asked, eyes widening.

"Well, if I were a betting woman," Nancy said, "I'd lay odds you'll go within forty-eight hours." She shrugged. "Of course, I could be wrong."

Maya looked up at Caleb, her eyes shining with a combination of nerves and excitement. Nancy replaced her hands on Caleb's, moved them slowly. "Now rub very gently, in soft, slow circles. It's going to soothe her through the contractions. See?"

He moved his hands over her. It was intimate. Almost sensual. When he glanced down at Maya, he saw that she had closed her eyes. This was the most relaxed he'd seen her since he'd been back here. "Am I doing it right?" he asked softly.

Her lips curved into a smile. "You're a whole lot better at this than Mom was."

"Yeah?"

"You're not doing the breathing, Maya."

"I'll hyperventilate and pass out."

"Then you're in the perfect place for it," Nancy said. "Now breathe. Hee hee hee, whoo. Come on."

"Hee-hee-hee-who," she breathed, only she managed to do it to the tune of Beethoven's Fifth, and Caleb burst out laughing.

"Oh, sure, encourage her!" Nancy said in exasperation.

Maya opened her eyes to grin up at him, her head moving up and down with his laughter. He looked back at her, and for just a moment their eyes locked. He stopped laughing. Her smile faded. And something inside her reached out to touch something inside him. At least, that was what it felt like.

"Now, Caleb," Nancy said, "I'm going to explain to you what happens when we get to the actual pushing."

He almost grimaced in pain at that thought.

Maya said, "Don't worry. As my mamma used to say before a spanking, 'Darlin', this is gonna hurt me a whole lot more than it's gonna hurt you.'"

"I wish it wasn't."

"My mamma also used to say to stop whining and be a Brand. Don't you worry, Caleb. I'll be fine."

He hated the black fear that crept up inside him when he though of the ordeal ahead. His mother had died, hemorrhaged to death with the doctors right there, helpless to save her no matter how they tried. And one of her children stillborn. The day of his birth had been a black day of despair and grief, rather than one of joy and celebration. He damn well didn't want the Montgomery family curse visiting itself on this woman...on these babies. But he didn't know what to do about it.

He noticed the nurse looking at him oddly, tried to shake the dread out of his expression, and forced a smile as he continued with his lesson in how to coach the woman who would be his wife through labor and delivery.

But later, when they'd finished and Maya had gone to visit the rest room before they left for home, the woman handed him a pamphlet. "Everything we've been over is on here. So you can review things before the big day."

"Great. I was beginning to regret not taking notes."

She smiled, but it didn't reach her eyes. "So what is it you're worried about, Mr. Montgomery?"

"Caleb. Please, after the things we've discussed today, I think we ought to at least be on a first-name basis."

She lifted her brows, gave a nod and waited. "You looked scared to death once or twice."

He nodded, licked his lips and glanced nervously in the direction Maya had gone. Not seeing her, he looked back at Nancy again. "I was a twin. My mother hemorrhaged—they couldn't save her."

"I'm sorry."

He held up a hand. "My twin brother was stillborn."

"I see," she said. "But, Caleb, that doesn't mean—"

"That's not all of it. My father was a twin, as well, and his brother didn't make it, either." He'd let his gaze sink slowly as he spoke, but now he lifted it again to see if there was any reaction in her eyes.

There wasn't. She was a nurse, though, and trained to hide her emotions from frightened patients, he told himself.

"Listen to me, Caleb. In the years since you were born there have been more advances in neonatal care than you can even imagine. We have babies born under three pounds today. Babies so tiny I've held them right in the palm of my hand." She cupped her hand to demonstrate. "Babies who did just fine. Now Maya's had ultrasound exams done. We already know that both babies are of good, solid size, and that they're healthy. Maya's healthy, too. And you've got to take her family history into account as well as your own. Her mother gave birth five times—the first time when she was only in her teens. And she was on her feet telling the other new moms in the ward to stop their whining in a matter of hours."

He smiled at that. He couldn't help it, it was such an accurate visual he was getting of Vidalia Brand.

"Maya's strong. The babies are strong. There's no reason to think they won't be just fine." She looked at him again, smiled. "But if it will make you feel any better,

I'll give Maya's doctor a call and bring her up to speed on your family history. Okay?''

He nodded. "That's good. I wanted to do it myself, but I didn't want Maya to know any of this."

Nancy nodded. "That's for the best. No sense getting her as terrified as you are."

"That's what I thought, too."

She nodded. "I'll keep it to myself—at least until after your kids are born safe and sound."

"Thanks. You're a good woman, Nurse Nancy."

She made a face, rolled her eyes. "Gee, that's the first time I've been called that." Her tone was sarcastic but teasing. Reaching up, she tucked the pamphlet into Caleb's shirt pocket. "See you in the delivery room, Dad," she said with a wink.

His stomach clenched all over again. "Bring smelling salts, in case I pass out, all right?"

"Oh, you wouldn't be the first," she assured him.

Which didn't make him feel any better for some reason.

Chapter 13

Maya sat beside Caleb in the dining room, which looked as if it had been polished up for a royal visit. A photographer toyed with his camera at the far end of the table. Bobby sat in a chair, tucked away in the corner. Lurking in the shadows like a happy frog who would snap into action if a fly happened by. And he didn't seem the least bit concerned. He seemed as if he knew full well that everyone would fall easily into line with his plan and be better off for it in the long run. The guy had spunk.

She didn't particularly like spunk today, feeling almost completely devoid of the stuff herself. Although the time she'd spent with Caleb at Nancy's house had been...it had been bliss. That was not a good thing, she reminded herself. She couldn't forget that this was a game. A political game. She would be Caleb Montgomery's wife because that was the role she needed to play for the good of all concerned. It didn't mean anything, and she couldn't let herself slip into believing that it did.

Everyone else seemcd to be lying low somewhere. Caleb's lawyers, the Levitz brothers, were apparently still out at the boarding house. Vidalia and the others had gone out to order a wedding cake. The house was empty, except for the five of them. Dirk Atwater, the well-known reporter, was adding cream to his coffee in the kitchen, while his photographer frowned at the overhead light, and changed his camera lens.

"If you get confused, just follow my lead, okay?" Caleb said in a low voice, leaning close, squeezing her hand.

She nodded. But she felt sick with nerves.

"And remember, the closer we stick to the truth, the better."

"Right."

"If you get confused about any details involving the wedding or arrangements, just make them up."

"I'm no good at making things up on short notice, Caleb," she said quickly.

"Well…then don't make it up. Fall back on what you dreamed about as a girl. Okay? Every young girl dreams about her wedding day and what her married life will be like, doesn't she?"

"Well…yes, sure, but—"

"Then use that. You'll be fine, I promise."

She nodded again. The reporter came in from the kitchen with his coffee, sandy blond hair styled with some kind of miracle mousse that made it look silky soft but prevented it from moving even a fraction of an inch out of place. His eyes were too blue to be real. Colored contacts, she thought. He was fairly well known in Oklahoma, did TV spots all the time in addition to his print columns. He looked like he should be an actor or a model.

He sat down with his coffee, looked from one of them to the other. "Are we ready?"

Caleb glanced at her, brows raised. She smiled and gave him a nod. "As ready as we'll ever be, Dirk. But before we begin, I do want to make one thing clear. Maya is very close to her due date. If anything said here seems to me to be upsetting her in any way, the interview is over."

The reporter's brow quirked just a bit, but he nodded. "Fair enough." He took a small tape recorder from his jacket pocket, set it on the table, clicked it on. "But, uh...I understood the baby wasn't due for a couple of weeks yet."

"Well, here's where you get the first of several scoops on your competitors," Caleb said, his gaze brushing over Maya before returning to the reporter. "We're having twins."

Dirk Atwater's eyes widened, then he grinned. "Twins!"

"Yeah. They run in my family."

"You never told me that," Maya said, sending Caleb a frown.

His smile faded, and he licked his lips. The reporter's eyes sharpened, and he watched every move they made so closely that Maya felt as if she were under a microscope. "I've been meaning to," Caleb said softly. "We've been so busy, with so much going on, there's barely been any time."

She nodded in agreement with that.

"At any rate," Caleb went on, "twins normally come early, and Maya's doctor expects them to make their entrance into the world any day now."

"Holiday babies," Dirk Atwater said, scribbling a note. Then he sat back in his seat. "You won't mind my mak-

ing the observation that you two seem...close. Far from
the relationship that's been depicted between you by some
of the tabloids.''

Maya frowned. ''I don't know how those people could
even pretend to know anything about Caleb and me.
They've never even spoken to us.''

''That's why we invited you here today, Dirk. We want
to set the record straight,'' Caleb put in.

''For the sake of your senate campaign?'' Dirk asked.

Caleb frowned. ''At this point, I don't even know
whether there will be a campaign.'' The reporter looked
skeptical. Caleb sighed. ''Right. I don't expect you to believe that. But for now, let's keep this on the subject, all
right?''

''All right. Fine. This young woman is carrying your
children, Mr. Montgomery. What do you intend to do
about that?''

Caleb smiled then, not at the reporter, but at her. ''I
intend to marry her, just as soon as we can make arrangements.''

The reporter blinked in surprise, looking from one of
them to the other. ''You're...getting married?''

Maya nodded at him. ''On Christmas Eve, as a matter
of fact.''

Dirk Atwater glanced at his photographer, who
shrugged at him. Then he looked back at Maya and Caleb
again. ''That's...tomorrow.'' And Maya nodded. ''So...
let me get clear on this,'' Atwater said. ''You're getting
married just to make things legal...to, uh, legitimize the
babies, correct? Then, Caleb, you'll head back to the mansion in Tulsa, while you, Ms. Brand, will continue on just
as before.''

Caleb started to speak, but Dirk held up a hand. ''If
you don't mind, sir, I'd like to hear Ms. Brand answer

this one." Caleb nodded, and Dirk focused on Maya. "So tell me, Ms. Brand. What happens after the wedding?"

Every eye turned on her. She fumbled, searched her mind, but damned if she knew what to say. She and Caleb hadn't talked about what would happen after the wedding. Not in any detail. But then she recalled what Caleb had told her—fall back on her dreams if she got confused. And that should be easy enough. Lord knew she'd nurtured those dreams for long enough that she knew them by heart.

She smiled at Dirk, got to her feet, belly first, and managed to accomplish the task even before Caleb leapt to his feet to help her. She walked to the window in the rear of the room, parted the curtain. "Come here, Mr. Atwater." He did. And she pointed. "See that level spot, at the top of the hill, right back there?"

Dirk nodded.

"That's the piece of this farm that belongs to me. It's where we'll build our home. A big cabin, made of pine logs. With a huge cobblestone fireplace, and knotty pine window boxes, where I'll grow pansies and geraniums. There will be a big room in the back for all my crafts and sewing. I'll give lessons in my spare time. No one in this town is as good at crafting as I am." She smiled, felt her cheeks heat just a little, but it was the truth.

"I didn't know that," Atwater said. And he looked around the room, taking in the décor—the wilderness scene handpainted on the blade of an old crosscut saw, hanging over the picture window. The embroidered samplers, the needlepoint table scarves. He glanced at her again, brows raised. "These are all yours?"

She nodded.

"You ought to see the baby quilts," Caleb put in, and

she thought she heard pride in his voice but reminded herself he was playing a part. For the reporter.

"There's going to be a huge front porch on the cabin," she told Atwater. "And a fenced yard in back, so the kids can't wander too close to the woods. In the summertime, that hillside is just alive with wildflowers and songbirds…and the deer come out at twilight to nibble the tender grasses." She sighed wistfully, visualizing it all just the way she'd always done. "And we'll have a dog. A big, oversized, long-eared, shaggy mutt of a dog."

She was smiling broadly as she let the curtain fall and turned to glance back at the table at Caleb. He was sitting there very still and very quiet, his face expressionless, and she felt her smile slowly die. Maybe she'd shocked him. Maybe her dreams didn't fit in with his plans at all.

"So this is for real, this marriage of yours? It's not just for appearance's sake?" Dirk Atwater turned away from the window to address Caleb.

Caleb stared at Maya, and she stared back.

Bobby got up and came over to the table. "Look at the two of them," he said to Atwater. "Does that look to you like it's for real?" The cameraman fired off a series of shots.

Maya felt her stomach clench and quickly averted her eyes.

But there was no stopping Bobby once he got started. "Over eight months ago, these two met by chance. Or maybe it was fate. The middle of a rainstorm, a flat tire, a man looking to get warm and dry walks into a charming little roadhouse and meets the girl of his dreams. It was love at first sight."

And as he spoke, Caleb never took his eyes off Maya. She wanted to look away, but found she couldn't.

"Through a series of misunderstandings and bad decisions," Bobby went on, "they fell out of touch. Ms. Brand didn't want to be labeled a gold digger—a fear that was justified, if the tabloids are any indication. And Mr. Montgomery didn't even know about the babies. Now these two have managed to get past all of that and put things together again. Not for the sake of the press, Mr. Atwater. They've done this *in spite of* the press. In spite of public opinion. In spite of irresponsible journalists who see fit to drag Miss Brand's family and her character through the mud to sell papers. In spite of the whole damned world, Mr. Atwater, these two star-crossed lovers have found their way back to each other. This is not a political scandal. This is a love story, Atwater. A Christmas story. A miracle."

Maya blinked back her senseless tears and wondered if Bobby were about to burst into a chorus of the "Star Spangled Banner" or "Silent Night." She thought Dirk Atwater might very well shed a tear of his own at any moment.

But then he pursed his lips, met her eyes and said, "So then there won't be any prenuptial agreement?"

Bobby's jaw dropped, and Caleb said, "Don't you think that's getting a bit too personal, Atwater? That's over the line."

Maya held up a hand. "Actually, I'm insisting on one." She sent a gentle smile Caleb's way. She'd been watching Bobby, and she thought she got it now. This art of "spinning." "I know you're against it, Caleb," she said, though she had no idea if he was or not. In fact, she rather thought he would be nuts not to ask for a prenup. "I just see no other way to prove to the world that all of this isn't an elaborate conspiracy to get my hands on your family's money."

"You don't need to prove anything to anyone, Maya," Caleb told her.

She sighed, nodded, but from the corner of her eye she saw Bobby's slight nod of approval. Good. She'd done her job, and maybe she ought to quit while she was ahead. "I'm a little tired," she said, rubbing the small of her back.

Caleb was beside her in a flash, arms sliding easily around her as he eased her back to her chair. The camera went off. "Do you need anything? A drink? Something to eat?"

Bobby cleared his throat. "I think this is going to have to conclude the interview. Dirk, you have the exclusive on the impending marriage and the twins until tomorrow morning. Then we'll issue a press release. That's all."

Atwater clicked off the tape recorder, nodded once and gathered up his notebook. "Thank you both," he said. "I appreciate this, and I think you'll see that when my story runs tonight." He shook Caleb's hand. Gave Maya a gentle smile. "You take care, Ms. Brand."

The photographer snapped another shot, and then they left.

Maya blew air through her lips and let her head fall backward in the chair. "God, I'm glad that's over."

"Oh, come on, don't tell me that was tough on you," Bobby chirped, smiling. "You sailed through it like a pro! Hell, where did you get all that stuff about the log cabin and the dog and the pansies? I couldn't have made that stuff up if I'd tried!"

She brought her head level again, saw Caleb searching her eyes. He said, "You fell back on your dreams, didn't you, Maya?"

She shrugged. "Maybe I'm just a good liar."

"I don't think so."

Looking away, she said, "So do you think he bought it?"

"We'll know in a few hours, when the evening edition hits the streets," Bobby said. "You two ought to go into town between now and then. Be seen together. Pick out some baby clothes or something. Great photo op, with all the press in Big Falls."

Maya tried not to grimace at the thought.

Caleb said, "No. I think maybe a quiet, healthy meal and then a long nap would be a better choice. Don't you, Maya?"

"Sounds like heaven to me," she said. "You must be reading my mind."

"I wish. Come on, let's get you someplace more comfy than this hard chair. Sofa or bed?"

"The easy chair will be sufficient. I can't be dozing with a wedding to plan."

Caleb brushed a lock of hair off her forehead. "Hey, trust your mom and sisters and Bobby and me to take care of all that, will you? You need your rest. You've got a pair of babies to deliver, you know."

She smiled a little nervously. "I want it simple, Caleb. No doves or violins or…or goose liver."

He made a silly pout. "Bobby, call the Pope and tell him we won't need him to perform the ceremony after all, will you?"

"Very funny," she said. But she saw the odd, speculative look Bobby sent them.

Caleb was already helping her to her feet, walking her into the living room and lowering her to the sofa. He tucked a stack of pillows behind her before ordering her to lie back, and then he stuck a few more under her feet. "I read that elevating the feet can ease the strain on the back.'' Even as he said it, he pulled off her shoes, let them thud to the floor.

"When you have time to do all this reading is beyond me," she muttered, deciding to give in to the pampering. She was achy and tired, and it felt good to be babied. That tiny voice of doubt whispered at her not to get too used to it, but she brushed it aside.

"Wait till you hear what I've learned about potty training." Caleb winked at her. And she thought that it wouldn't be so bad to live with this guy. At least…if that were what he intended.

She wondered if it was. Wished it could be. Hated herself for daring to wish such a big wish.

She fell asleep on the sofa in spite of her determination not to, and the nap was easily a couple of hours long. But the commotion in the kitchen woke her up at once. The deep booming voice belonged to some man who had no qualms about speaking at full volume. "Are you out of your mind! What are you thinking?"

"Hey, just a gol'darn minute, mister fancy-suit! Who in all hades do you think you are, storming into my kitchen yellin' like a lunatic, anyway!" Vidalia's tone was just as loud and twice as mean.

Maya started to get to her feet just as Kara reached the foot of the stairs. "What's going on out there?" Kara asked.

"Damned if I know," Maya said. "Help me!" She held out a hand. Kara took it and pulled her to her feet. The yelling was still going on when the two of them walked into the kitchen. A man in a calf-length black wool coat stood just inside the door, having apparently just come in from outside. He still had snow on his shiny shoes and at the bottom of his gleaming brass-handled walking stick. He had a face like a mountain of solid granite, after it had been blasted through to make room for a road to pass. Chiseled and lined and hard...but only on one side. The other side seemed oddly lax. The man towered a good six feet tall, even though he was leaning over just slightly, weight on the walking stick. He was waving a newspaper around in his other hand and saying, "Get out of my way, woman! This doesn't concern you!"

Vidalia was in his face, her forefinger poking him repeatedly in the chest to emphasize her words, "It's my house, mister, and you'd better believe anything in it concerns me!"

Behind her, Caleb shrugged. "You gotta admit, she has a point, Dad."

Maya gasped, and the three of them turned around, spotting her there. Caleb quickly took Kara's spot beside her, his arm sliding protectively around her shoulders, his gaze doing a quick scan of her face. One she was getting used to. He was always looking at her like that, as if checking to be sure she was okay. As if he could see in her eyes if she wasn't.

"Maya, I'd like you to meet my father, Cain Caleb Montgomery the Second." She looked from Caleb to the older man, who was scowling hard. "Dad, this is Maya. Soon to be your daughter-in-law and the mother of your first grandchildren."

"Over my dead body," the old man growled.

Vidalia leaned up into his face. "*That* can be arranged."

He glared at her, one eye narrowing slightly more than the other.

"Mother, please," Maya said, moving out of Caleb's embrace to place a calming hand on her mother's shoulder. Her mother moved aside at Maya's urging, and Maya stood before her future father-in-law. A more intimidating presence she couldn't even begin to imagine. Even with the obvious damage the stroke had dealt him, he was an imposing man. But she lifted her chin and looked him in the eye. "I understand your being upset about this, Mr. Montgomery. But I promise you, I would never do anything to hurt your son or your family."

His brows went up. "I'm not sure if you're a good actress, woman, or if you're as clueless as you pretend to be, but trust me, the harm has already been done. And continues to be done."

"Father—" Caleb began, a deep threatening tone in his voice.

"No, Caleb, let him speak. Please. I want to hear how he thinks I've harmed your family."

"Our reputation! Our line! By God, girl, we can't have a girl of your background muddying up our family tree!" He shook the newspaper again. "Illegitimate, they say! Father was a bigamist, for landsakes! Ties to organized crime. Mother who—"

"Mother who what?" Vidalia asked, gripping the front of his shirt in her fists.

He stopped talking, looked down at the woman. "You? You're the saloon-owning mother?"

"You're damn straight I am, mister, and I'm about to forget my manners and toss your sorry carcass out into the nearest snowdrift."

He blinked down at her, his eyes wide.

"Mom," Maya said, "at least this one didn't call you a barmaid." Not that she expected it to help.

"Dad," Caleb said firmly, "your mother was a waitress at a truck stop when your father met her. Or have you forgotten that?"

"My father wasn't running for the U.S. Senate when he met her."

"That's totally irrelevant."

"That's the only thing that *is* relevant! Don't you know what this girl's background is going to do to your campaign, son? And this," glancing down at the newspaper he tossed it onto the table, "this fairy tale Bobby's trying to sell the public—it's never going to work. Voters don't care about sappy stories, they care about their bank accounts." He shook his head slowly, then closed his eyes and pressed a hand to them.

Vidalia gripped his arm. "Sit down, you foolish old windbag, before you fall down." She guided him to a chair. "Kara, get some of Selene's calmin' tea brewing. That with the chamomile and valerian root." As Kara shot into action, Vidalia eyed the older man. "You had a stroke last spring, didn't you?"

He looked up, defensively. "I'm completely recovered from that."

"Maybe. Didn't learn anything from it, though, did you?"

Maya pulled out a chair and sat down beside the old man. Caleb sat beside her and turned the newspaper around so he could examine the story. Maya watched him reading it over and saw his lips pull into a smile. Then he pushed it toward her. "It's good," he told her. "It's very good."

"Good? Bah, it's fiction! Any fool can see through that sorry excuse for a cover story," his father said.

Kara put a teacup down in front of the older man, and then Selene appeared with a big amethyst in one hand and a bowl of mixed herbs in the other. "I heard yelling. What's up?" She set the amethyst in the middle of the table. The glittering purple stone winked and glimmered.

"My father arrived," Caleb said. "You can call him Cain. Dad, this is Selene, Maya's sister, the one you haven't insulted yet tonight. The two you have are Kara, her other sister, and Vidalia, her mother."

He lifted his brows. "Vidalia? Like the onion?" He stopped short of sniffing in derision.

"That's right. They named me that because I'm so good at making arrogant jackass men cry like babies."

"Easy, Mom," Selene called from the range, where she was fiddling around. "The negative vibes are going to be cleared out of this room in just a few seconds." She poured the remaining water from the tea kettle into a saucepan, lit the burner underneath it and stirred it slowly while sprinkling her herbs into the water.

"What the hell is this? You have some kind of witch doctor in the family, too?"

"Careful, or she'll turn you into a toad," Caleb told his father. "Drink your tea."

His father sipped. "Bad enough about the stripper in the family! Now we have voodoo!" His brows went up, and he licked his lips; then he sipped some more of the tea.

"We do not have any strippers in this family, Mr. Montgomery," Vidalia huffed.

"Actually, Maya's older sister is a highly successful model," Caleb said.

His father grimaced but kept sipping his tea. "I don't care if she's an Oscar-award-winning actress," he muttered. "This marriage can't happen. I won't let it happen."

"You don't have a choice in the matter, Father."

"Son, don't you see what's going to happen here? You'll lose your shot at the Senate."

"I'd rather lose my shot at the Senate than lose my shot at being a father to these babies."

His father's head came up, and his eyes seemed frozen. "Babies? There are two?"

Maya saw the look Caleb sent his father. There was a message in it, one his father seemed to see and read. He said, "Yes, twins. It was in the article."

The old man's gaze slid toward Maya, then lower to her belly, and she could have sworn there was something new there. A hint of...could that be concern? Worry? At least it wasn't blatant hostility.

"I got so wrought up I never finished reading the whole thing," he said.

Steam was rolling off Selene's brew now, and she was waving a hand at it as if to send it around the room. It gave off a pleasant, woodsy aroma. Then there was a tap on the door. Bobby came in, Mel right behind him. Both of them were smiling as they shouldered their way into the crowded kitchen.

Kara looked at them. "Where did you two meet up?"

"Just now in the driveway," Mel quickly told her. She had a bag of groceries in her hands, which she handed off to Vidalia, before bending to tug off her snowy boots. "Bobby says he has good news." She got out of the way, sniffing the air as she went to check out Selene's concoction.

"I sure do. Dirk Atwater's paper ran a telephone poll in the same issue as the story. Caleb, your numbers have gone through the roof since they last ran this same poll, two weeks ago. Then you were neck and neck with the other likely candidates. Now you're leading them by more than thirty percent."

Caleb's brows rose. That was his only reaction. His father, on the other hand, looked stunned. "You've got to be kidding me,'' he said. ''The voters are actually falling for this nonsense?''

''Voters have hearts, Cain,'' Bobby told the older man. ''I tried to tell you that years ago, but you never wanted to hear it.''

''Well the voters in this family have stomachs,'' Vidalia said firmly. ''And if I hope to feed them, I'm going to need the bunch of you to take your hides out of my kitchen.''

Maya nodded and started to get to her feet, but Caleb put a hand on her shoulder and shook his head. ''Stay put. Have some tea. Relax,'' he told her. ''I'm gonna take my father over to the boarding house, get him settled in. I think I, uh...need to have a talk with him. Get some things...straight.''

She nodded. ''Don't be hard on him, Caleb. He's your father, no matter what.''

Caleb glanced at his father, who must have overheard that remark. Maya wondered if the man was still scowling at her but didn't turn to look.

''Maya, we have all the arrangements in place. I don't want you fussing or worrying about anything at all. All you have to do is wake up in the morning. We're getting married at ten o'clock.''

She felt her brows shoot upward. ''But...how did you pull everything together so fast?'' She looked from Caleb to her mother and back again.

''Your mom can fill you in on the details. Okay?''

She nodded. ''O-okay. I guess. Caleb, there's so much I want to talk to you about before we...you know...do this thing.''

''I know.'' He looked at her so intensely she could almost feel the touch of his eyes. ''I know. I'll come back early, I promise. We'll have time to talk. All the time you want. Okay?''

She nodded. Then sucked in a breath of surprise when he leaned down and pressed a kiss to her mouth. It was quick, brief, but not a peck. It was firm and moist. A kiss that…seemed to *mean* something. But what?

Then he was gone, Bobby and his father with him.

"See that?" Selene said, still wafting her steam with her hands. "Cleared away the negativity so well that it even chased the old grouch away!"

"He's not as bad as he seems," Maya said.

"No one could be as bad as he seems," Vidalia said.

"Gee, what did I miss?" Mel asked.

Kara grinned. "It's just as well you did miss it, Mel. Otherwise that old goat would have been carrying his walking stick in a new place."

"Kara!" Vidalia scolded—or tried to, but it was ruined when the grin she tried to suppress broke through.

Everyone laughed. Then Maya said, "So my wedding is all planned?"

Vidalia smiled at her. "I'm under strict orders from that man of yours to get your approval on everything first. But I'm supposed to do that without giving you the slightest cause for stress or tension." She shrugged. "Guess he's never been around too many brides before if he thinks that's possible." She turned to pull her notebook from the top of the fridge and, flipping it open, sat down at the table. "It's amazing what that man manages to do with a few phone calls. I'm telling you, hon, having all that money and clout is not a bad thing."

Neither, Maya thought, was being so popular in the polls. For some reason, though, that news didn't make her as happy as it should. Because it meant he would probably decide to run after all, even though he'd said repeatedly that he hadn't made that decision yet. He would make it now. He would run, and he would win. And he would have to spend half his time, or maybe more, in Washington, D.C., and the other half in the state capital, or traveling around doing...political stuff. If she did get her dream house, she would be in it alone.

Well, she thought, a hand on her belly, not entirely alone. Just not with him. And for some reason that felt like the same thing.

Then again, he hadn't promised they would be together constantly. Even live together at all. That was one of the things they needed to talk about. Their living arrangements. Because she had no intention of moving away from her family. Especially when they might be all she and the kids had, if Caleb turned out to be the kind of man who would break his word, let her down. The kind of man who wouldn't be there when she really needed him.

More and more, she doubted Caleb was that kind of man at all.

If only she could be sure....

Chapter 14

"Maybe...it can work after all."

Cain Caleb Montgomery II spoke the words as if they were being forced from his lips. And he had a grimace on his face while he did it. Caleb had been sitting before the fire in the parlor of Ida-May Peabody's boarding house, talking with his father for the better part of an hour, hearing all the same arguments and keeping his father's teacup filled with tea steeped from the little packets Selene had handed him on his way out of the Brand house tonight. He didn't like the gray tinge to his father's skin. He didn't like the dizzy spell the old man had had earlier. And he didn't like it that his father refused to admit to feeling even slightly less than peak.

Now all those things faded to background worries as shock took precedence. He stared at his father, wondering if he'd heard him wrong. Maybe he'd fallen asleep and just dreamed it. "Did you just say you might have been wrong?"

His father glared at him. "Don't expect to be hearing it again any time soon."

He sipped the tea, his third cup, and for just a moment Caleb wondered what sorts of herbs mystical Selene had put into it, and whether they were fully legal.

"That woman, the mother with the onion name..."

"Vidalia," Caleb corrected.

"That's right, Vidalia. She's tough. I gave her my worst, and she didn't even flinch. Most females would've been weeping." He puckered his lips in thought, rubbed his chin. "I like that about her. If your Maya has any of her mother's gumption, she might just make you a decent wife. She doesn't know how to dress or act, and that hair will have to go, but all that can be corrected. She seems bright enough to learn as she goes. I suppose she has all the raw material to be molded and shaped into—"

"I don't want her molded or shaped into anything, Father. I like the way she dresses, and I like the way she acts, and I'd fight any man who tried to get near her hair with a pair of scissors."

His father's brows went up, and he studied his son's face. "She'll never survive in our world as she is, son. She'll have to change, adapt to it."

Caleb looked away, because he didn't want to argue with his father. Not tonight. Not when that statement made so much sense, even if nothing else his father said tonight had. His world would be difficult for Maya. Maybe impossible for her.

But he wasn't even clear on things in his own mind just yet. No, there was no sense upsetting his father by arguing with him, especially when the old man wasn't feeling up to par.

"How...er...are the babies?" his father asked, his tone gruff.

For the second time tonight the old man had surprised him. Caleb got to his feet and walked to the fireplace, bent to toss a log onto the flames and stayed there, hunkered down, as it began to burn. "The doctor says they're both fine and strong. No sign of any problems."

"You're worried, though."

Turning, he looked at his father over his shoulder. "Hell, yes, I'm worried. They're twins. Like I was…like you were." He felt too much showing in his eyes, so he jerked his head around, focused on the flames again.

He heard his father get up, heard his steps but didn't turn. A hot tear burned behind Caleb's eye, but he blinked against it. Then a hand fell on his shoulder. "I've been there, you know."

Caleb's brows came together. Stunned, he turned to look at his father.

"It's like a nightmare, where you can only watch what happens, but you can't move to stop it, or do a damn thing to help. You feel the dread right down deep in your gut, but you're paralyzed."

Blinking, Caleb said, "That's exactly what it feels like."

"I know." Lowering his head, shaking it, his father went on. "We knew there were problems with one of you long before the time for the birthing came, son. The doctors felt all along that one of the twins was not developing at a normal rate." He lowered his head. "It felt like a personal insult to me. Hell, man, I never failed at anything before! And when your mother didn't make it, either…Caleb, I was never the same. I felt responsible. If not me, then who? I was her husband. I was supposed to protect her, take care of her."

Caleb rose slowly. "So you blamed me for it."

Meeting his son's eyes, Cain nodded. "Maybe…maybe

a part of me did, son. That's true. But that ended long, long ago. Since then it's just been...a spin.''

"A spin?"

Cain nodded. "All my rubbish about the strong surviving, the weak falling by the wayside, sacrifice for the greater good. Hell it was how I dealt with the loss. By putting a spin on it. By pretending it was a sign of strength. Because if I could make myself believe that about you and the brother you never had, then maybe I could make it true about myself and my brother, as well." He clasped Caleb's shoulder hard. "But it's not true and never was. Your twin didn't survive because he didn't develop normally. As for my own, I'll probably never know. But that doesn't mean these twins of Maya's have to suffer the same fate, son. If they're both strong and healthy this late in the game, then chances are—"

"They're going to be fine. Both of them. They have to be."

His father drew a breath, sighed. "My great-grandmother had twins, and both survived. Did you know that?"

"No."

They stood side by side now, both staring at the fire. "Maya, she's strong. Healthy. Comes from good stock, if that harridan mother of hers is any indication," Cain told his son.

Caleb nodded. "The woman gave birth five times without problems," he said.

"That's good. That bodes well." Cain didn't turn. He said, "Your mother used to quilt. Did I ever tell you that?"

Caleb looked at him in surprise.

"I read in that article that Maya does that sort of thing, too. Just thought you'd like to know it was something she had in common with your mother. She was talking about giving it up. Said it was too rustic a hobby for a woman in her position. She never did, though. Just kept it to herself.'' Turning, he set his empty cup down. ''Guess I'll head up to bed now. Big day tomorrow, with the wedding and all.'' He started toward the stairs.

''Dad.''

The old man stopped but didn't turn around.

''Thanks.''

''Good night, son.''

''Night.'' Caleb sat down again, alone now with his thoughts. His fears. And the new, confusing things circling his mind like sharks. He was glad his father had reached out to him tonight, tried, in his way, to mend old wrongs. But he couldn't help but think he should have been having a long conversation with someone else tonight.

With Maya.

Because, dammit, there was so much he needed to work through where she was concerned. So much he was confused about. Mostly he wanted to know why she'd agreed to marry him. Had it been for the reasons he'd laid out? Because, frankly, he'd been making those up as he went along. It scared the hell out of him to admit it, even to himself, but he had to know. They were at zero hour. Mostly he'd just wanted to lock on to her and the babies in some way that assured him they wouldn't just vanish from his life, fall through his tenuous grasp someday. Coming out here, he'd discovered that they were precious to him…*she* was precious to him. He could understand feeling that need to hold on to the babies. They were his, after all. But why that desperate need to cling to Maya Brand?

She was the mother of his kids. That had to be stirring

some kind of primal instincts to life inside him. There were probably all kinds of psychological reasons why a man would feel drawn to a woman who was about to bear his children.

Weren't there?

And why didn't it feel as if that was the answer? Why was he suddenly dreading the thought of taking her with him, into his world, watching her evolve into the perfect political wife, seeing her change...and maybe cut her hair? Or...give up quilting?

He stayed up by the fire for a long time, thinking, searching his mind. But all he kept seeing when he imagined the future was a dark-colored log cabin on a hillside above a wildflower-strewn meadow. A couple of kids, and a big shaggy dog bounding through the blossoms. Maya on the front porch, in the sunshine. A doe and a pair of spotted fawns feeding out back.

He fell asleep, and the images wove into dreams. Vivid, achingly wonderful dreams.

Maya had pleaded exhaustion and gone to her room just to get out of the sight of her mother and sisters before the tears came. And once they started, they didn't seem to want to stop. She buried her face in her pillows and thumped her mattress repeatedly with her fist, but it didn't help.

After twenty minutes she forced herself to sit up, reached for a tissue and caught a glimpse of herself in the vanity mirror. Red puffy eyes, wild hair, streaks on her face and a runny nose looked back at her. "You are a basket case, Maya Brand," she told herself. "Why don't you get a grip?"

"Because you're going to become a wife and a mother of two all in the space of the next few days, darlin'." Her mother's voice made her jerk her head around. Vidalia sat in the chair beside the bed. In her hands she held a big bowl of vanilla ice cream, with chocolate syrup drizzled over the top, and a generous dollop of whipped cream...and two spoons.

Maya sniffled. "How long have you been sitting there?"

"Long enough for the ice cream to get just soft enough. I figured I'd let you cry it out. It's cleansing, a good cry. Sometimes you just need to let it rinse you clean."

She held out the bowl.

Maya eyed it. "I'm not hungry," she said.

"Since when do we eat ice cream because we're hungry?" Vidalia asked, and set the bowl in her daughter's lap.

Maya picked up the spoon and took three consecutive bites.

"You came upstairs before I got to tell you about the wedding plans that man of yours managed to put together."

She sniffed, ate another bite, looked at her mother.

"He spoke to Reverend Mackensie, and the reverend says he'll personally take care of getting the church ready. He even offered to have the full choir turn out, and Mrs. Sumner is practically begging to be allowed to play the organ." Vidalia sneaked a quick taste of the ice cream with her own spoon. "And get this, Mrs. Mackensie and the Ladies' Auxiliary volunteered to see to it the flowers arrived and take care of the decorations. Well, you know, Mrs. Mackensie's sister is the only florist in town, so I suppose that makes sense, but—"

"But, Mom, the church ladies don't even like me."

"Oh, honey, they do now."

Maya thrust out her lower lip. "I don't think I want them at my wedding."

"That's what Caleb told them. He said he just wanted use of the church, thank you very much. Said he had his own florist in mind, and that he didn't want anyone there who wasn't specifically invited. Told the reverend his next sermon ought to be on loving thy neighbor and the dangers of false pride." She smiled. "The reverend laughed! He said it was about time someone put that bunch in their place, and he thought Maya Brand was just the one to do it."

Maya's eyes widened as she stared at her mother.

"It's true, hon. Oh, don't you see, child? You're getting what you've always wanted. Respectability. Why, you're marrying into a family who could buy and sell this town and everyone in it. Every person who ever snubbed you is gonna be kissing up full force, just hopin' to get invited to have a cup of coffee with you."

Maya's face puckered, and her lower lip quivered. "Y-you're right. That's wh-what I've always w-wanted. But I wanted to earn it...not marry into it."

"You'd already earned it, Maya. That's the point. Those women are forced now to give you the respect you already deserved. You should be happy to see them so firmly put in their places."

"I...know I should."

Her mother tilted her head to one side. "Well, then, how come you're crying?"

"I don't know!" she wailed, and the tears flooded her face, and she shoveled in some more ice cream.

"Darlin'," her mother said after a moment, "I do know. And so do you, deep down. And you'd best get busy thinking it through and figurin' it out, because you're gonna be married in a few hours, and it would be a darned good notion to have your head on straight when you do.''

Blinking several times, sitting up straighter, she thought very hard. Her mother snatched tissues from the box and wiped Maya's face, her nose.

''Well?''

Maya stared down at the melting ice cream in the bowl. ''I'm afraid I'm not good enough to be a senator's wife.''

''You're a liar. You're good enough to be any thing you want to be, and you know it. Now think some more. What's really wrong?''

Maya frowned. ''Maybe it's...that I think *he* may not think I'm good enough—''

''Bullcookies. He wouldn't be marrying you if he thought that way. Try again.''

''His...father. Yes, that's it, his father hates me, and—''

''His father is a teddy bear trying to act like a grizzly. I can't believe a daughter of mine didn't see through that stuff and nonsense at first glance.''

Licking her lips, Maya nodded. ''I did. He's just lonely and feeling left out.''

''Uh-huh.''

Drawing a deep breath, Maya sighed, took a big bite of ice cream and thought some more. ''Maybe it's...that I don't know what's going to happen. I mean, I don't want to move away from here. But he's going to have to, if he becomes a senator. And I don't want to go with him, but I don't want to be left behind, either.''

''Why not?''

Her brows went up. Another bite. ''Well, I...I...the kids. It would be hard on the kids, and hell, I don't want to be raising them all alone. I mean, I've seen how hard that is.''

"We've been just fine alone, Maya. You know you could do it, and do it in spades, if you had to."

"But this is different. I mean…okay, it's not that I don't think I could raise the kids alone, I mean, I could. Of course I could. I know I could."

Vidalia nodded and dipped her spoon in for another bite.

"It's just that I don't want to be alone."

"You were fine alone, a year ago," her mother pointed out.

"That was before I met Caleb…" Maya blinked and went very still, with a spoonful of ice cream halfway to her mouth. She lowered the spoon. "Oh, no," she whispered. "What if I love him?" She turned to stare at her mother through eyes gone wide with horror. "Landsakes, Mom, what if I *love* him?"

Maya's mother sat beside her, stroking her hair and talking to her until she finally fell asleep. A restless, fitful sleep, but still, she needed the rest. And she did rest, just fine, until about 1:00 a.m., when something woke her. She wasn't sure whether it was the howling wind outside or the sensation of being soaking wet from the waist down. She only knew that the house was freezing cold and pitch dark, and that her water had broken.

"Mom?" she called.

And then a giant hand closed tight around her middle, squeezing her front and back, inside and out, and she gripped her belly and yelled louder, pain and fear driving the single word out of her with far more force than before. *"Mamma!"*

An insistent, howling sort of cry shook Caleb out of sleep. At first, in his drowsy state, he thought it was

The Brands Who Came for Christmas

Maya's voice, crying out to him for help. He came awake with a start, surprised that when he opened his eyes, the only light to be seen was the orange red glow of the coals in the fireplace, a few feet from him. And the cry he'd heard was only the wind, shrieking abnormally outside. Blinking away the sleep haze, Caleb realized he'd fallen asleep on the sofa in the living room of Ida-May's boarding house. Still, there was usually a light left on down here at night.

Sitting up, he rubbed his shoulders, suddenly chilled. Then he reached for the big lamp on the end table.

Click.

Nothing. He tried again, but it was no use. Either the bulb was blown or…

"…or the power's out," he said aloud. And that was when that wailing wind outside drew his attention again. And there was rattling, too. He half expected to see a death wagon come thundering into the room with a banshee at the reins, singing her funereal dirge.

He shook that image away with another shiver, a full body one this time. "It's the wind," he muttered. And he went to the fireplace, added three chunks of wood, then rose again and tried the wall switch. Still no lights. But as the flames grew, they illuminated the room for the most part. He could see around him. Orange and yellow, leaping shadows.

Then another light appeared. A small flame, floating closer out of the shadows, until it morphed into Ida-May herself, carrying an old-fashioned kerosene lamp. "Caleb?" she asked, squinting at him, then nodding in answer to her own question. "Power's out," she told him. "And it's storming to beat all." She set the lamp on a high shelf and quickly went to the hearth to light another lamp—one Caleb hadn't even noticed sitting there. Come to think of it, there was a candelabra on that marble stand in the corner.

Caleb went for that, brought it to the fireplace and reached for the matches there on the mantel. "Does this happen often?" he asked, lighting the candles one by one.

"Oh, once or twice a year at most. This is a big one, though. My goodness, listen to it rage!"

He didn't need to listen to hear the fury of the storm. The wind whistled and moaned, and branches skittered against the windows and walls. He went to the nearest window, parted the curtain and tried to look outside. Dark as pitch. The entire town was black, and even the whiteness of the snow didn't break it. "Looks like the whole town's blacked out." Then he turned. "I need to check on Maya."

"Oh, my, yes!"

Footsteps thundered, and in moments Bobby reached the bottom of the stairs, with Cain at his side. In the fireglow, the old man's face looked downright mean. "Dad, here, take the sofa." Caleb helped his father to a seat, then yanked a blanket off the back and draped it over his shoulders.

"It's colder than the hubs of hell in this place." Cain growled, pulling the blanket closer and hunching into it.

"The power's out, Mr. Montgomery," Ida-May explained. "But we have the fireplace. You'll be warm as toast in no time." Then she looked at Bobby. "Someone should wake the others, those two lawyer fellows and Ol' Hank. Have them come down here where it's warm."

"I'll get them," Bobby said. "Along with some more blankets."

"Why's the power out?" Cain demanded. "And what's that infernal racket?" Then, blinking, he looked toward the windows, then at Caleb. "Snowstorm?"

"Yeah, the whole town is without power, by the looks of things." Caleb tried the telephone, but there was only dead air. He clicked the cutoff several times, to no avail. Then he went to the foot of the stairs and called up them, "Bobby, bring your cell phone down."

Cain was shaking his head. "How bad is it out there, son?"

"I don't know, Dad."

The old man pursed his lips. "That Brand girl...she hadn't ought to be out there at that farm without heat, or even a telephone."

"I know."

"I have a radio, some batteries. I'll get them," Ida-May said, and taking one of the lamps, she hurried away. Caleb went to the door, yanked his coat off the rack and pulled it on. "I'm gonna take a look outside. Maybe it's not as bad as it sounds."

"Good idea, son."

He stepped out onto the porch, pulling the door closed behind him. The howling here was louder, almost deafening, and a rhythmic thumping worried him. He pulled up his collar and went to the door, opened it. The wind hit it, yanked it from his hand and slammed it against the wall. Caleb ducked his head, brought his hands up in front of his face and, squinting, stepped out onto the stoop. Icy barbs of snow slashed at his face like razors. The snow on the ground was level with the top step and still coming. He tried to see up and down the road, but only snow, gray with darkness, shadowy drifts looking like miniature mountains and wind-driven snow were visible. Everything was covered, every rooftop and porch, every vehicle and tree. Telephone poles, those he could make out in the darkness, were tilted and leaning. Wires, laden with snow, drooped low.

He back onto the porch and forced the door closed against that insistent wind. It was an effort, but he managed it. He took off his coat, shook the snow off it, stomped off his shoes and went back inside. "It's a freaking nightmare out there."

His father and Bobby were pushing all the chairs nearer the fireplace. Martin and Jacob Levitz, Caleb's lawyers, stood huddled over the radio as Ida-May turned the dial from static to static. The boarding house's permanent resident, a grizzled fellow Caleb only knew as "Ol' Hank," sat in a rocker looking confused.

Finally Ida's radio dial hit paydirt. "...the unexpected blizzard is raging through Big Falls and surrounding areas with winds up to sixty-five miles per hour and temperatures well below freezing. Twenty-four inches of snow have already been dumped in the area, with another eighteen inches possible before morning. Residents are advised to remain in their homes if at all possible. Use fireplaces, woodstoves, kerosene heaters if you have them. If not, light all the burners on your propane or natural gas ranges. If you have none of those, then you need to dress warmly, stay dry and keep moving until daylight. All roads are closed. Emergency personnel cannot get through. Phone service is out in three counties, and power in more, though the full extent of the outage is not known at this time. Rescue personnel will be out in force at dawn, when the storm is expected to abate. If you need emergency assistance, hang a red flag from a front window or door of your home."

Caleb swallowed hard and looked at his father. "I have to get to Maya."

"Son, they said to wait until dawn." He glanced at the old-fashioned pendulum clock on Ida-May's mantel. "It's only five or six hours away, at the most. Surely she'll be all right until then.''

He met his father's eyes. ''What if she isn't?''

''Caleb, you could get killed out there in this mess. It's a good five miles out to the Brand farm.''

''Dad, the nurse we saw yesterday predicted she'd give birth within forty-eight hours. Anything could be happening out there.''

''Come on, Caleb, what makes you think—''

''I don't know. I don't know. I just...I feel it in my gut. I have to get out there.'' He paused, searching his father's face. ''What if it were my mother out there? What would you do, Dad?''

Thinning his lips, the old man nodded. ''All right.'' Then he turned. ''Caleb's going to need flashlights, with good batteries, and some damn warm clothes.''

''Flashlight, hell,'' Ol' Hank grumbled. ''What the boy needs is one o' them there snow machines. You know, like Joe Petrolla's got.''

Caleb blinked and turned slowly to Hank. ''A snowmobile?''

''Yep, that's what I mean. A sno-MO-bile.''

''Hank, does this Joe...fellow live near here?''

''Lives a half mile south. Turn right at the light, if you can find the light—it's the only light in town, you know. Turn right onto Oak Street. It's the first house on the left.''

''I know where that is,'' Caleb said, remembering every trip through this town. Picturing the street in his mind, hoping to hell he could find it in the pitch dark, in a blizzard.

''Caleb, there are guardrails along the edge of the road between here and there,'' Ida-May said. ''Only on the left hand side, though, cause that's where the steeper drop is. You go out, and you find those guardrails. Let 'em guide you so you don't get off track. Hold right on to 'em, till you get to the traffic light. You hear?''

He nodded. ''That's good advice, Ida-May, thank you.''

She nodded, picking up a lamp. ''Now you come on upstairs with me. My late husband's clothes are still packed in the closet. We'll get you bundled up proper.''

Chapter 15

The sounds of thundering feet in the upstairs hallway of the Brand farmhouse, immediately following Maya's shout, were loud enough to drown out the noise of the storm outside. In between the pounding feet, there were bangs and bumps and crashes, and voices asking what was wrong with the lights, and more rattling and clanking, and more footfalls. It only went on for a matter of perhaps two minutes, but Maya felt as if it was taking her family *hours* to complete the simple task of getting from their rooms to hers.

But then they were all stumbling through the bedroom door. Selene in her floor-length black silk nightgown looked even more like a Gothic heroine due to the black wrought iron candelabra she carried, with its spiderweb design. Her silvery hair spilled over her shoulders, and she looked so damn skinny Maya suddenly wanted to growl at her. Right behind her came Mel, with a baseball bat in one hand and a flashlight in the other. She wore flannel pajamas, and her short dark hair stuck up in several directions. A fighting mad hen with wet feathers. She made Maya want to laugh. Behind her, Vidalia burst in, wearing her red satin bathrobe with the black lace collar and cuffs. Maya had always referred to this as her dom-inatrix robe. She carried an old tin and glass hurricane lamp, its globe in need of cleaning, but it gave off some light all the same. Her masses of raven curls were bound in one long braid that twisted down her back. The fourth one in was Kara. She had no light and came bursting into the room so fast she ran into Vidalia, who bumped into Mel, who shouldered Selene, who fell onto the bed and managed not to set the blankets on fire with the candles.

There were several "oomphs" and "ughs," and then Kara said, "Sorry. What's going on?"

"Power's out."

"Big snowstorm."

"Maya yelled."

Three voices gave three answers. Then Maya gave the fourth. "I'm in labor."

There was one brief moment of stunned silence, and then everyone started bustling at once. Kara muttered something about boiling water, and Mel said something about dialing 911, and Selene said, "I think I have a spell for this somewhere!"

Then Vidalia shouted, just once. *"Stop!"*

And everyone went still and silent. "That's better. Now calm down, all of you. Mel, take this lantern, go on out to the barn and get the generator fired up." She handed the hurricane lamp to Mel. "Dress warm, now. There's no big hurry. First babies take their time. Kara, you go on downstairs and call Caleb over at Ida-May's. Tell him it's time. And, Selene, you go on out with Mel and start up the van. Pull it right up to the door here. We'll let it get nice and warm.'' She smiled and took Selene's candles, setting them on the bedside stand. ''You'll find some more lamps and candles in the kitchen closet, third shelf. Matches with them, as always. Go on now. I'll stay here and mind your sister.''

Nodding, they shuffled out, Mel's flashlight guiding the way.

Maya tried to slow her breathing, tried to be calm. It wasn't easy. She was actually trembling. Drawing a breath, she sat up and flung back the covers. ''I'm soaking wet,'' she said. ''I think my water broke.''

''Not to worry, hon. I'll just get you some clean, dry things.'' Vidalia went to the dresser, pulling open the top drawer, and hauling out an oversized flannel granny gown with pink flowers all over it.

''That thing's big enough to shelter the homeless,'' Maya moaned.

''And just think, this will be the last night you'll need to wear it. Come on, now, up on the edge of the bed.''

Maya moved with no small effort, and her mother helped her peel off her wet nightgown. She brought a washcloth and towels for Maya to wash herself up, and helped her into the clean, warm nightie. Then she wrapped her in the extra blanket and set her in a chair beside the bed.

It took all of five minutes. And then the next contraction came, and it pulled tight, and Maya wrapped her arms around herself and bowed her head, and made a sound from down deep in her chest.

Vidalia was peeling the wet blankets and sheets off the bed, but she stopped, and her head came up. ''Is that the second contraction?''

''Mmm.'' Maya managed that and nothing more, but accompanied it with a fierce nod.

"And the first was when you called out?"

"After," Maya told her. And she knew damn well it hadn't been very long. She pried her eyes open, saw her mother look at the wind-up clock on the bedside stand. She didn't look away until Maya sighed her relief and sat a little straighter. Her mother finished stripping the bed, carried the bundle of covers to the bathroom and came back with fresh linens. How she managed to be so fast and efficient in almost total darkness was beyond Maya. She thought her mother could probably do just about anything. Thank God she was here!

"There now," Vidalia said. "I'll throw fresh blankets on there, and it will be all ready and waiting for you when we come home from the hospital."

Maya licked her lips. "Dammit, I was supposed to get married today," she moaned.

"Watch your mouth, dear."

"I don't want my babies illegitimate."

"Oh, for heaven's sake, child, it's the twenty-first century. What kind of a modern woman are you if you still think a baby needs its father's name to be considered legitimate? I mean, really, who made that rule? When did the mother's name become so unimportant?"

"Mom, this isn't exactly the time for feminism or politics."

A throat cleared, and Maya looked to the doorway, seeing Kara and Selene standing there, looking frightened. "Um…Mom, can we talk to you a minute? Out here?" Kara asked.

Vidalia lifted her brows. Maya held up a hand. "No. Whatever's wrong, you spit it out right here, right now. I've got a right to know."

Kara looked at Maya. Then she looked at Vidalia. Vidalia heaved a mighty sigh, and gave a nod. "Go on, what is it?"

"Mom, there's a blizzard going on out there. No power, no phones, at least two feet of snow piled up, and some of the drifts out there are higher than my head. Wind's blowing something fierce. I can't even see from the house to the barn."

Frowning, Vidalia went to the window, parted the curtain. "Where's Melusine?"

"She went out anyway. Bundled up and said she thought she could make it to the barn, get the generator started," Selene said softly. "We told her not to go, but you know Mel."

"Lord have mercy," Vidalia whispered.

Maya bit her lip, but the cry was wrung from her anyway. Tears sprang to her eyes this time, the pain was so intense. Her sisters huddled around her, and Vidalia looked at the clock. "Four minutes," she said. Shaking her head slowly, she looked at the ceiling. "Lord, if you're still owin' me any favors, now would be a fine time to pay up on 'em." Then, she stood straighter, lifted her chin. "All right, all right, we have what we have, we may as well deal with it. Kara, get that mattress cover from the hall closet, and get it onto this bed. Bring extra blankets, too. Selene, did you gather up the lamps and candles?"

"They're right here. I brought the whole box." As she spoke, she turned back into the hallway, bent to pick up a large cardboard box and brought it into the bedroom.

Vidalia went to the round pedestal table by the window and, taking the tablecloth by its edges, gathered it at the top, lifting a dozen framed photos, trinkets and knick-knacks all at once. She set them in an out-of-the way corner. "I want you to put every one of those lights right here, in this bedroom window, and fire them up. We'll need the light to work by, and if they're bright enough, they might help Mel keep her bearings.''

''What if they don't, Mom?'' Selene was already unloading candles and kerosene and oil lamps from the box onto the table.

''Don't you worry, Selene. Vidalia Brand is not goin' to let any blizzard take one of her girls. Now you just do what I told you, quick as you can. There's work to be done. I need rubbing alcohol, scissors, that ball of string from Maya's sewing basket....''

Caleb thanked God for Ida-May's suggestion about clinging to the guardrails at least a hundred times before he made it to the traffic light. The snow was blinding, the wind constantly driving his body off track. He could have veered off course and not even known it. It was impossible to tell the road from the ditches. There was nothing but snow. White, ice-cold snow, crotch-deep and stubborn as hell. With every step he took, his legs and borrowed boots were pushing massive amounts of the stuff. It was unbelievable.

He had to let go of the guardrail and cross the street now. The rail was on the left-hand side, and the street he wanted was on the right. He turned, aimed the flashlight Ida-May had given him, hoping to pinpoint a spot on the other side so he could have something to aim for. But the light couldn't cut through the wall of slanting snow. He started forward anyway, but a gust caught him and sent him stumbling sideways. He fell over, snow in his face, even inside the fur-trimmed hood of the late innkeeper's parka. Shaking himself, Caleb rose to his hands and knees, got slowly to his feet. He was off track, turned around already. He'd lost his sense of which way he'd been facing, which way he wanted to go.

Tipping his head back, he turned in a slow circle, aiming the flashlight upward, until finally he saw it reflected back at him from the traffic light above. And when he found it, he realized he could just manage to make out the shapes of the cables that held it suspended above the street. He'd been on the left, so the shortest stretch of cable was where he'd been. The longest stretch was a map pointing the way to the other side of the road.

Bowing against the wind, he walked, stopping every three or four steps to look up at the traffic light and its cables to keep his bearings. And eventually he reached the spot where the cable ended. Again he shone the light. What now? Nothing to go by, no guardrails. He battled his way forward, facing directly into the biting wind now, took a few steps, then a few more. And at last his light gleamed on what turned out to be the reflective numbers on the door of a house. He was looking for the first house on the left. Joe Petrolla's place. He didn't know if this was the first house, or if it were on the right or the left. It was as close as he could guess, though.

His entire body shaking, he managed to get up the sidewalk to the front door, and then he banged as hard as the oversized mittens would allow.

It was only moments before the door opened and a man in a plaid housecoat pulled him inside, then slammed the door closed behind him. "Great jumpin' Jehoshaphat, who in their right mind would be out on a night like this? You all right, fella?"

Shivering, Caleb yanked off the mittens, so he could loosen the scarf and the strings that held the hood—no easy task, since they were caked with snow and ice. But after a few seconds his cold fingers managed to accomplish it, and he pushed the hood down. "I'm Caleb—"

"I know who you are!" the man said. "Honey, it's that politician fella from the newspapers. The one who's gonna marry Maya Brand!"

Caleb hadn't noticed the woman huddled near a pot-bellied wood stove on the other side of the room. He did now. "Well, I'll be," she said.

"Listen, I don't have a lot of time to explain, but I'm looking for Joe Petrolla. Are you him?"

The man frowned and shook his head. "No. Name's Cooper. Tom Cooper. This is my wife, Sarah."

"How far am I from this Petrolla's house?"

The man scratched his head, looked at his wife.

"Only Petrolla I even knew moved to Texas five years back," the wife said.

Caleb closed his eyes, lowered his head.

"Must have been some important, to bring you clear out here on a night like this," Tom Cooper said.

"It is important. The roads are blocked, power's out, as you probably already know, and the phones are dead. Maya is all alone out there at the farmhouse, and I don't have any way of even knowing if she's all right." He bit his lip. "Just yesterday a nurse predicted she'd have the babies within a day or two at most."

"Someone ought to go on out there and check on her," Tom Cooper said slowly.

His wife, who'd crossed the room, smacked him on the arm. "Well what did you think this young man was doing, Thomas, taking a stroll?" She rolled her eyes and looked at Caleb. "What did you want from this Petrolla, anyway?"

"Ol' Hank, at the boarding house, told me the guy had

a snowmobile. I thought I'd stand a better chance of making it out to the farm if I could borrow it."

She sighed heavily. "Well, we don't have a snowmobile."

"You'd never make it on a snowmobile in this storm anyway," her husband said.

Then the wife's head came up. "Could you make it with the bulldozer, Tom?"

Tom blinked twice and turned a horrified stare at his wife. "What the—do you think I'd just hand over--that thing cost more than this house, woman!"

"Tom's in the construction business," she said, as if that explained his reaction. "His equipment is as precious to him as if it were attached." She turned a narrow glare on Tom. "But there is a pregnant woman and twin babies at stake here, so of course he'll realize there's only one right thing to do."

Cooper set his jaw and shook his head.

"Mr. Cooper, you said you knew who I was," Caleb told the man. "So that must mean you know what I'm worth."

The man's brows drew together in a brief frown, then rose as his mind processed this new data.

"Tom, please...if you help me tonight, I'll buy you a brand-new dozer tomorrow. Any kind, any size, any price, you name it."

Tom Cooper rubbed his chin. "Don't need a dozer," he said slowly. "Got one." Then, tilting his head to one side, he said, "Could use a backhoe, though."

"Deal. You have my word, and your wife is our witness. The minute the roads are cleared, you go out and you order the biggest, shiniest backhoe in existence, and I'll foot the bill." Caleb thrust out a hand.

Tom pursed his lips, then reached out and shook on it.

Turning, he said, "Hon, I'm gonna need my wool union suit and my Carhartt overalls."

"Hey, wait a minute. I didn't say anything about you going with me," Caleb said. "It's not safe out there."

Tom lifted his brows. "You ever run a dozer, mister?"

Caleb shook his head.

"Didn't think so. I'll be ready in ten minutes." He glanced at the window, shook his head. "Nope, you'd have never made it out there on a snowmobile. Never."

"I wanted to do this in the hospital! I wanted a freaking epidural!" Maya's voice carried all through the house. But as the contraction eased and she relaxed back on the pillows, her focus changed again. "How long has it been?"

"Only an hour," Vidalia said.

"Mom, you gotta go after Mel. Dammit, if I could, I'd go myself."

"Mel's the toughest of any of us," Vidalia said. She couldn't hide her fear from Maya, though, or from anyone else. It showed on her face. She was terrified for Mel.

"Let me go. Mom, she's right. We have to get to Mel," Kara said.

"I can do it," Selene put in. "You have to let one of us try, Mom."

Vidalia looked again at the window. "Just give her a few more minutes. I don't want to risk either of you getting lost out there." She wiped the sweat from Maya's brow with a soft cloth.

Kara had brought up the small portable kerosene burning heater from the basement, and it was almost too warm in the small bedroom now. Or maybe it only seemed that way to Maya.

She clasped her mother's hand. "You have to let one of them go, Mom. Mel might be in trouble."

"Maya—"

"Listen...oh, hell...." The pain was coming again, she clenched her jaw and her fists, and spoke through it. "Tie a rope...to the porch rail. Tie...the other end...around her waist."

Vidalia nodded hard. "Do your breathing, Maya. Come on, breathe through it."

She panted out the breaths as she'd been taught, while her mother joined her. When it passed, Vidalia stroked her hair. "Good girl, you're doing fine, honey." Then she turned. "Your sister's right. Kara, I want you to get the rope from the hall closet. Tie one end around your waist and the other to the porch rail. Go out as far as you can reach and see if there's any sign of Mel. Bundle yourself, girl. Cover every bit of skin, take the flashlight and don't linger. You get out there, and if you don't see her, you get right back in."

"Why not me?" Selene demanded.

"Because you're younger and you're smaller. The wind would whip you around like a dandelion seed. I want you to stay on this end, every bit as bundled as Kara. You keep watch that the rope doesn't come loose. And don't you even think of leaving that porch, you understand me?"

Selene scowled, but nodded. She moved to the head of the bed and leaned over to kiss Maya's cheek. "Be okay, hon. I won't be long."

"Hey, I've got your childbirth herbs in my pillowcase, your protection incense burning and your power stone being crushed to dust in my fist, sis. What could go wrong?"

Kara came to the other side. "Will you two be okay without us?" she asked.

"Mom's done this a few times, don't forget," Maya said breathlessly. "Go on, bring Mel back."

Kara nodded, and she and Selene hurried out of the room.

Another pain hit, and Maya's head came off the pillow at the intensity of it. *"Is it supposed to hurt this much?"* she growled.

"Breathe, baby. That's it. You trust me, when we ask you about this later, you're gonna tell us it was nothing at all. This part leaves your mind like it never happened."

Panting through clenched teeth, Maya said, "That's bull."

"If it were bull, darlin', you'd be an only child." Vidalia smiled gently at her. "In fact, I think everyone would be. Well, everyone except for twins and triplets and such special little angels as those."

The pain ebbed. Maya stopped panting, blew a sigh, dropped her head to the pillows once more. "Can you see out the window, Mom?"

"It's damn near black as pitch," Vidalia said, but she went to the window all the same and stood looking out. "Well now, wait a minute…what in the world?"

"What is it?" Maya twisted her head to try to see, but couldn't.

"Why…there's a light, way off to the north. Looks to be coming this way, too. Who on earth…?"

"Is it Mel? Maybe she got turned around and wandered—"

"No, it's too far away to be Mel. Besides, that little flashlight wouldn't shine so far, not in this weather."

Maya closed her eyes. Maybe it was Caleb. God, she wanted him so much right now. And it made no damn sense whatsoever, but there it was. He'd been her first thought when she'd felt the initial pangs. And he'd been on her mind constantly ever since. She'd been lying here foolishly fantasizing that he would show up, like some knight in shining armor. That he would fight his way through a storm that even emergency workers couldn't penetrate just to be with her. She kept envisioning him bursting through the bedroom door.

She was hopeless. If he had a clue how she really felt about him, he would probably take his offer of marriage and run screaming back to Tulsa just as fast as his feet could take him. She'd always been so practical. When had she turned into this emotional, needy, lovesick basket case?

But she knew the answer to that. She'd been that way since she first laid eyes on Caleb Montgomery. And she didn't think there was any cure in sight.

And yes, she needed him tonight, and no, he wasn't here. But she knew now that she couldn't judge him by that. If he knew what was happening, he would be here. If there were a way to get here. His not being here didn't mean he would turn out to be a man like her father was, or that he would let her down or walk out on her children. It didn't mean that at all.

"Whoever it is, they're coming this way," Vidalia said.

"I hope it's a team of paramedics with radios and a whole suitcase full of drugs," she said, as yet another contraction tightened its fist around her.

"You are such a liar," her mother told her. "You hope it's Caleb." She licked her lips, shook her head slowly. "And frankly, daughter, so do I."

The bulldozer moved at the speed of molasses, and with every snowdrift it crushed beneath its tracks, Caleb felt more certain that something was wrong. Terribly wrong.

His stomach was tied up in knots, and the cold wasn't the only thing causing his shivering.

What if something happened to those babies?

What if something happened to Maya?

A shaft of red-hot pain sliced right through his frozen body to lay open his heart. Damn, he was a mess, wasn't he?

"Shouldn't we see the house by now?" He leaned close to Tom Cooper, and shouted the question. Between the noise of the dozer and that of the storm, he wasn't sure the man could hear him even then. Besides, they were both wrapped in hoods and scarfs and a solid half-inch layer of snow at this point.

Cooper turned slightly and yelled back, "Maybe. If there were any lights on."

Hell, if there were no lights on, then what the hell did that indicate? Nothing good, he bet. A brief image of Maya lying frozen in her bed, still and white, her skin like glass, crystals forming on her eyelashes, floated into his mind. Like Sleeping Beauty, he saw her. He squeezed his eyes tight and gave his head a hard shake to rid himself of that image.

She was okay. She had to be okay, and the babies, too.

Cooper held up one mitted paw, sort of pointing.

Caleb squinted into the cutting snow to try to see what he did and finally made out a dim speck of light in the distance. "Go toward it!" he yelled.

It probably was an unnecessary instruction.

The dozer belched and bucked, inch by inch, nearer the light. And the light didn't move. More and more it seemed to be coming from ground level, and the fear in Caleb's belly churned tighter. Then the spotlights mounted on the dozer were pointing directly at the smaller light, so it vanished altogether. But the edge of the house came into view, and he could see lights at last in one of the upper windows.

"Thank God," he whispered. "Thank God." At least it looked as if someone were alive in there.

The dozer rocked closer, and its lights picked out a lone form, struggling against the wind...with what looked like a rope tied around it. Turning to face the dozer, the form waved its arms frantically, held its hands flat out, made a pushing motion.

"Stop, Tom," Caleb shouted. "Shut her down, but keep the lights on."

Cooper did so. Caleb climbed off the machine, amazed at how difficult it was to bend or unbend anything. Every joint in his body seemed to have frozen over. His legs sank hip deep in snow as soon as he hit, but he waded forward, fumbling in his big pocket for the flashlight, grabbing it as clumsily as a bear cub in boxing gloves, and finally flicking it on.

The figure with the rope around it was bundled beyond recognition, until he got all the way up in her face. Then her eyes, peering over the top of a scarf gave her away as a Brand woman, and her height told him which one.

"Kara? What are you doing out here?" he said, loudly, over the wind.

"Caleb?" she asked. "Oh, thank God!" She hugged him, totally ineffective in all the layers of clothing.

"What's wrong?" he shouted again, clasping her shoulders, and backing her up just a few inches.

"It's Mel! She went out to the barn—for the generator—but she never came back."

His heart did a little spasm in his chest. "How long?" he shouted.

"Almost two hours!"

He didn't like it. Damn, Mel out in this for two hours? Why the hell hadn't someone gone out after her sooner?

"Go back to the house," he yelled. "I'll find her."

Kara shook her head. "Not without my sister!"

He started to get mad, then remembered the faint light he'd seen before. It hadn't been Kara's. It had been further out than that. He patted Kara's shoulders. "Wait here!" Then he dragged himself back out to the dozer, where Tom Cooper waited. "Turn off the lights and come with me."

Cooper cut the lights, clambered down, and the two of them hunched their backs against the storm and made their way through the snow once more. When they reached Kara, Caleb said, "I think I saw her. I'm going out. You two stay right here. If I'm not back in ten minutes, Cooper, you take this girl back to the house, whether she wants to go or not. It's at the other end of her rope."

Cooper nodded. Kara argued, but Caleb didn't take time to listen. He started out through the drifts, praying to God he would see that little beam of light again.

And then he did. Ten feet from the barn, with an inch of snow already covering it. He raced closer, dropped to his knees, and pawed the snow away rapidly, digging out the light, and the gloved hand that clung to it. Mel's hand. Then her arm, shoulder and the rest of her. Lifting her upper body, he shook her. "Mel! Mel, come on! Talk to me!"

There was a very slight movement of her lips. Maybe a moan, but if so, it was lost in the wind. At least he knew she was alive. He gathered her up into his arms, turned and started back the way he'd come. He homed in on the glow spilling from the upstairs window and trudged with everything he had.

He reached Kara and Tom Cooper with what felt like the last ounce of strength in his body. He was so cold he couldn't even feel his hands or feet anymore.

Cooper took Mel from his arms, turned toward the house. Caleb took a step toward it, as well, and Kara put a hand on his chest to stop him. "We still need the generator," she said.

Cooper turned back. "Don't walk it, Caleb! Take the dozer. No one out there to run over by accident now!"

With a sigh of relief, he nodded. "Get back to the house, Kara. I'll be in with the genny in a few minutes."

She looked him in the eye and said, "Hurry, Caleb. We need you in there." Then she turned and trudged away.

In only seconds she was swallowed up by the storm. Drawing himself up, Caleb started toward the dozer.

Chapter 16

He hadn't thought about how he was supposed to get the generator to the bulldozer. The thing was huge, and it would have taken two or three men at the very least, to pick it up. But he discovered chains on the back of the dozer, attached them to the machine, and even thought to make sure it had gasoline in its tank, so he wouldn't have to make this trek again to syphon some from one of the cars. The tank was full, though, so he remounted the bull-dozer and ground it into motion. And he thanked his lucky stars Tom Cooper hadn't just handed it over earlier to-night or he'd never have gotten here. He'd been watching for five miles, and he still just barely managed to make it go where he wanted. There was a definite knack to this thing.

He dragged the generator right up to the front door, then shut the dozer down, got off, and, finally, after what seemed like an endless, freezing journey, he stumbled on frozen stumps into the house.

Cooper met him at the door "I'll start the genny and get her plugged in the second I get thawed out here. You'd best get out of those things. You're needed elsewhere."

He thought of Mel and rapidly, clumsily, started tugging at the snow-encrusted scarf and mittens. The parka's zipper was frozen, and there was so much snow frozen to his legs that he could barely tell where the boots ended and the overalls began. Snow scattered everywhere, but eventually he got shed of most of the layers and limped into the living room on numb feet.

Mel lay on the sofa, her clothes on the floor, her body wrapped in blankets. Kara and Selene worked fiercely, rubbing her hands and feet. Mel's hair was wet but thawed out. The fireplace burned full blast, giving off blessed heat that began to make his own hands and feet burn as the feeling came back to them.

"How is she?" he asked, leaning over the other two.

Mel's eyes opened. Her teeth were chattering and her body shaking, but she managed a weak smile. "I'll b-b-be fine. Thanks t-t-to you."

"Hey, that's what brothers-in-law are for, isn't it?"

"Caleb...I...need to tell you something." Mel was so cold her teeth were chattering. "I...the photographs. It...was me. I sent them."

He leaned closer to her, looked right into her eyes and said, "Then I know who to thank, don't I?"

Her smile was wavering, but heartfelt, he thought. Then she frowned. "W-what are you waiting for? You should be upstairs," she told him.

Caleb frowned. "Upstairs?" Then he glanced at the other two.

But before either of them could speak, a heart-ripping shriek tore through the house and right into his soul. He thought it might have cracked a few windows. A rush of dizziness hit him so fast, he almost fell down. "Maya?" he asked stupidly.

"You better get up there, Caleb," Selene said. "We'll take care of Mel."

Caleb didn't want to think what he was thinking, but he didn't take time to verify it. Instead he lunged to the stairs, and his half-functioning, damp sock-clad feet stumbled and slammed into steps on the way up. They would hurt like hell later, when the feeling came back.

"God, Mamma, why does it have to hurt so much!" Maya's voice cried brokenly.

He lurched down the hall, burst into her bedroom and stared in shock at the scene being played out in front of him.

Maya lay propped up on pillows. Her knees were bent and pointed at the ceiling, and her bare feet pressed down into the mattress. Her mother, looking about as terrified as Caleb felt, was at the foot of the bed. Then, looking up at her daughter, pasting a calm and confident smile in place, Vidalia Brand said, "All right now, honey, it's time. When the next contraction comes, I want you to push."

For one brief instant he thought he might pass out cold. He shook that away and thought he might throw up instead, from sheer terror. But he shook that off, too. The look of unmitigated fear on Maya's pale face was all it took to snap him out of it. It was fairly easy to size up the situation. The babies were coming, and they were coming now. There was no choice about it. His own fears didn't matter. Hers did. His job here was to get her through this. Not add his own worries to hers.

"Now, Maya Brand," he said, "I thought I told you I wanted to be in the delivery room. What are you thinking of, trying to get started on this without me?"

Maya's head turned fast, and her eyes met his. And he saw something that almost floored him all over again. The look in her eyes when she saw him standing there…he'd never seen anything like that before. He'd never felt so wanted, or so needed. Or so loved.

He felt himself grow an inch or two taller.

"Caleb," she whispered, sounding exhausted already. "My God, you're here. You're really here."

"I'm here." He moved closer, trusting his legs not to buckle.

Maya's eyes widened. "Caleb, my sister…Mel… she's—"

"Safe and sound on the sofa downstairs. Kara and Selene have everything in hand down there. And a friend of mine ought to have that generator running in a few minutes or so. I want you to stop worrying about all that. You've got plenty to do right up here."

She heard his voice and thought it was her mind, weaving more fantasies. She'd been lying in the bed, in pain, terrified for her babies, for her sisters, for herself…wishing with everything in her that Caleb would walk through her door and somehow make her believe everything was going to be okay. So powerful was the image in her mind that when she turned her head and saw him there, she almost didn't believe he was real. And then she did, and everything she'd been feeling for him seemed to spill from her pores and beam from her eyes.

His face changed—something moved over his features. But she couldn't tell what. Then he was moving closer, and she noticed his odd gait—he was limping or—

"Caleb, what's wrong?"

He shook his head, pausing to warm his hands over the

small portable heater. "Nothing a little warming up won't fix," he told her.

Vidalia frowned at him. "How in the world did you manage to get out here, Caleb Montgomery?"

He winked. "Would you believe I hitched a ride on a sleigh with a guy in red and eight tiny reindeer?"

"It's a day early for that," Vidalia said. Then Maya saw her mother look down at Caleb's feet, saw her brows draw together in concern. She started to twist around to have a look for herself, but another contraction hit.

Caleb came to the bedside, and the second his hand was within reach, she clutched it in hers. Cold. His hand was still so cold.

"Time to push, honey," her mother told her. "You remember the drill."

"Come on," Caleb said, sliding an arm around her shoulders to brace her up. His face was close to hers. "Push now. That's it, one, two, three, four..."

When Caleb reached ten, she stopped pushing. Rested. He let her lie back and stroked her hair away from her face. Vidalia ran to the bedroom door and shouted down the stairs. "We need a bowl of ice chips up here," she called.

By the time she was back in position again, another pain had Maya in its grip, and she pushed again while Caleb held her and counted.

Selene arrived with the requested bowl of ice chips and set them on the bedside stand. In her other hand she held a pair of wool socks. "Put these on, Caleb," she said, handing them to him. "We warmed them by the fire for you. Your feet look about frozen."

"That was really sweet of you. Thanks." He tugged the damp socks off, and quickly pulled the warm ones on, just barely finishing before the next contraction came.

It went on and on. Caleb holding her, counting with her, wiping the sweat away from her brow, feeding her ice chips in between. She pushed until she thought she couldn't push anymore. She felt her body being torn apart. And then, finally, a rush of relief.

She fell back on the bed, breathless and limp. Panting, she looked at Caleb, and saw his gaze directed toward her mother, at the bed's foot. His look was intense, and for the first time, she saw the fear in his eyes showing through the confident facade. The only sound from the foot of the bed was that of her mother's hurried movements.

"Mamma?" Maya whispered. She tried to lift her head from the pillows to see. Her heart seemed to slow to a stop in her chest, and she held her breath. Caleb's hand tightened around hers.

Then, softly, a hoarse and snuffly cry. Like the bleat of a newborn lamb. And then her mother was at her side, holding a tiny, messy, squirming, red-faced bundle, wrapped in a small blanket. "A boy," Vidalia said. "Your son, Caleb." And she handed the baby into Caleb's waiting arms.

Maya couldn't take her eyes off the baby. Her mother helped her sit up farther, plumping the pillows behind her, which she'd pretty well flattened, as Caleb sat on the edge of the bed holding the baby. He hadn't said a word. Not a word.

As soon as Maya was upright, Caleb gently placed the baby into her arms. Filmy, unfocused eyes squinted at her, and when she touched the tiny hand, it gripped her finger and her chest contracted with a kind of wonder and joy she'd never experienced. Lifting her head, she looked at Caleb.

His face was wet. His eyes, his cheeks. He met her gaze, and smiled at her. "My God, Maya, look what you did. You're…incredible.'' And then, leaning closer, he brushed his lips over hers, very gently. She closed her eyes, sighed very softly. His hand threaded in her hair, and he kissed her again. Then he drew back and just stared at her, as if he'd never quite seen her before.

She looked at the baby. ''Cain Caleb Montgomery the Fourth,'' she said softly. ''Such a big name for such a little thing.''

Caleb lowered his forehead to hers, and the tears on her cheeks mingled with those on his.

The sound of a motor reached Maya, and only then did she tear her eyes away from her baby. Then the lights flickered on, blinked off, came on again, and stayed this time.

''Thank the Lord,'' Vidalia said. ''Now, darlin', if it's okay, can I take my grandson for just a bit?''

Maya nodded, and Caleb gathered the baby from her arms and handed him carefully to Vidalia. She turned toward the doorway, and for the first time Maya looked beyond Caleb to see that Kara and Selene were crowded there, peering in. They were both damp eyed, too.

''Well come on in here and close the door, this little one needs to be kept very warm just now,'' Vidalia said.

''Mel's resting,'' Kara explained. ''Tom Cooper's gonna sit with her so we can help out up here.''

''I turned the furnace way up, Mom, and I brought diapers and baby clothes, and blankets,'' Selene said.

''Yeah, and even a little hat.'' Kara held up the tiny little cotton skullcap. ''They always put hats on them in the hospitals.''

Vidalia looked at the baby, obviously not relishing the idea of handing him over. But then another contraction came, and Maya, caught by surprise, cried out. Vidalia shot her a worried glance and handed the newborn off to

Selene, complete with a set of instructions, which she spoke rapidly even as she resumed her position at the foot of the bed.

"Oh, God, not yet," Maya moaned. "I can't do this again." It hit her that that was exactly what was about to happen.

"Yes, you can. Come on, Maya, you can. I know you can," Caleb told her.

Panting, she waited for the pain to pass, then looked up at him. "I need to sit up. I need something to brace against."

He didn't hesitate. He lifted her shoulders and positioned himself on the bed behind her, just the way they had done at the childbirth class. He bent his knees so she could brace her hands on his thighs, and his chest was solid behind her.

"Better?" he asked.

She let her head fall back against him and nodded. "I think…oh, God!"

"Another one? Okay, okay, it's all right. Breathe through it." His hands were on her belly, rubbing circles that were supposed to be soothing. But it was his breath, and his voice, so close to her ear that gave her the most relief, the most comfort. He was here. He was actually here for her, when it had been all but impossible to be. He was not like her father, and he would never be. He might not love her, but he would always, she sensed, be there for her. And for her children.

He held her like that all through the wee hours. He breathed with her, talked to her, held her. A few feet away, her sisters took turns holding the baby, their body heat his incubator. And as the sun came up, breaking through the storm clouds, and climbing steadily higher, Maya pushed with all the strength she had left in her.

And finally the second baby emerged into the world.

She collapsed against Caleb. And his arms tightened around her. She heard the fear in his voice when he spoke. "Vidalia…? Is he…?"

Opening her eyes, Maya looked up at Caleb's face, seeing the stricken expression. Fear hit her hard, and she shifted her gaze to the foot of the bed, where her mother was working. But she couldn't see the baby.

But then Vidalia smiled, and she knew it was okay. Everything was okay. The baby started to cry gustily as Vidalia wrapped it in a blanket and held it close to her. "You men just tend to jump to conclusions, don't you?" she asked Caleb as she brought the little bundle and placed it in Maya's arms. "Your daughter is just fine," Vidalia whispered.

"Oh…a girl?" Maya breathed. "A little girl? Just like Selene said…."

"Was there ever any doubt?" Selene asked softly. "Help ought to be here soon. At first light Mr. Cooper headed back to town. Said he'd go straight to the sheriff's department and let them know the situation."

Maya frowned tiredly. "How was he going to do that?"

"Same way he got out here with Caleb," Kara said. "On his bulldozer."

Maya blinked in shock, tipping her head backward to stare up at Caleb. "You came all the way out here last night on a bulldozer?"

He shrugged. "Hey, I was looking for a snowmobile, but I figured I'd better take what I could get."

"But it must have taken over an hour—and in that storm…God, Caleb, it was a crazy thing to do."

"Walking would have been crazier," he told her. And his eyes got that look again. All…deep and potent. "But

I would have, if that was the only way to get to you last night.''

Her brows came down. ''How did you know?''

He shook his head. ''I didn't…. I just had a feeling that I had to get here. That you needed me.''

''I was sending a telepathic 911,'' Seléne confessed from across the room.

But Caleb's gaze never moved from Maya's, as she whispered, ''So was I, Caleb. I was wishing for you so much…and you came. You came.''

''I always will,'' he promised her. And for the first time, she believed it with all her heart.

Chapter 17

She'd been resting in the hospital all day. Heck of a way to spend Christmas Eve. Caleb had been in and out a half-dozen times, each time seeming a little more tense. He brought flowers the first time, candy the second, a pair of giant teddy bears the third. He kept saying he had a very busy schedule today, but that he couldn't stay away from her and the babies for more than a couple of hours at a time.

She wished he wouldn't say things like that unless he really meant them—at least, the way she wanted him to mean them. She was sure he was utterly sincere where the babies were concerned, but she was sure he could bear to be away from her just fine, if need be.

At any rate, he certainly was heroic. She'd had the TV on for the past hour, and the coverage of the storm told her more than she'd already known about how bad it had been last night. He'd literally risked his life to get to her.

Her admiration for him—her love for him—grew even deeper at the knowledge.

The door opened, and she looked up, wondering which of her frequent visitors would appear there. Selene, Kara, her mother, Caleb—or Mel, who was in a room down the hall recovering from her brush with hypothermia. Aside from a touch of frostbite, she was going to be just fine. They'd promised she could go home today. Maya and the babies would be released on Christmas morning.

But the visitor was none of those people. It was, instead, Cain Caleb Montgomery II. He hesitated in the doorway, peering in at her, leaning on his cane. "I can come back later, if you're resting," he said.

"No, no, please come in."

He did, his cane thumping the floor with every other step.

"Have you seen the babies yet?"

He looked at her with a smile...an actual smile. She hadn't seen one on him until then. "I've been in the nursery for the past half hour." The smile grew. "They let me hold them. I didn't want to put them down."

"I'm glad I'm not the only one," she said. "Come in and sit down, Mr. Montgomery."

"Oh, now. You call me Cain." He sat down, pursed his lips. "Actually, I'm hoping that, down the road, you might want to call me Dad, instead. I mean, you know, since you're marrying my son."

Her hand touched her chest involuntarily—in response to a small flutter there. "I haven't called anyone that in years."

"Yes, well..." He cleared his throat. "I owe you an apology, Maya. I came here judging you, insulting you and your family, and the truth was, I was only reacting out of fear that you were going to take my son away from me. Instead, you've given me…oh, such a precious gift.''

She didn't know how to respond to that, so she said nothing.

"I want you to know that Caleb and I have had a long talk. I've told him already that whatever he decides to do or not do with his life, is fine with me. Just so long as I have plenty of time with his…his family.''

"Oh, my goodness.'' She had to dab at her eyes. "That must have meant so much to him. And it does to me, too. Thank you Cain…Dad.''

His smile was quick and bright. "Well, I won't keep you. We have lots to do tonight, after all. But, um…I have a little gift for you first. Two, actually, but, um—''

Caleb came in then, glanced at his father, then at Maya, and smiled warmly.

"Good, good, you're here. You should be,'' Cain said. "Would you kindly get the package I left outside the door there, son?''

Caleb frowned, but did as his father asked. He came back with a huge package wrapped in gleaming gold foil, with elaborate ribbons. "It's for Maya,'' Cain said.

Caleb brought the package to her and laid it across her lap on the bed.

"My goodness, it's almost too beautiful to open.''

But she opened it anyway. She tore the paper aside and took the cover off the large box it had concealed.

And then she felt her mouth fall open and tears spring to her eyes as she stared down at the wedding gown of ivory satin and lace. She looked up at Cain, who hurried forward and took the dress from the box by its shoulders, holding it up so she could see it better. The full skirt spilled free, and Maya caught her breath. "I don't know what to say. It's…it's beautiful. The most beautiful gown I could imagine.''

"I knew you were planning to have the ceremony before the birth,'' Cain said. ''So I thought you probably didn't have a dress—at least, not one that would fit you now.''

"Well, you were right,'' Maya said, still admiring the gown.

"This was…this was Caleb's mother's.''

Her gaze shifted to Cain. "Oh…oh, my…'' Pushing aside her covers, sending the box and wrappings to the floor, Maya got to her feet, went to the older man and kissed him softly on the cheek. ''Thank you. You don't know how much this means to me.''

He grinned and handed Caleb the dress. ''I'll go now, so you can give her the other present.''

"Thanks, Dad. Or should I say Grandpa?''

"Grandpa is a title I'll bear with great pride.'' He winked at his son and limped out the door, with a decided bounce in his step.

Caleb opened the small closet and carefully arranged the dress on a hanger. Then he turned to where Maya was still standing.

"You should be lying down. Resting.''

"I've been lying down all day, Caleb. I'm fine, really.''

He smiled. ''You sure are.''

Feeling her cheeks heat, she averted her face, walked to the chair beside the bed and sat down. Caleb went to the bed, sat on its edge. ''I want to talk to you about our…um…our arrangement.''

Her head came up fast. ''You do?'' Worry gnawed at her. Had he changed his mind? Had he decided he didn't want to marry a woman he didn't love after all?

"Things have changed, Maya. And…well, I just don't

think it would be fair to let you go through with this marriage without being perfectly honest with you.''

Lifting her chin, bracing herself, Maya looked him in the eye. ''All right. I'm listening.''

Drawing a breath, he took her hands in his. ''First of all, I've decided not to run for the Senate. In fact, I'm pulling out of politics altogether.''

It was not what she'd expected to hear.

''I thought I'd go into private practice. Open a law office right here in Big Falls. How would you feel about that?''

She knew she was gaping, but she couldn't seem to stop. Shaking herself, she finally let her relief show. ''I'd feel...wonderful. God, Caleb, that's almost everything I've been hoping for.''

''Really?'' He smiled. ''Why didn't you say so?''

She shook her head. ''I...I didn't want to start making career decisions for you, Caleb. I don't have the right to do that.''

He came off the bed, still holding both her hands. ''You have every right. Maya....'' He hesitated, bit his lip. ''Maya, you said that was *almost* everything you'd been hoping for. What else was there?''

She looked away fast. ''Nothing. It doesn't matter, Caleb.''

One hand rose, palm gentle on her cheek, turning her to face him again. ''Come on, Maya, tell me the truth. Please. Because...I'm hoping for more, too.''

She felt her eyes widen as she searched his. ''Caleb?''

''I'm in love with you, Maya. I don't want to marry you for the sake of the babies, or to save your reputation or mine, or anything else. I want to marry you because I don't ever want to have to spend a day of my life without you. And I'm sitting here like a big idiot hoping to God you feel the same way about me.''

Her lips trembled, and tears spilled onto her cheeks. ''I do, Caleb. I have all along.''

He cupped her face and kissed her, long and slow and deeply. And when he straightened away again, he took a small velvet box from his pocket. ''This is the other gift Dad mentioned.'' He opened the lid to reveal a glittering diamond engagement ring, its large teardrop-shaped stone utterly flawless. ''This was my mother's, as well. And I know she'd want you to wear it.''

Taking the ring from its nest, he slipped it onto Maya's finger. ''Will you marry me, Maya? For real?''

''Yes,'' she whispered. ''Yes, Caleb, I will.''

He kissed her softly again. ''In an hour?''

''I…'' Her eyes flew open. ''An hour?''

''What did you think I'd been running around planning for all day?''

''But…*an hour?*''

''What's wrong, darling? Do you need help getting ready that soon?''

''Maybe a little,'' she said, her tone sarcastic.

He grinned at her, gave her a devilish wink and one last kiss, then went to the door and pulled it open. ''Would all my pending in-laws please come in now?''

One by one, her sisters came in the door. Selene, and then Mel, and then Kara. Her mother came in last and let the door go.

''No, no, no. That's not everybody,'' Caleb said, snatching the door before it closed all the way, opening it wide once more. ''I said *all* my pending in-laws.''

Several confused frowns were aimed at him. And then it became clear.

Edain Brand, the prodigal daughter, walked through the

door, looking even more beautiful than she had when she'd left home two years before.

"Edie? Oh my God, Edie?"

Kara, Selene and Mel mobbed her with hugs, and when they parted, Edie faced Vidalia.

Their eyes met, and for just one brief second Maya wondered if the old tension would rise up yet again between them. But then Vidalia smiled, and opened her arms, and Edie rushed into them.

Maya met Caleb's eyes across the room. "You did this, didn't you?"

"Merry Christmas," he said.

Edie and Vidalia pulled apart, and Edie went to Maya, hugged her gently, and said, "I can't believe I'm an aunt twice over."

"It's so good to have you home, Edie."

"It's good to be home, hon."

They separated, and again Maya looked toward the door. Caleb blew her a kiss and slipped quietly out of the room.

An hour later, Caleb waited in the elaborately decorated hospital chapel as his bride walked toward him. His children were held in the loving arms of their grandmother and grandfather, and every time he looked at them, he felt his chest swell with pride.

When he looked at their mother, it was more like awe. He couldn't believe he'd gotten so lucky. But maybe... maybe luck had nothing to do with it. Selene kept insisting that it was no coincidence that caused him to have a flat tire in front of the OK Coral almost nine months ago. She kept saying it was something far more powerful. Something like fate.

When Maya stood beside him and slipped her hand into

his, smiling up into his eyes with love shining from hers, he thought maybe his bride's kid sister was wiser than any of them.

He slid a glance toward where Selene was sitting.

She gave him a nod as if she knew exactly what he was thinking.

Epilogue

So that's the whole story. Well, not the whole story, but that's how it began. I'm sitting here now on the wide front porch of my log cabin. The snow finally melted; spring came as it always does. From here, I can look down on the farmhouse on the far side of the wildflower-dotted meadow below. It's within shouting distance. Not that shouting is ever needed. My mom and sisters are up here as often as Caleb and the babies and I are down there. But we always were a close family. Always will be, too.

Edie's still here. She's been quiet and moody, and I think Mom has been letting her get away with that for the past few months, but her patience is wearing thin. Any day now I expect her to tell Edie enough is enough and it's time to stop licking her wounds and tell us what went wrong out there in La-La-Land.

My dream house is almost exactly the way I pictured it. I say "almost" because I never pictured it this big and sprawling, but I guess that's what happens when you marry a millionaire. Caleb got rid of the Lexus sports coupe, though. Bought a minivan for me and an Explorer sports utility for him. Eddie Bauer Edition, of course, but that's okay. He managed to rent office space in town, just around the corner from Sunny's Place, and he hung up a shingle that says Montgomery Law Office. He takes all kinds of cases —and many of his clients can't afford to pay him. But he says that, luckily, he *can* afford to represent them.

He's a hell of a guy, my husband.

Here he comes now, walking across the meadow from Mom's house, a baby in each arm. Look at him, smiling and talking to them as if they can understand every word. Sometimes, the way they look at him, I almost think they can. We named our little girl after my mom. Vidalia. But we call her Dahlia for short. You know, like the flower. Mom insisted. Said as much as she might deny it, it wasn't easy growing up with an onion for a name. As for little Caleb, we call him Cal, just to avoid confusion. Tough having three men in the family with the same name. And Caleb's father is around enough so that he finally broke down and rented a house in town, so he has a permanent residence out here. He could stay with us when he visits, of course, but he's too stubborn to want to appear dependent. Still, he's out here more than he's in Tulsa. He took Caleb's decision not to run for office far better than either of us expected him to. The old goat is so madly in love with his grandchildren that there isn't much Caleb or I can say or do to upset him. But if he brings any more toys to the house, I don't know where we'll put them.

Caleb's halfway to the house now. He just looked up and caught my eye. And the breeze is ruffling his hair. Gosh, when he looks at me like that, my stomach still clenches up. I love that man more than I ever thought possible. He healed my old wounds for me...and I like to think I helped mend some of his. And he gave me something more precious than gold—those babies. And his love.

At any rate we're happy—deliriously happy with our little family. And I think we will be for a long, long time.

* * * * *

You're not going to believe this offer!

In October and November 2000, buy any two Harlequin or Silhouette books and save $10.00 off future purchases, or buy any three and save $20.00 off future purchases!

Just fill out this form and attach 2 proofs of purchase (cash register receipts) from October and November 2000 books and Harlequin will send you a coupon booklet worth a total savings of $10.00 off future purchases of Harlequin and Silhouette books in 2001. Send us 3 proofs of purchase and we will send you a coupon booklet worth a total savings of $20.00 off future purchases.

Saving money has never been this easy.

I accept your offer! Please send me a coupon booklet:

Name: _____

Address: _____ City: _____

State/Prov.: _____ Zip/Postal Code: _____

Optional Survey!

In a typical month, how many Harlequin or Silhouette books would you buy <u>new</u> at retail stores?

☐ Less than 1   ☐ 1   ☐ 2   ☐ 3 to 4   ☐ 5+

Which of the following statements best describes how you <u>buy</u> Harlequin or Silhouette books? Choose one answer only that <u>best</u> describes you.

☐ I am a regular buyer and reader
☐ I am a regular reader but buy only occasionally
☐ I only buy and read for specific times of the year, e.g. vacations
☐ I subscribe through Reader Service but also buy at retail stores
☐ I mainly borrow and buy only occasionally
☐ I am an occasional buyer and reader

Which of the following statements best describes how you <u>choose</u> the Harlequin and Silhouette series books you buy <u>new</u> at retail stores? By "series," we mean books within a particular line, such as *Harlequin PRESENTS* or *Silhouette SPECIAL EDITION*. Choose one answer only that <u>best</u> describes you.

☐ I only buy books from my favorite series
☐ I generally buy books from my favorite series but also buy books from other series on occasion
☐ I buy some books from my favorite series but also buy from many other series regularly
☐ I buy all types of books depending on my mood and what I find interesting and have no favorite series

---

Please send this form, along with your cash register receipts as proofs of purchase, to:
In the U.S.: Harlequin Books, P.O. Box 9057, Buffalo, NY 14269
In Canada: Harlequin Books, P.O. Box 622, Fort Erie, Ontario L2A 5X3

(Allow 4-6 weeks for delivery) Offer expires December 31, 2000.   PHQ4002